Kaput & Zösky

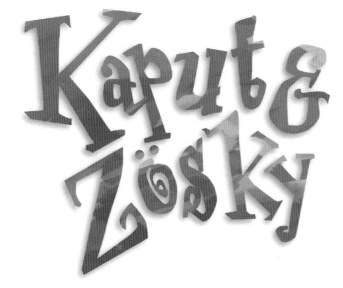

Kaput & Zosky

Lewis Trondheim

WITH ART BY ERIC CARTIER

:01
First Second
NEW YORK & LONDON

Translated by EDWARD GAUVIN

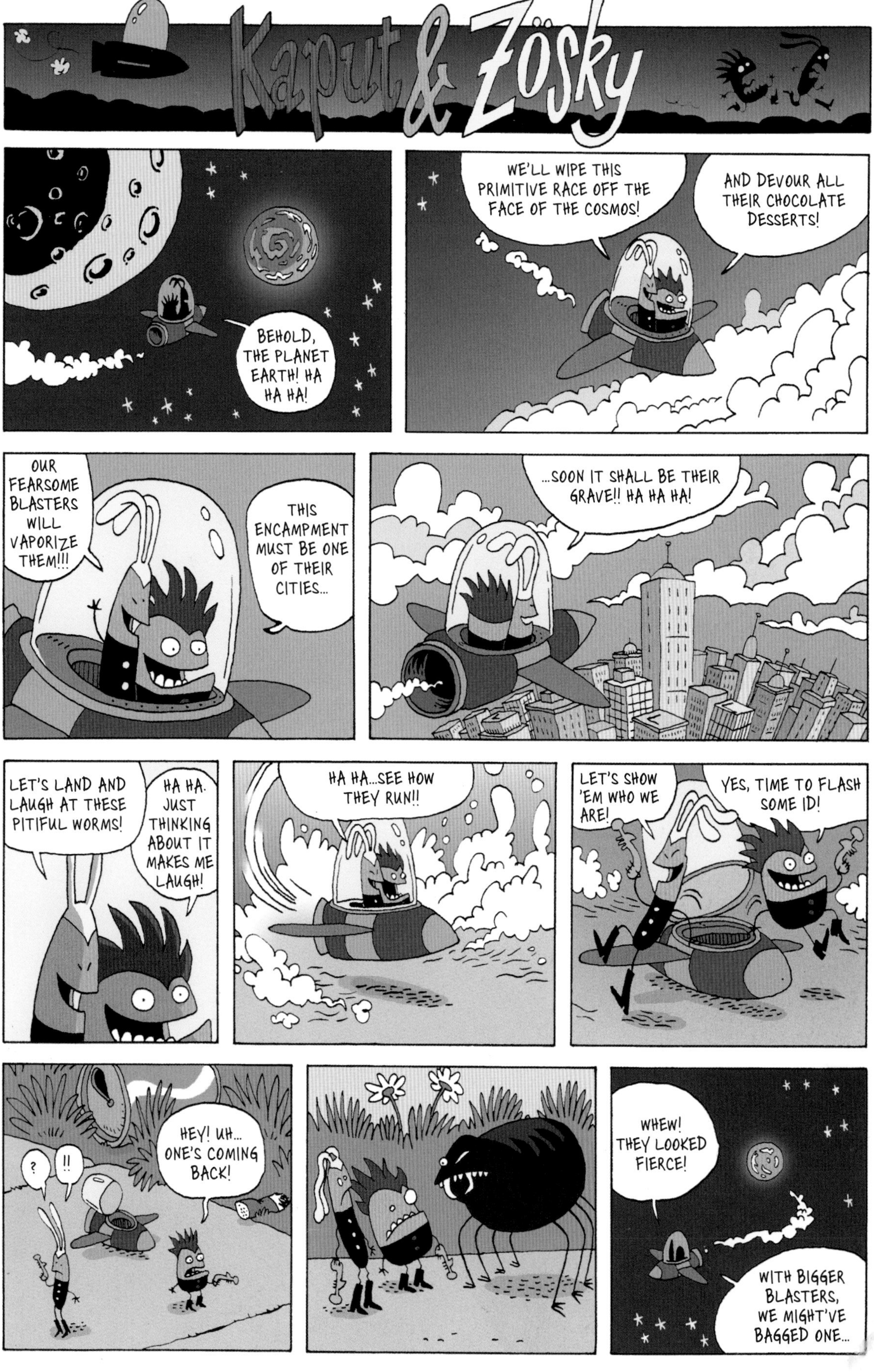
Kaput & Zösky
BEHOLD, THE PLANET EARTH! HA HA HA!
WE'LL WIPE THIS PRIMITIVE RACE OFF THE FACE OF THE COSMOS!
AND DEVOUR ALL THEIR CHOCOLATE DESSERTS!
OUR FEARSOME BLASTERS WILL VAPORIZE THEM!!!
THIS ENCAMPMENT MUST BE ONE OF THEIR CITIES...
...SOON IT SHALL BE THEIR GRAVE!! HA HA HA!
LET'S LAND AND LAUGH AT THESE PITIFUL WORMS!
HA HA. JUST THINKING ABOUT IT MAKES ME LAUGH!
HA HA...SEE HOW THEY RUN!!
LET'S SHOW 'EM WHO WE ARE!
YES, TIME TO FLASH SOME ID!
?
!!
HEY! UH... ONE'S COMING BACK!
WHEW! THEY LOOKED FIERCE!
WITH BIGGER BLASTERS, WE MIGHT'VE BAGGED ONE...

the Cosmonaut

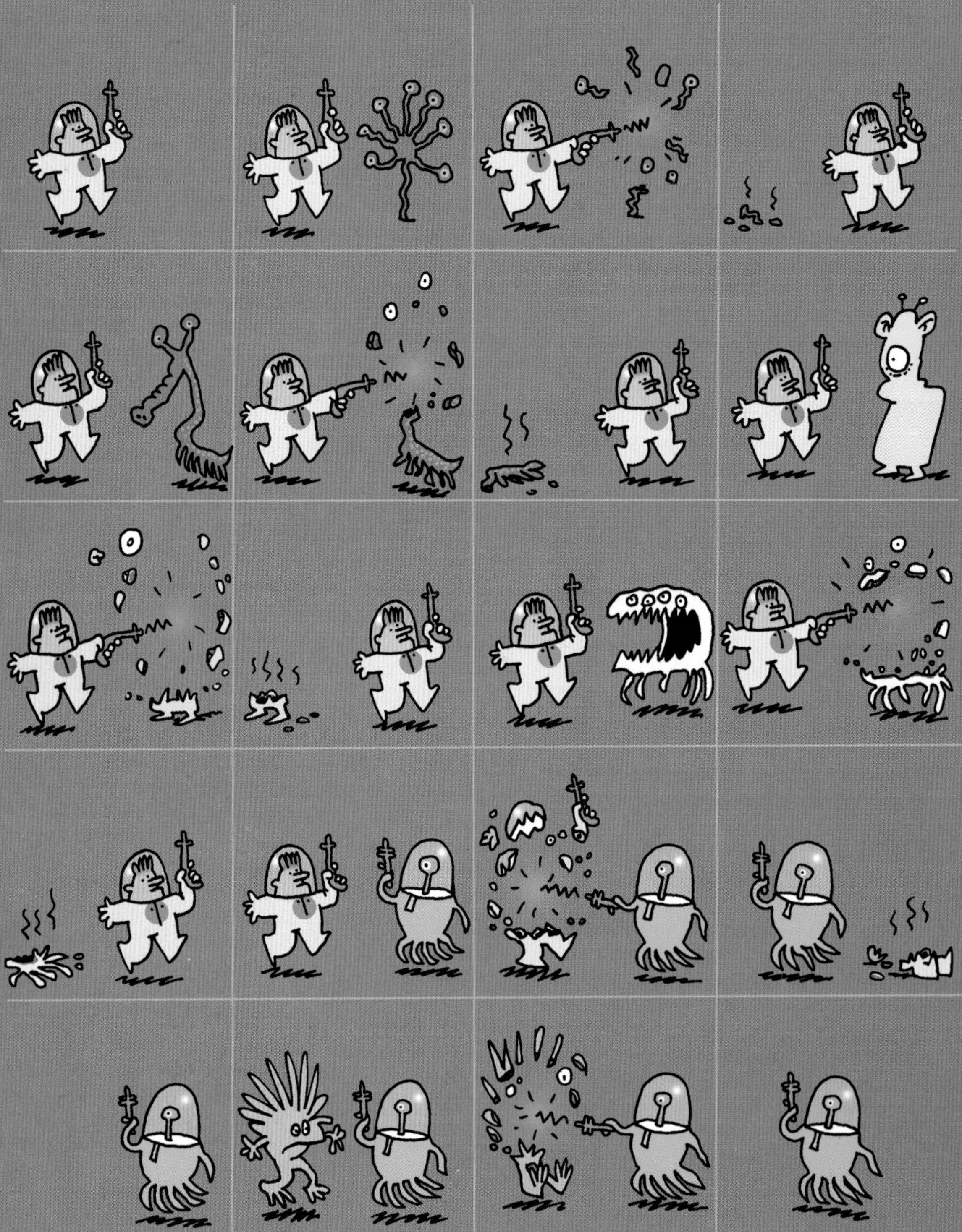

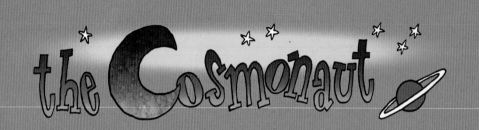

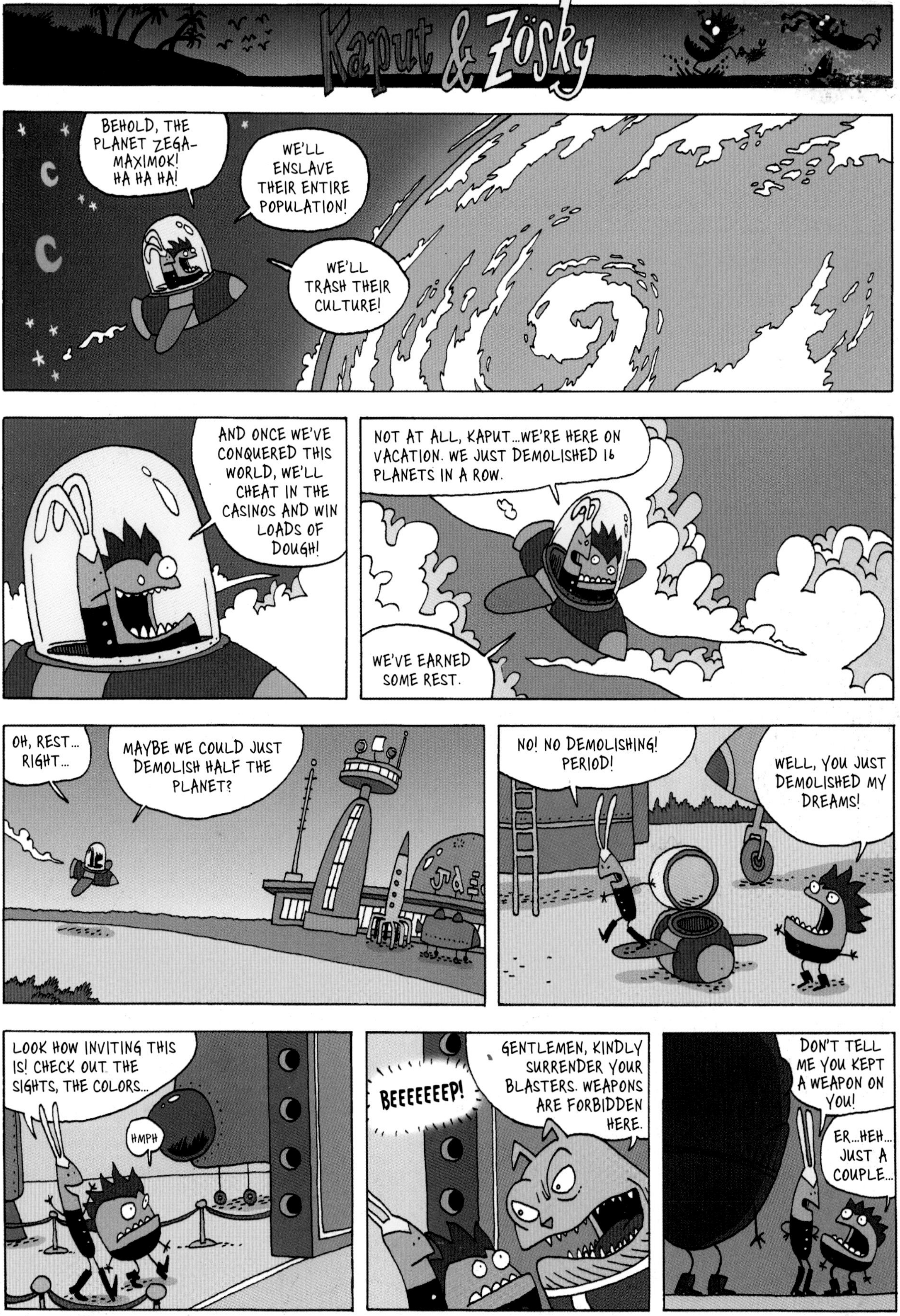
Kaput & Zösky
BEHOLD, THE PLANET ZEGA-MAXIMOK! HA HA HA!
WE'LL ENSLAVE THEIR ENTIRE POPULATION!
WE'LL TRASH THEIR CULTURE!
AND ONCE WE'VE CONQUERED THIS WORLD, WE'LL CHEAT IN THE CASINOS AND WIN LOADS OF DOUGH!
NOT AT ALL, KAPUT...WE'RE HERE ON VACATION. WE JUST DEMOLISHED 16 PLANETS IN A ROW.
WE'VE EARNED SOME REST.
OH, REST... RIGHT...
MAYBE WE COULD JUST DEMOLISH HALF THE PLANET?
NO! NO DEMOLISHING! PERIOD!
WELL, YOU JUST DEMOLISHED MY DREAMS!
LOOK HOW INVITING THIS IS! CHECK OUT THE SIGHTS, THE COLORS...
HMPH
BEEEEEEEP!
GENTLEMEN, KINDLY SURRENDER YOUR BLASTERS. WEAPONS ARE FORBIDDEN HERE.
DON'T TELL ME YOU KEPT A WEAPON ON YOU!
ER...HEH... JUST A COUPLE...

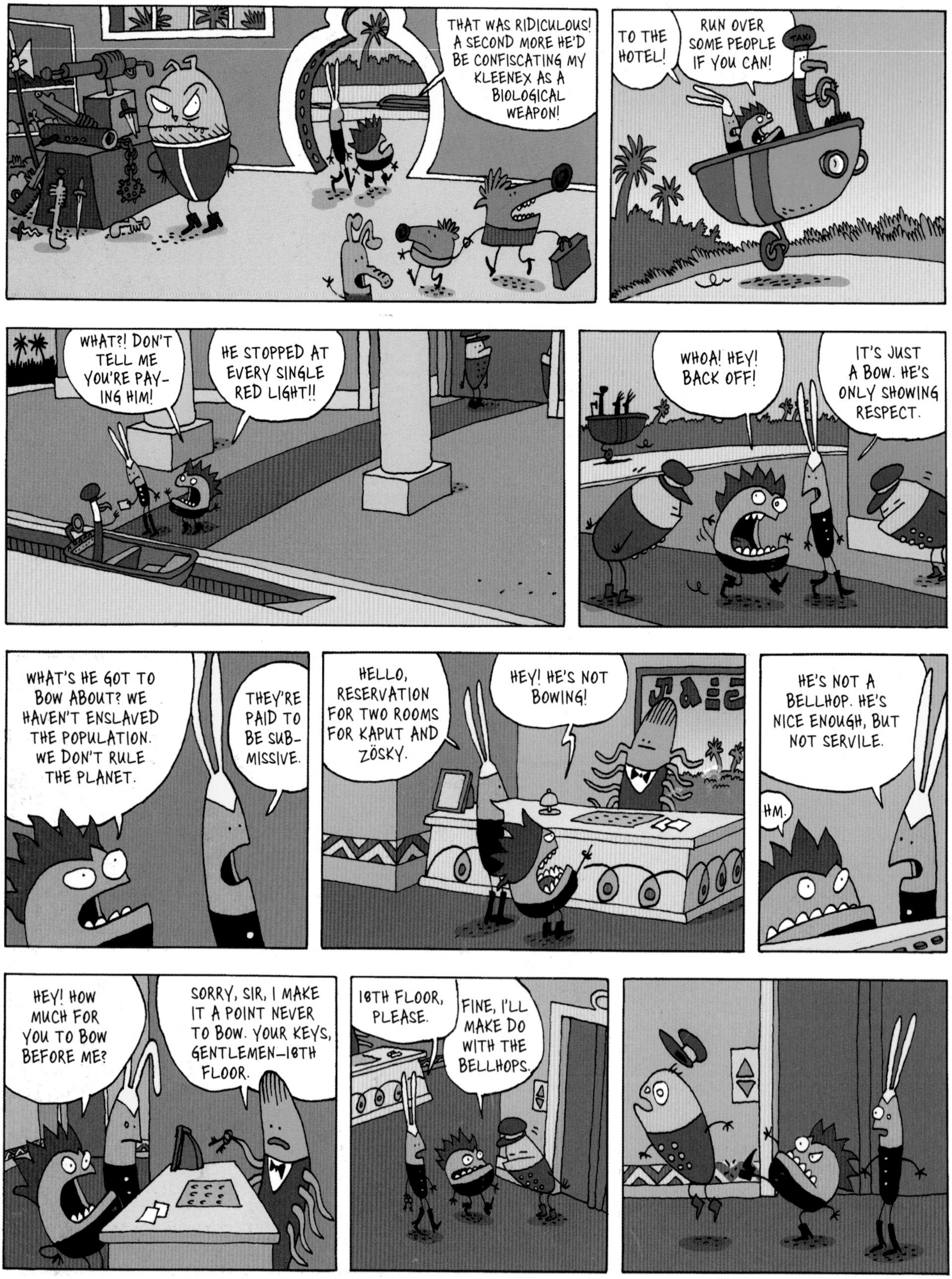
THAT WAS RIDICULOUS! A SECOND MORE HE'D BE CONFISCATING MY KLEENEX AS A BIOLOGICAL WEAPON!
TO THE HOTEL!
RUN OVER SOME PEOPLE IF YOU CAN!
TAXI
WHAT?! DON'T TELL ME YOU'RE PAY-ING HIM!
HE STOPPED AT EVERY SINGLE RED LIGHT!!
WHOA! HEY! BACK OFF!
IT'S JUST A BOW. HE'S ONLY SHOWING RESPECT.
WHAT'S HE GOT TO BOW ABOUT? WE HAVEN'T ENSLAVED THE POPULATION. WE DON'T RULE THE PLANET.
THEY'RE PAID TO BE SUB-MISSIVE.
HELLO, RESERVATION FOR TWO ROOMS FOR KAPUT AND ZÖSKY.
HEY! HE'S NOT BOWING!
HE'S NOT A BELLHOP. HE'S NICE ENOUGH, BUT NOT SERVILE.
HM.
HEY! HOW MUCH FOR YOU TO BOW BEFORE ME?
SORRY, SIR, I MAKE IT A POINT NEVER TO BOW. YOUR KEYS, GENTLEMEN—18TH FLOOR.
18TH FLOOR, PLEASE.
FINE, I'LL MAKE DO WITH THE BELLHOPS.

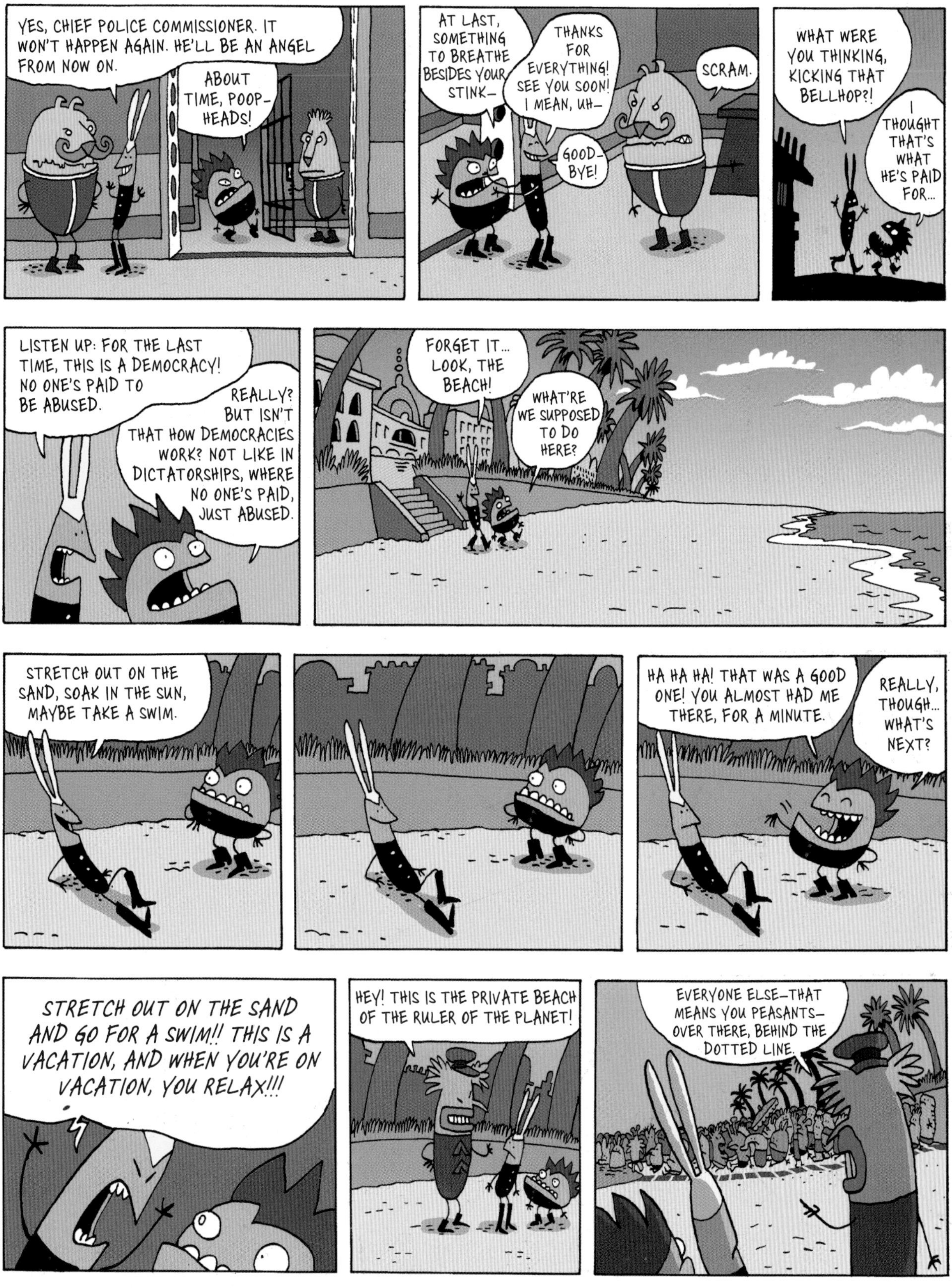
YES, CHIEF POLICE COMMISSIONER. IT WON'T HAPPEN AGAIN. HE'LL BE AN ANGEL FROM NOW ON.
ABOUT TIME, POOP-HEADS!
AT LAST, SOMETHING TO BREATHE BESIDES YOUR STINK—
THANKS FOR EVERYTHING! SEE YOU SOON! I MEAN, UH—
GOOD-BYE!
SCRAM.
WHAT WERE YOU THINKING, KICKING THAT BELLHOP?!
I THOUGHT THAT'S WHAT HE'S PAID FOR...
LISTEN UP: FOR THE LAST TIME, THIS IS A DEMOCRACY! NO ONE'S PAID TO BE ABUSED.
REALLY? BUT ISN'T THAT HOW DEMOCRACIES WORK? NOT LIKE IN DICTATORSHIPS, WHERE NO ONE'S PAID, JUST ABUSED.
FORGET IT... LOOK, THE BEACH!
WHAT'RE WE SUPPOSED TO DO HERE?
STRETCH OUT ON THE SAND, SOAK IN THE SUN, MAYBE TAKE A SWIM.
HA HA HA! THAT WAS A GOOD ONE! YOU ALMOST HAD ME THERE, FOR A MINUTE.
REALLY, THOUGH... WHAT'S NEXT?
STRETCH OUT ON THE SAND AND GO FOR A SWIM!! THIS IS A VACATION, AND WHEN YOU'RE ON VACATION, YOU RELAX!!!
HEY! THIS IS THE PRIVATE BEACH OF THE RULER OF THE PLANET!
EVERYONE ELSE—THAT MEANS YOU PEASANTS—OVER THERE, BEHIND THE DOTTED LINE.

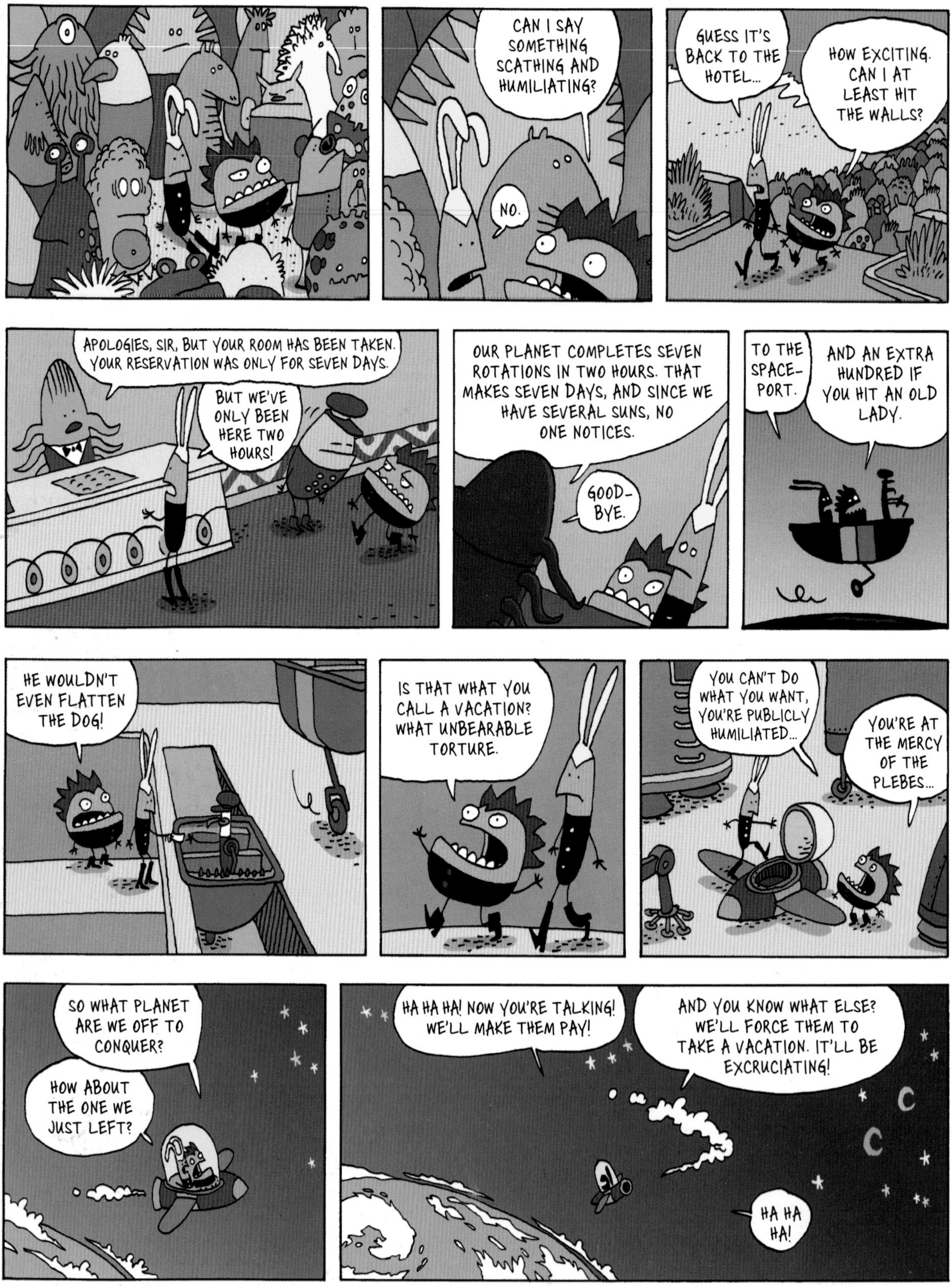
CAN I SAY SOMETHING SCATHING AND HUMILIATING?
NO.
GUESS IT'S BACK TO THE HOTEL...
HOW EXCITING. CAN I AT LEAST HIT THE WALLS?
APOLOGIES, SIR, BUT YOUR ROOM HAS BEEN TAKEN. YOUR RESERVATION WAS ONLY FOR SEVEN DAYS.
BUT WE'VE ONLY BEEN HERE TWO HOURS!
OUR PLANET COMPLETES SEVEN ROTATIONS IN TWO HOURS. THAT MAKES SEVEN DAYS, AND SINCE WE HAVE SEVERAL SUNS, NO ONE NOTICES.
GOOD-BYE.
TO THE SPACE-PORT.
AND AN EXTRA HUNDRED IF YOU HIT AN OLD LADY.
HE WOULDN'T EVEN FLATTEN THE DOG!
IS THAT WHAT YOU CALL A VACATION? WHAT UNBEARABLE TORTURE.
YOU CAN'T DO WHAT YOU WANT, YOU'RE PUBLICLY HUMILIATED...
YOU'RE AT THE MERCY OF THE PLEBES...
SO WHAT PLANET ARE WE OFF TO CONQUER?
HOW ABOUT THE ONE WE JUST LEFT?
HA HA HA! NOW YOU'RE TALKING! WE'LL MAKE THEM PAY!
AND YOU KNOW WHAT ELSE? WE'LL FORCE THEM TO TAKE A VACATION. IT'LL BE EXCRUCIATING!
HA HA HA!

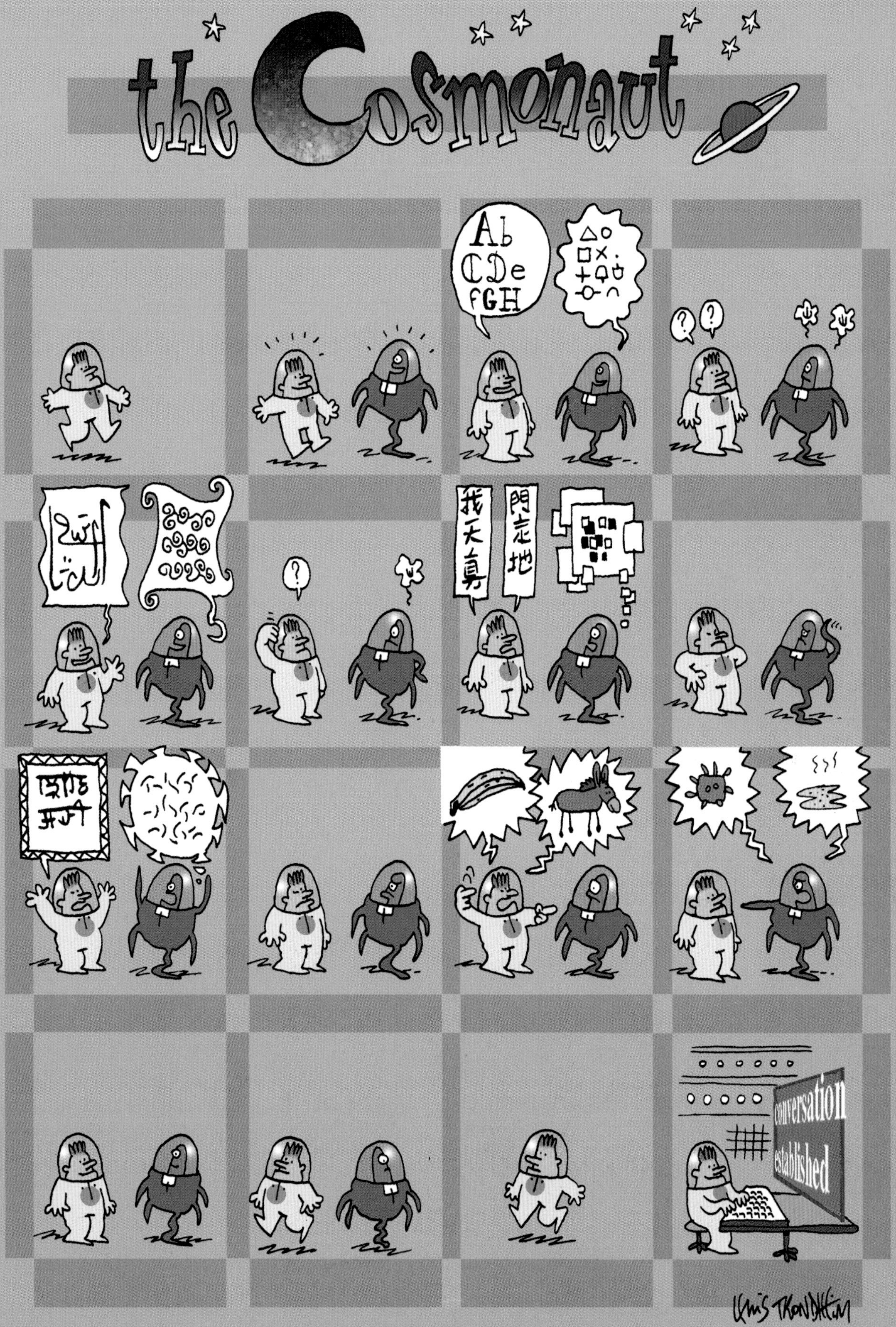
the Cosmonaut
Ab CDe fGH
conversation established

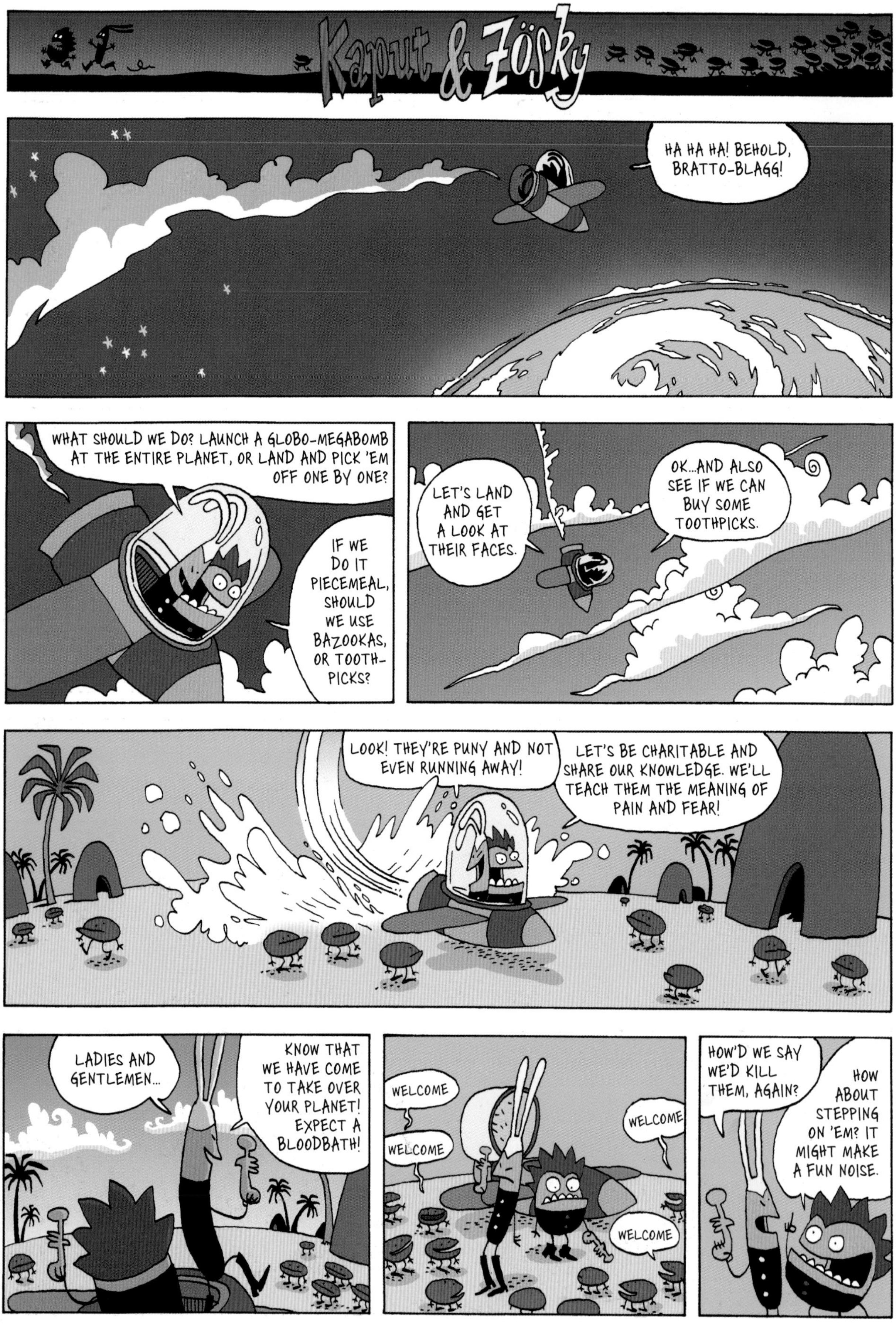

Kaput & Zösky
HA HA HA! BEHOLD, BRATTO-BLAGG!
WHAT SHOULD WE DO? LAUNCH A GLOBO-MEGABOMB AT THE ENTIRE PLANET, OR LAND AND PICK 'EM OFF ONE BY ONE?
IF WE DO IT PIECEMEAL, SHOULD WE USE BAZOOKAS, OR TOOTH-PICKS?
LET'S LAND AND GET A LOOK AT THEIR FACES.
OK...AND ALSO SEE IF WE CAN BUY SOME TOOTHPICKS.
LOOK! THEY'RE PUNY AND NOT EVEN RUNNING AWAY!
LET'S BE CHARITABLE AND SHARE OUR KNOWLEDGE. WE'LL TEACH THEM THE MEANING OF PAIN AND FEAR!
LADIES AND GENTLEMEN...
KNOW THAT WE HAVE COME TO TAKE OVER YOUR PLANET! EXPECT A BLOODBATH!
WELCOME
WELCOME
WELCOME
WELCOME
HOW'D WE SAY WE'D KILL THEM, AGAIN?
HOW ABOUT STEPPING ON 'EM? IT MIGHT MAKE A FUN NOISE.

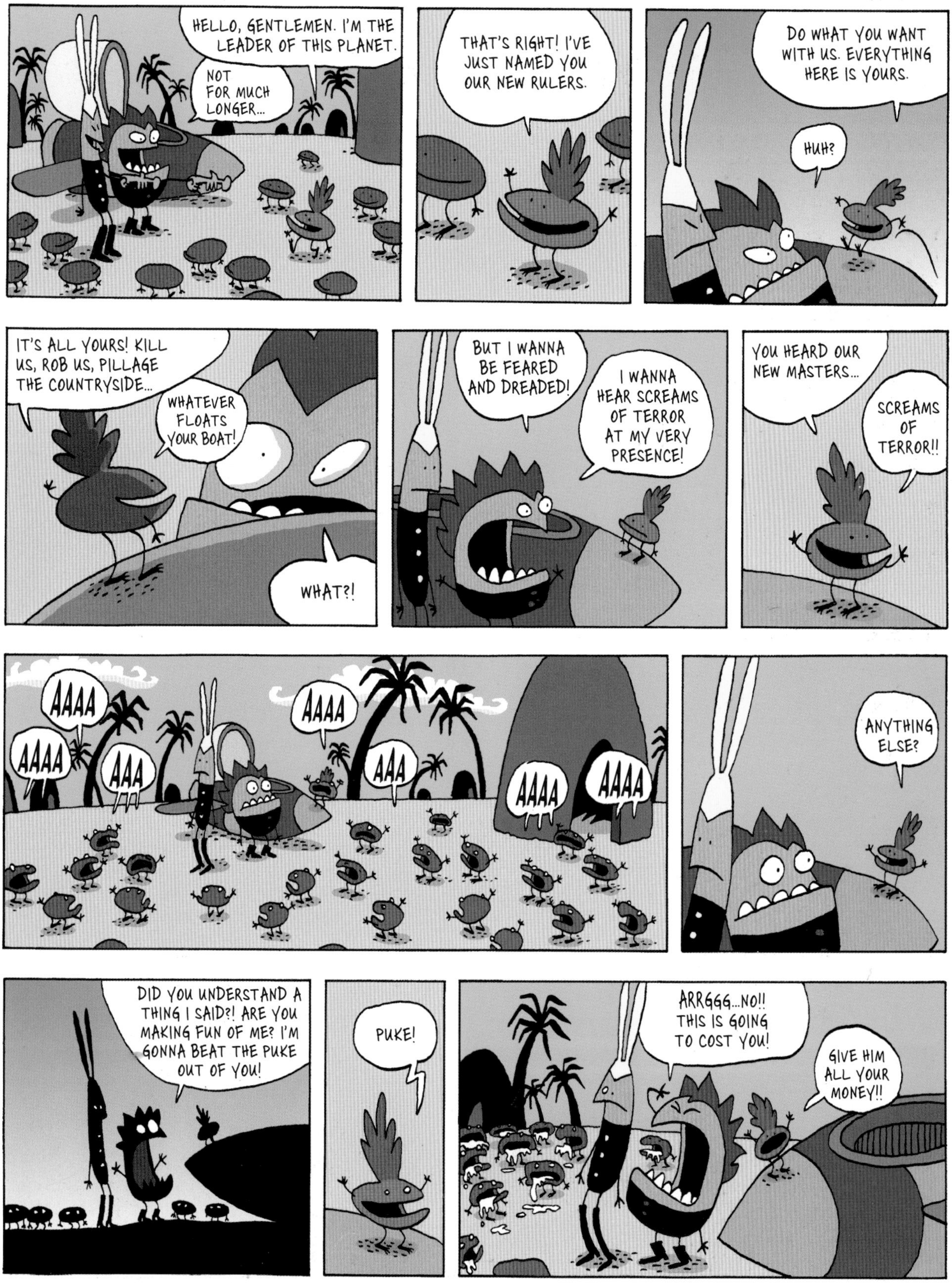
HELLO, GENTLEMEN. I'M THE LEADER OF THIS PLANET.
NOT FOR MUCH LONGER...
THAT'S RIGHT! I'VE JUST NAMED YOU OUR NEW RULERS.
DO WHAT YOU WANT WITH US. EVERYTHING HERE IS YOURS.
HUH?
IT'S ALL YOURS! KILL US, ROB US, PILLAGE THE COUNTRYSIDE...
WHATEVER FLOATS YOUR BOAT!
WHAT?!
BUT I WANNA BE FEARED AND DREADED!
I WANNA HEAR SCREAMS OF TERROR AT MY VERY PRESENCE!
YOU HEARD OUR NEW MASTERS...
SCREAMS OF TERROR!!
AAAA
AAAA
AAA
AAAA
AAA
AAAA
AAAA
ANYTHING ELSE?
DID YOU UNDERSTAND A THING I SAID?! ARE YOU MAKING FUN OF ME? I'M GONNA BEAT THE PUKE OUT OF YOU!
PUKE!
ARRGGG...NO!! THIS IS GOING TO COST YOU!
GIVE HIM ALL YOUR MONEY!!

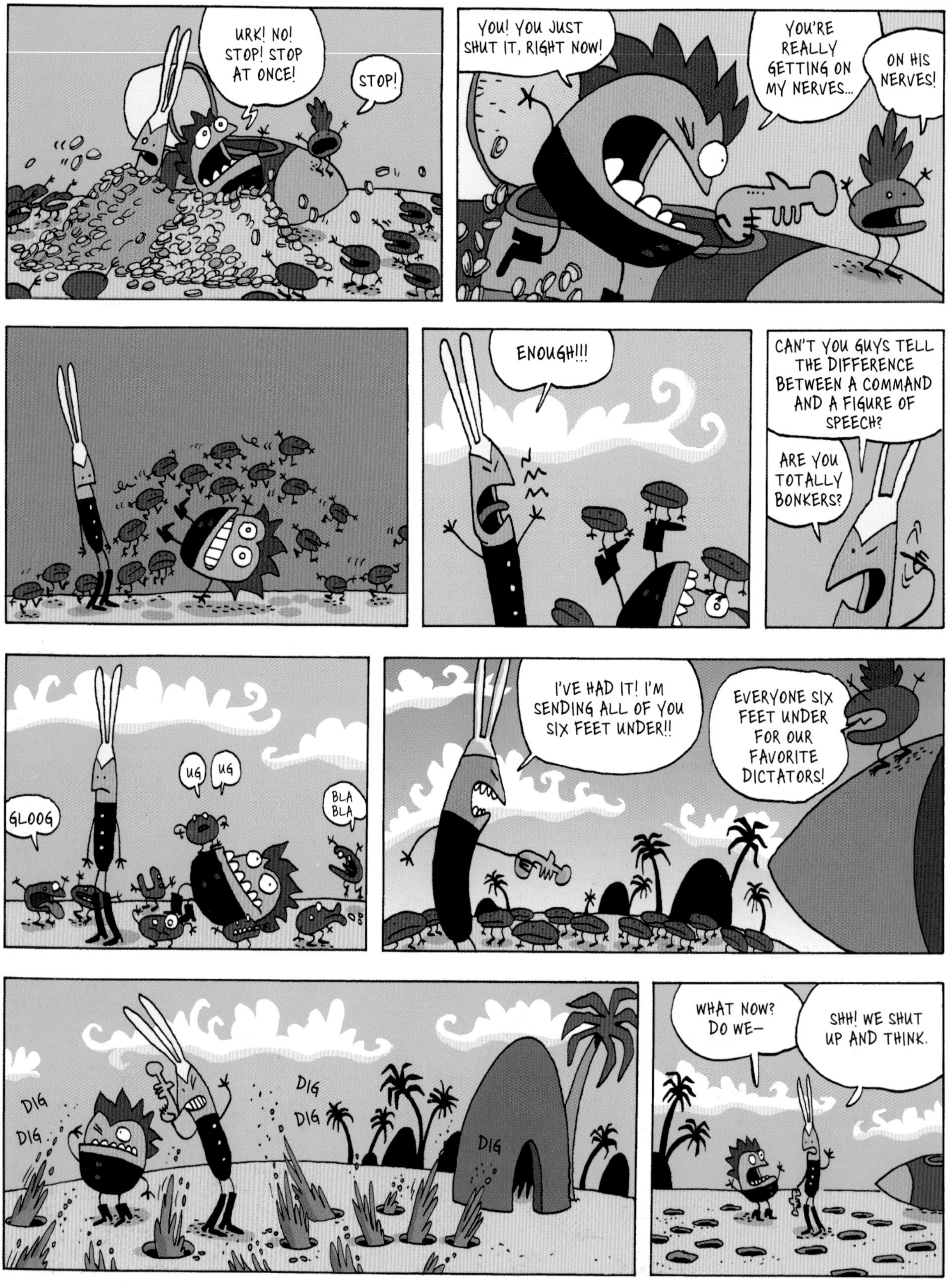
URK! NO! STOP! STOP AT ONCE!
STOP!
YOU! YOU JUST SHUT IT, RIGHT NOW!
YOU'RE REALLY GETTING ON MY NERVES...
ON HIS NERVES!
ENOUGH!!!
CAN'T YOU GUYS TELL THE DIFFERENCE BETWEEN A COMMAND AND A FIGURE OF SPEECH?
ARE YOU TOTALLY BONKERS?
GLOOG
UG
UG
BLA BLA
I'VE HAD IT! I'M SENDING ALL OF YOU SIX FEET UNDER!!
EVERYONE SIX FEET UNDER FOR OUR FAVORITE DICTATORS!
DIG
DIG
DIG
DIG
DIG
WHAT NOW? DO WE–
SHH! WE SHUT UP AND THINK.

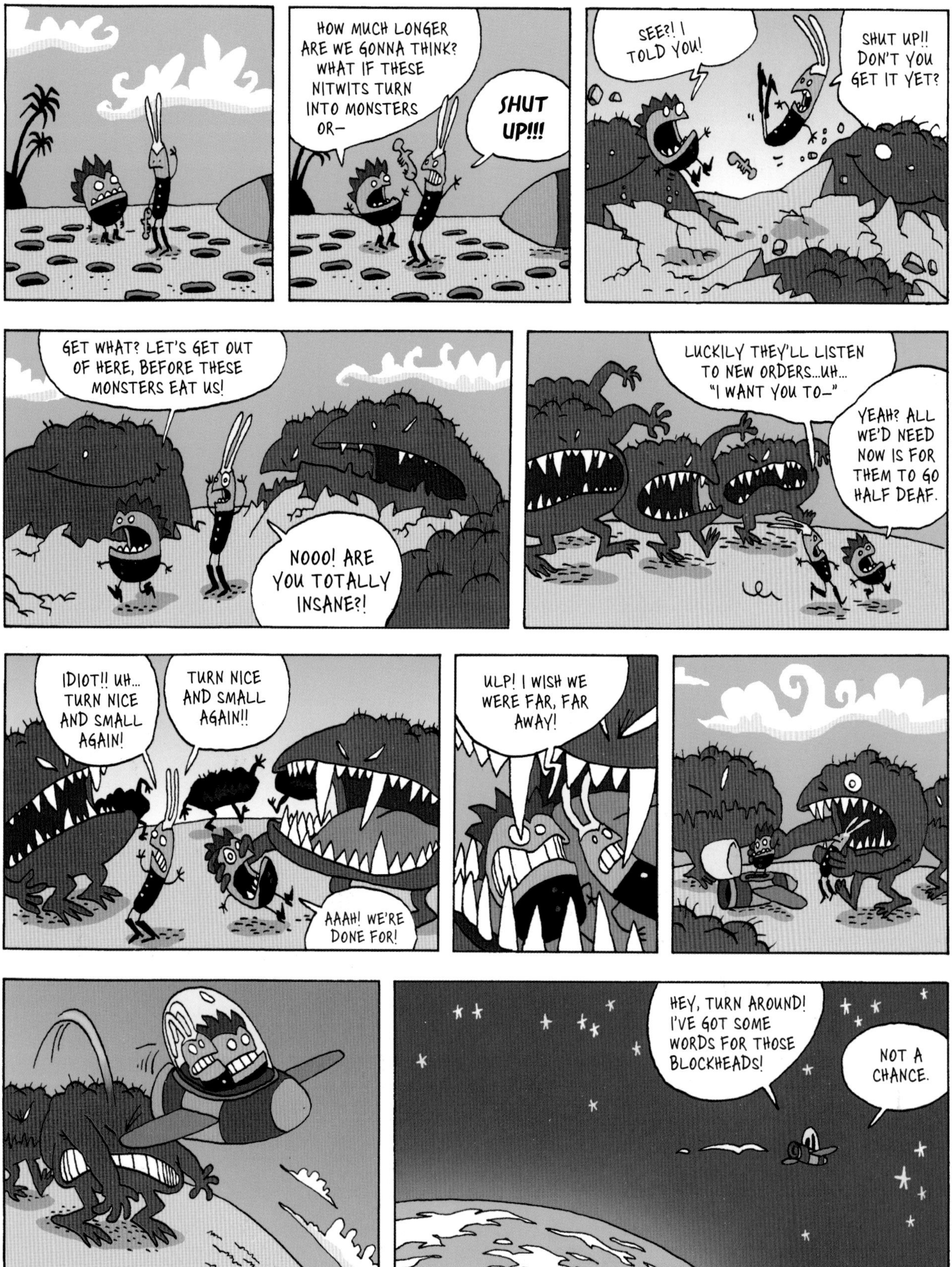
HOW MUCH LONGER ARE WE GONNA THINK? WHAT IF THESE NITWITS TURN INTO MONSTERS OR—
SHUT UP!!!
SEE?! I TOLD YOU!
SHUT UP!! DON'T YOU GET IT YET?
GET WHAT? LET'S GET OUT OF HERE, BEFORE THESE MONSTERS EAT US!
NOOO! ARE YOU TOTALLY INSANE?!
LUCKILY THEY'LL LISTEN TO NEW ORDERS...UH... "I WANT YOU TO—"
YEAH? ALL WE'D NEED NOW IS FOR THEM TO GO HALF DEAF.
IDIOT!! UH... TURN NICE AND SMALL AGAIN!
TURN NICE AND SMALL AGAIN!!
AAAH! WE'RE DONE FOR!
ULP! I WISH WE WERE FAR, FAR AWAY!
HEY, TURN AROUND! I'VE GOT SOME WORDS FOR THOSE BLOCKHEADS!
NOT A CHANCE.

the Cosmonaut

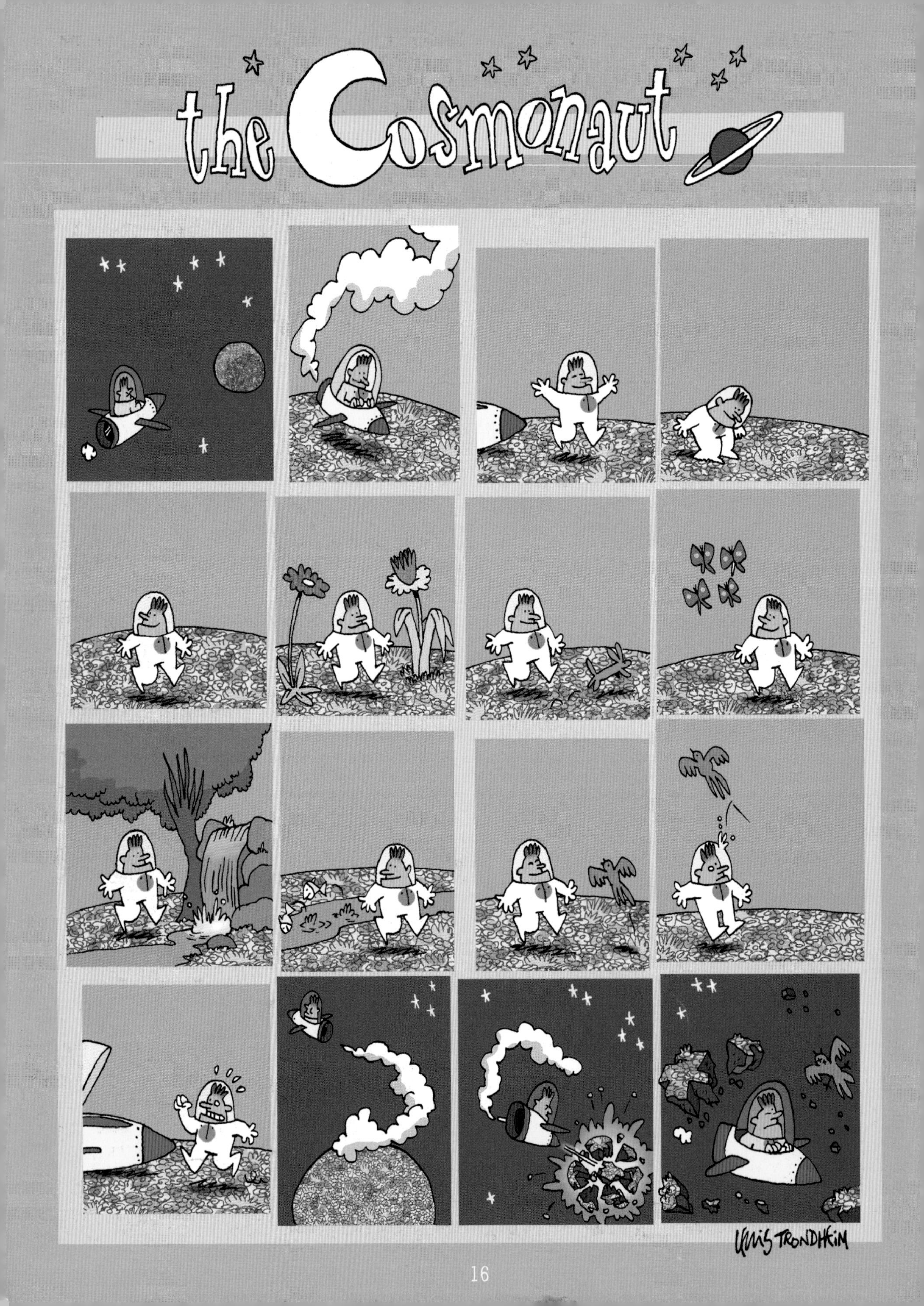
LEWIS TRONDHEIM

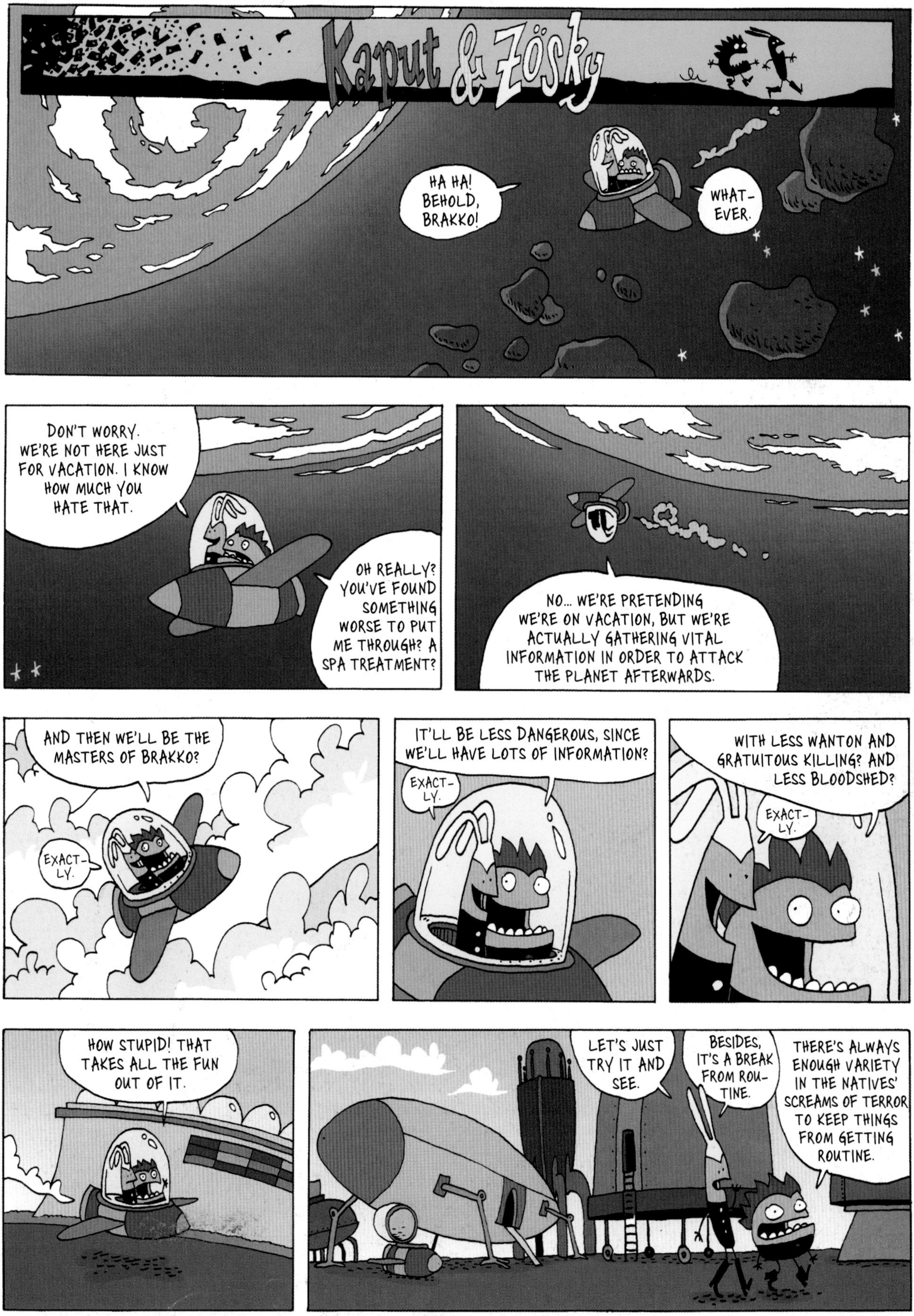
Kaput & Zösky
HA HA! BEHOLD, BRAKKO!
WHAT-EVER.
DON'T WORRY. WE'RE NOT HERE JUST FOR VACATION. I KNOW HOW MUCH YOU HATE THAT.
OH REALLY? YOU'VE FOUND SOMETHING WORSE TO PUT ME THROUGH? A SPA TREATMENT?
NO... WE'RE PRETENDING WE'RE ON VACATION, BUT WE'RE ACTUALLY GATHERING VITAL INFORMATION IN ORDER TO ATTACK THE PLANET AFTERWARDS.
AND THEN WE'LL BE THE MASTERS OF BRAKKO?
EXACT-LY.
IT'LL BE LESS DANGEROUS, SINCE WE'LL HAVE LOTS OF INFORMATION?
EXACT-LY.
WITH LESS WANTON AND GRATUITOUS KILLING? AND LESS BLOODSHED?
EXACT-LY.
HOW STUPID! THAT TAKES ALL THE FUN OUT OF IT.
LET'S JUST TRY IT AND SEE.
BESIDES, IT'S A BREAK FROM ROU-TINE.
THERE'S ALWAYS ENOUGH VARIETY IN THE NATIVES' SCREAMS OF TERROR TO KEEP THINGS FROM GETTING ROUTINE.

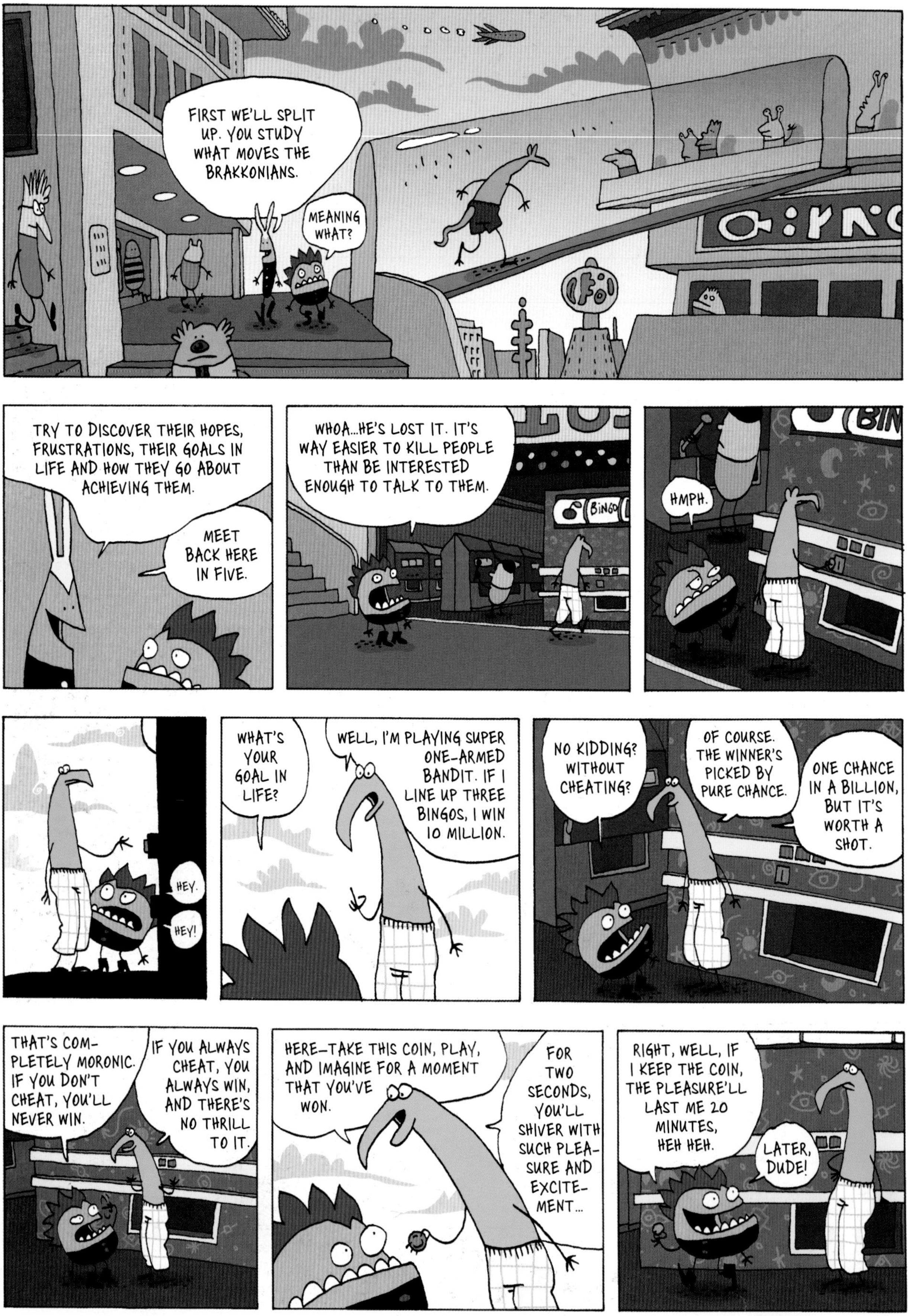

FIRST WE'LL SPLIT UP. YOU STUDY WHAT MOVES THE BRAKKONIANS.
MEANING WHAT?
TRY TO DISCOVER THEIR HOPES, FRUSTRATIONS, THEIR GOALS IN LIFE AND HOW THEY GO ABOUT ACHIEVING THEM.
MEET BACK HERE IN FIVE.
WHOA...HE'S LOST IT. IT'S WAY EASIER TO KILL PEOPLE THAN BE INTERESTED ENOUGH TO TALK TO THEM.
BINGO
HMPH.
HEY.
HEY!
WHAT'S YOUR GOAL IN LIFE?
WELL, I'M PLAYING SUPER ONE-ARMED BANDIT. IF I LINE UP THREE BINGOS, I WIN 10 MILLION.
NO KIDDING? WITHOUT CHEATING?
OF COURSE. THE WINNER'S PICKED BY PURE CHANCE.
ONE CHANCE IN A BILLION, BUT IT'S WORTH A SHOT.
THAT'S COMPLETELY MORONIC. IF YOU DON'T CHEAT, YOU'LL NEVER WIN.
IF YOU ALWAYS CHEAT, YOU ALWAYS WIN, AND THERE'S NO THRILL TO IT.
HERE—TAKE THIS COIN, PLAY, AND IMAGINE FOR A MOMENT THAT YOU'VE WON.
FOR TWO SECONDS, YOU'LL SHIVER WITH SUCH PLEASURE AND EXCITEMENT...
RIGHT, WELL, IF I KEEP THE COIN, THE PLEASURE'LL LAST ME 20 MINUTES, HEH HEH.
LATER, DUDE!

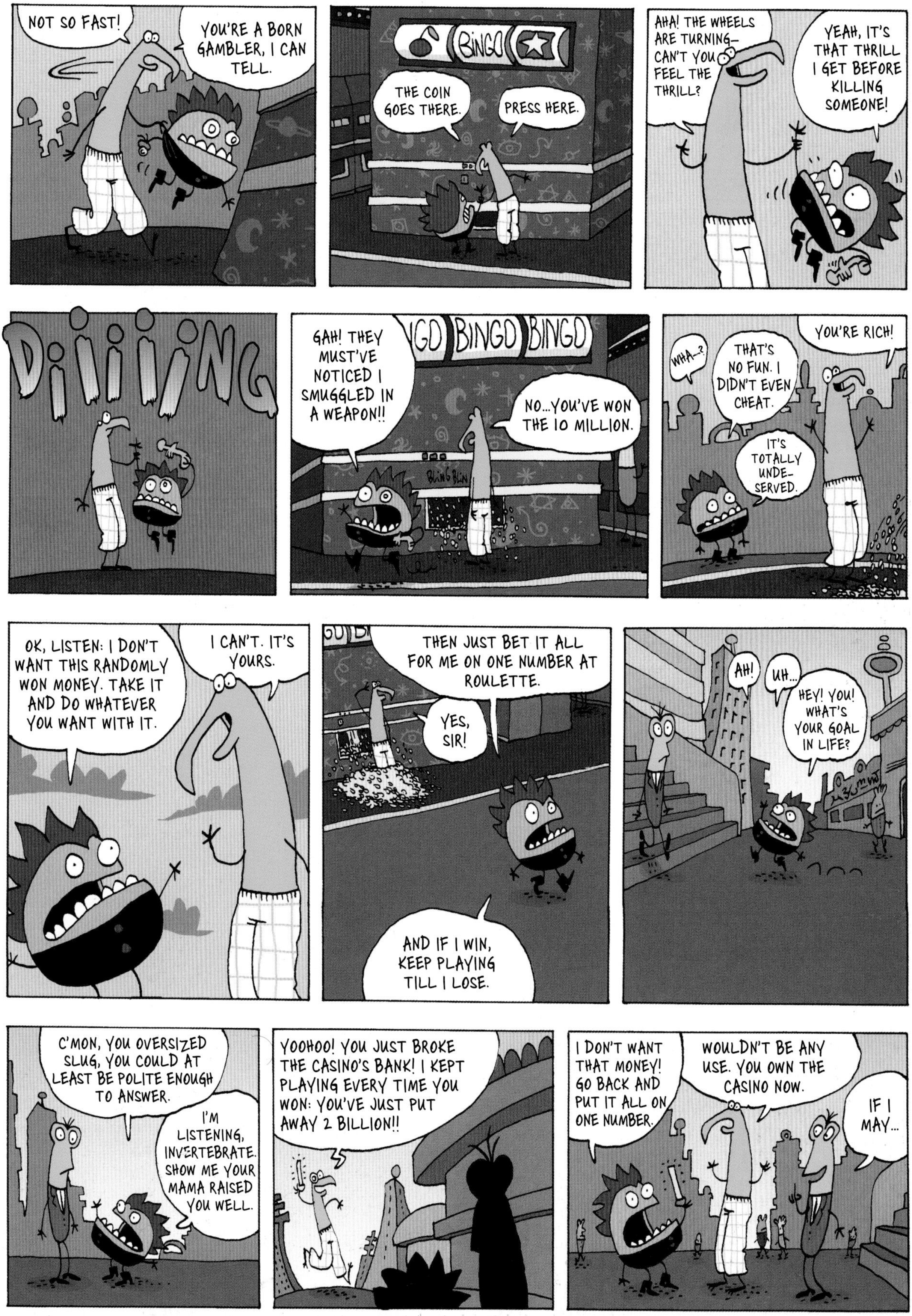
NOT SO FAST!
YOU'RE A BORN GAMBLER, I CAN TELL.
BINGO
THE COIN GOES THERE.
PRESS HERE.
AHA! THE WHEELS ARE TURNING— CAN'T YOU FEEL THE THRILL?
YEAH, IT'S THAT THRILL I GET BEFORE KILLING SOMEONE!
DIIIIING
GAH! THEY MUST'VE NOTICED I SMUGGLED IN A WEAPON!!
NO...YOU'VE WON THE 10 MILLION.
WHA—?
THAT'S NO FUN. I DIDN'T EVEN CHEAT.
YOU'RE RICH!
IT'S TOTALLY UNDE-SERVED.
OK, LISTEN: I DON'T WANT THIS RANDOMLY WON MONEY. TAKE IT AND DO WHATEVER YOU WANT WITH IT.
I CAN'T. IT'S YOURS.
THEN JUST BET IT ALL FOR ME ON ONE NUMBER AT ROULETTE.
YES, SIR!
AND IF I WIN, KEEP PLAYING TILL I LOSE.
AH!
UH...
HEY! YOU! WHAT'S YOUR GOAL IN LIFE?
C'MON, YOU OVERSIZED SLUG, YOU COULD AT LEAST BE POLITE ENOUGH TO ANSWER.
I'M LISTENING, INVERTEBRATE. SHOW ME YOUR MAMA RAISED YOU WELL.
YOOHOO! YOU JUST BROKE THE CASINO'S BANK! I KEPT PLAYING EVERY TIME YOU WON: YOU'VE JUST PUT AWAY 2 BILLION!!
I DON'T WANT THAT MONEY! GO BACK AND PUT IT ALL ON ONE NUMBER.
WOULDN'T BE ANY USE. YOU OWN THE CASINO NOW.
IF I MAY...

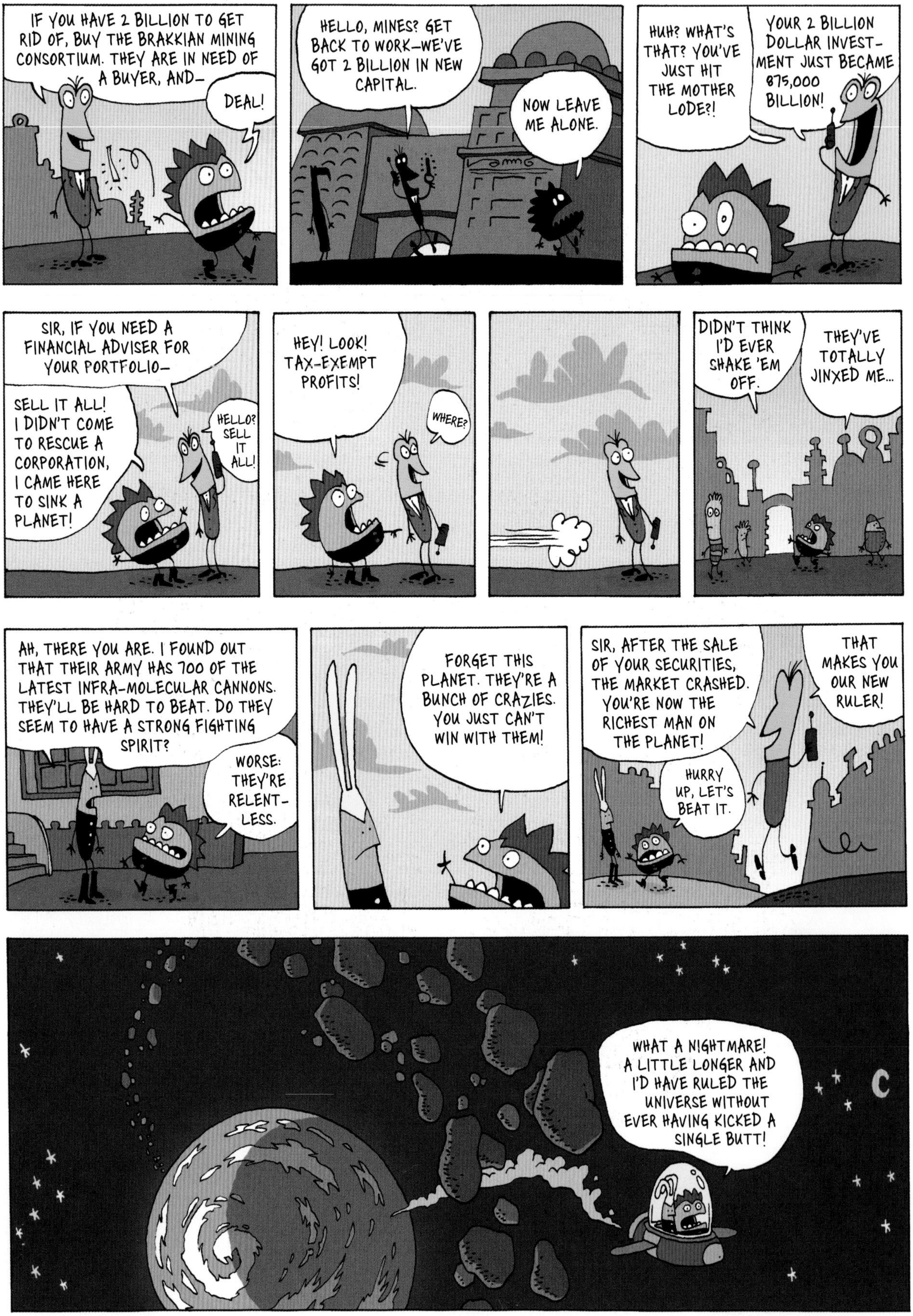
IF YOU HAVE 2 BILLION TO GET RID OF, BUY THE BRAKKIAN MINING CONSORTIUM. THEY ARE IN NEED OF A BUYER, AND—
DEAL!
HELLO, MINES? GET BACK TO WORK—WE'VE GOT 2 BILLION IN NEW CAPITAL.
NOW LEAVE ME ALONE.
HUH? WHAT'S THAT? YOU'VE JUST HIT THE MOTHER LODE?!
YOUR 2 BILLION DOLLAR INVEST-MENT JUST BECAME 875,000 BILLION!
SIR, IF YOU NEED A FINANCIAL ADVISER FOR YOUR PORTFOLIO—
SELL IT ALL! I DIDN'T COME TO RESCUE A CORPORATION, I CAME HERE TO SINK A PLANET!
HELLO? SELL IT ALL!
HEY! LOOK! TAX-EXEMPT PROFITS!
WHERE?
DIDN'T THINK I'D EVER SHAKE 'EM OFF.
THEY'VE TOTALLY JINXED ME...
AH, THERE YOU ARE. I FOUND OUT THAT THEIR ARMY HAS 700 OF THE LATEST INFRA-MOLECULAR CANNONS. THEY'LL BE HARD TO BEAT. DO THEY SEEM TO HAVE A STRONG FIGHTING SPIRIT?
WORSE: THEY'RE RELENT-LESS.
FORGET THIS PLANET. THEY'RE A BUNCH OF CRAZIES. YOU JUST CAN'T WIN WITH THEM!
SIR, AFTER THE SALE OF YOUR SECURITIES, THE MARKET CRASHED. YOU'RE NOW THE RICHEST MAN ON THE PLANET!
THAT MAKES YOU OUR NEW RULER!
HURRY UP, LET'S BEAT IT.
WHAT A NIGHTMARE! A LITTLE LONGER AND I'D HAVE RULED THE UNIVERSE WITHOUT EVER HAVING KICKED A SINGLE BUTT!

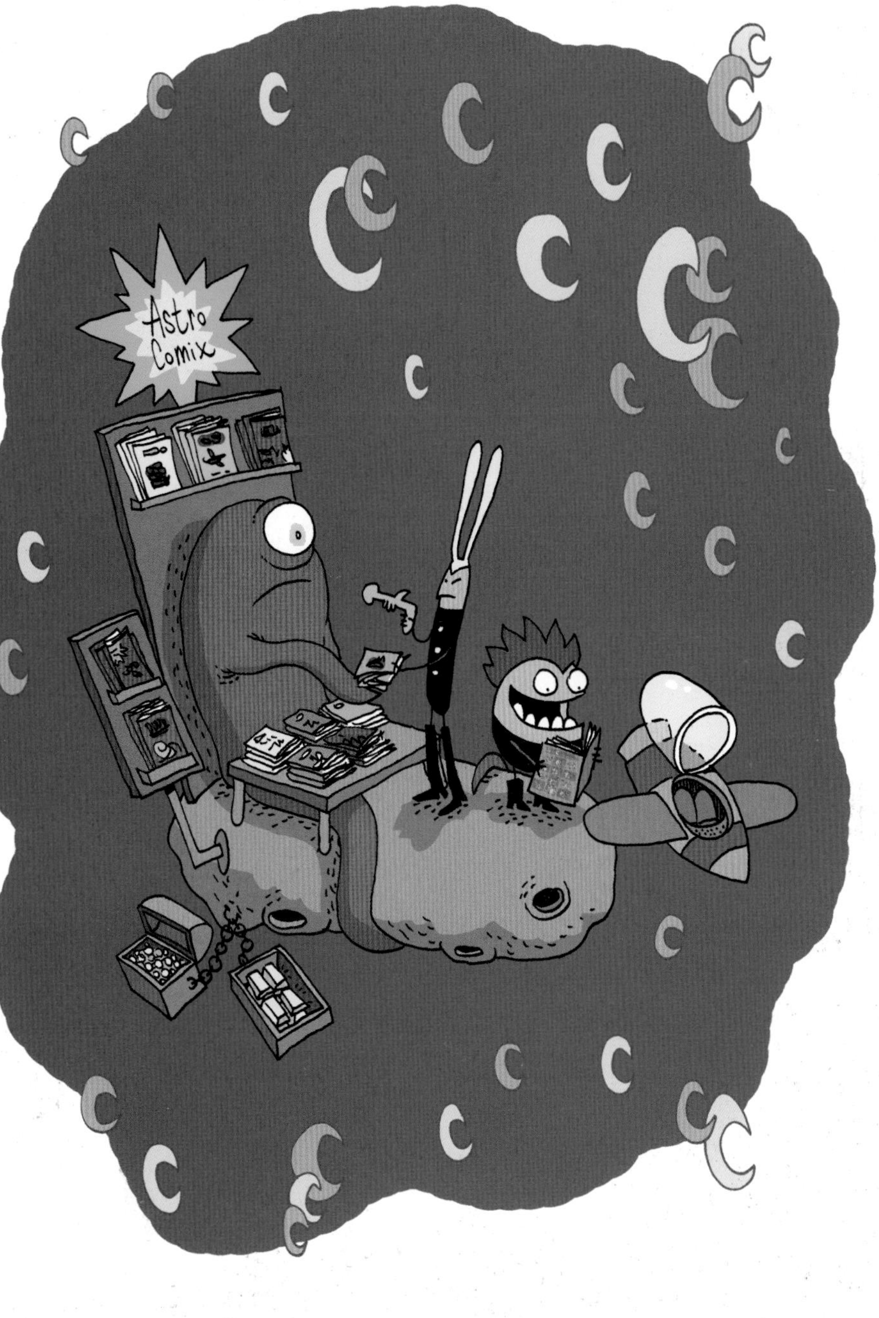
Astro Comix

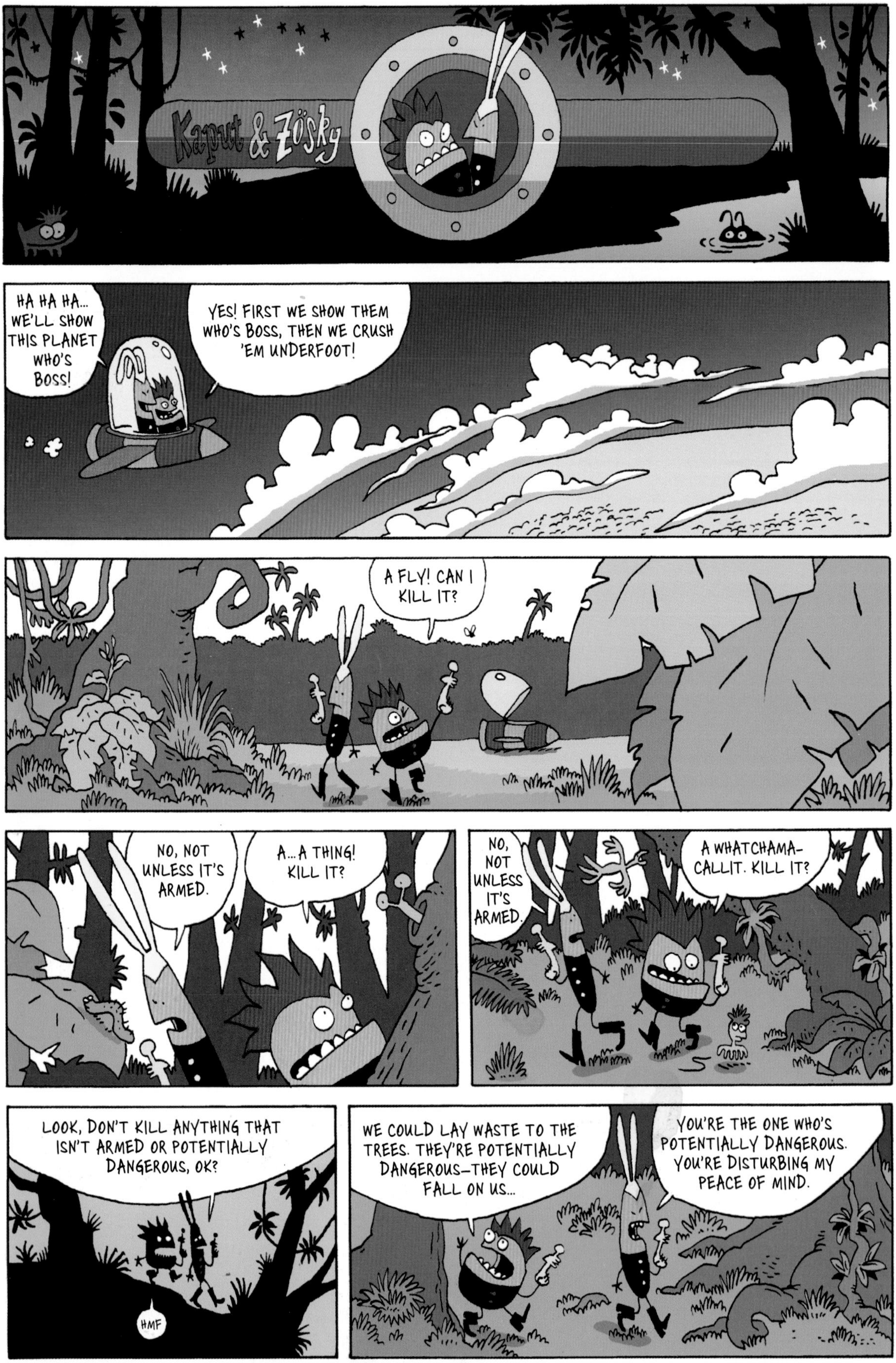
Kaput & Zösky
HA HA HA... WE'LL SHOW THIS PLANET WHO'S BOSS!
YES! FIRST WE SHOW THEM WHO'S BOSS, THEN WE CRUSH 'EM UNDERFOOT!
A FLY! CAN I KILL IT?
NO, NOT UNLESS IT'S ARMED.
A... A THING! KILL IT?
NO, NOT UNLESS IT'S ARMED.
A WHATCHAMA-CALLIT. KILL IT?
LOOK, DON'T KILL ANYTHING THAT ISN'T ARMED OR POTENTIALLY DANGEROUS, OK?
HMF
WE COULD LAY WASTE TO THE TREES. THEY'RE POTENTIALLY DANGEROUS—THEY COULD FALL ON US...
YOU'RE THE ONE WHO'S POTENTIALLY DANGEROUS. YOU'RE DISTURBING MY PEACE OF MIND.

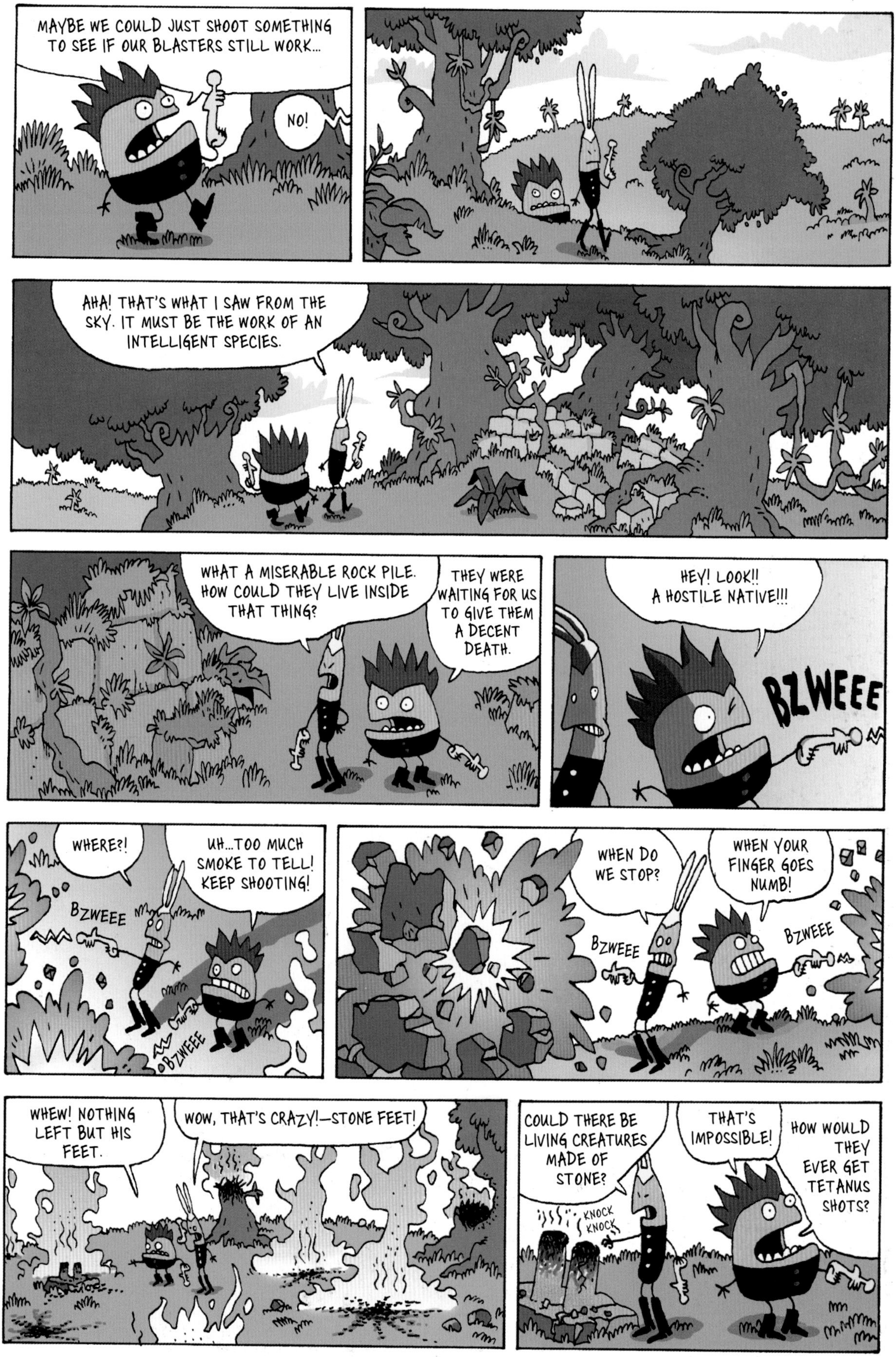
MAYBE WE COULD JUST SHOOT SOMETHING TO SEE IF OUR BLASTERS STILL WORK...
NO!
AHA! THAT'S WHAT I SAW FROM THE SKY. IT MUST BE THE WORK OF AN INTELLIGENT SPECIES.
WHAT A MISERABLE ROCK PILE. HOW COULD THEY LIVE INSIDE THAT THING?
THEY WERE WAITING FOR US TO GIVE THEM A DECENT DEATH.
HEY! LOOK!! A HOSTILE NATIVE!!!
BZWEEE
WHERE?!
UH...TOO MUCH SMOKE TO TELL! KEEP SHOOTING!
BZWEEE
BZWEEE
WHEN DO WE STOP?
WHEN YOUR FINGER GOES NUMB!
BZWEEE
BZWEEE
WHEW! NOTHING LEFT BUT HIS FEET.
WOW, THAT'S CRAZY!—STONE FEET!
COULD THERE BE LIVING CREATURES MADE OF STONE?
KNOCK KNOCK
THAT'S IMPOSSIBLE!
HOW WOULD THEY EVER GET TETANUS SHOTS?

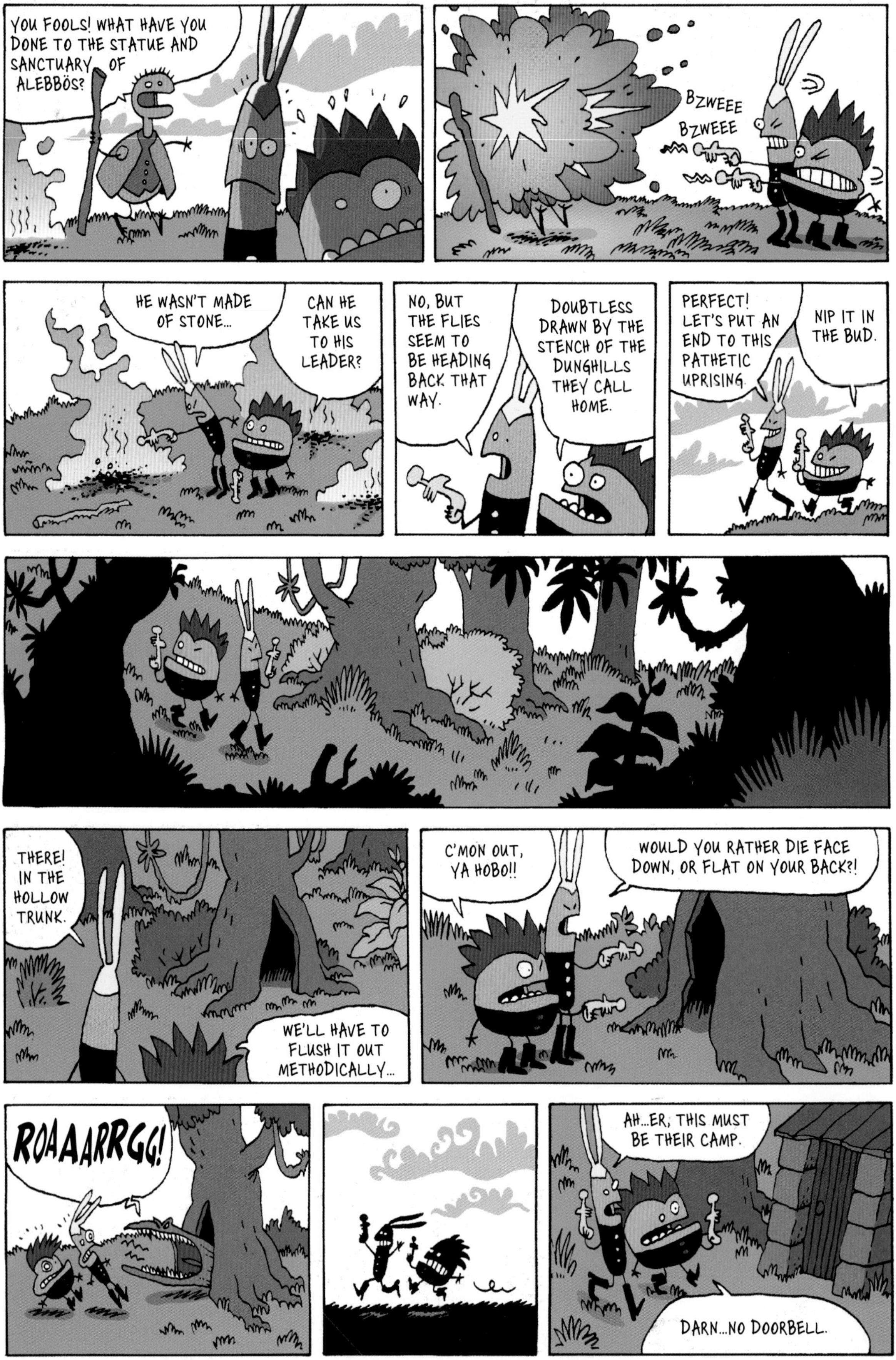
YOU FOOLS! WHAT HAVE YOU DONE TO THE STATUE AND SANCTUARY OF ALEBBÖS?
BZWEEE
BZWEEE
HE WASN'T MADE OF STONE...
CAN HE TAKE US TO HIS LEADER?
NO, BUT THE FLIES SEEM TO BE HEADING BACK THAT WAY.
DOUBTLESS DRAWN BY THE STENCH OF THE DUNGHILLS THEY CALL HOME.
PERFECT! LET'S PUT AN END TO THIS PATHETIC UPRISING.
NIP IT IN THE BUD.
THERE! IN THE HOLLOW TRUNK.
WE'LL HAVE TO FLUSH IT OUT METHODICALLY...
C'MON OUT, YA HOBO!!
WOULD YOU RATHER DIE FACE DOWN, OR FLAT ON YOUR BACK?!
ROAAARRGG!
AH...ER, THIS MUST BE THEIR CAMP.
DARN...NO DOORBELL.

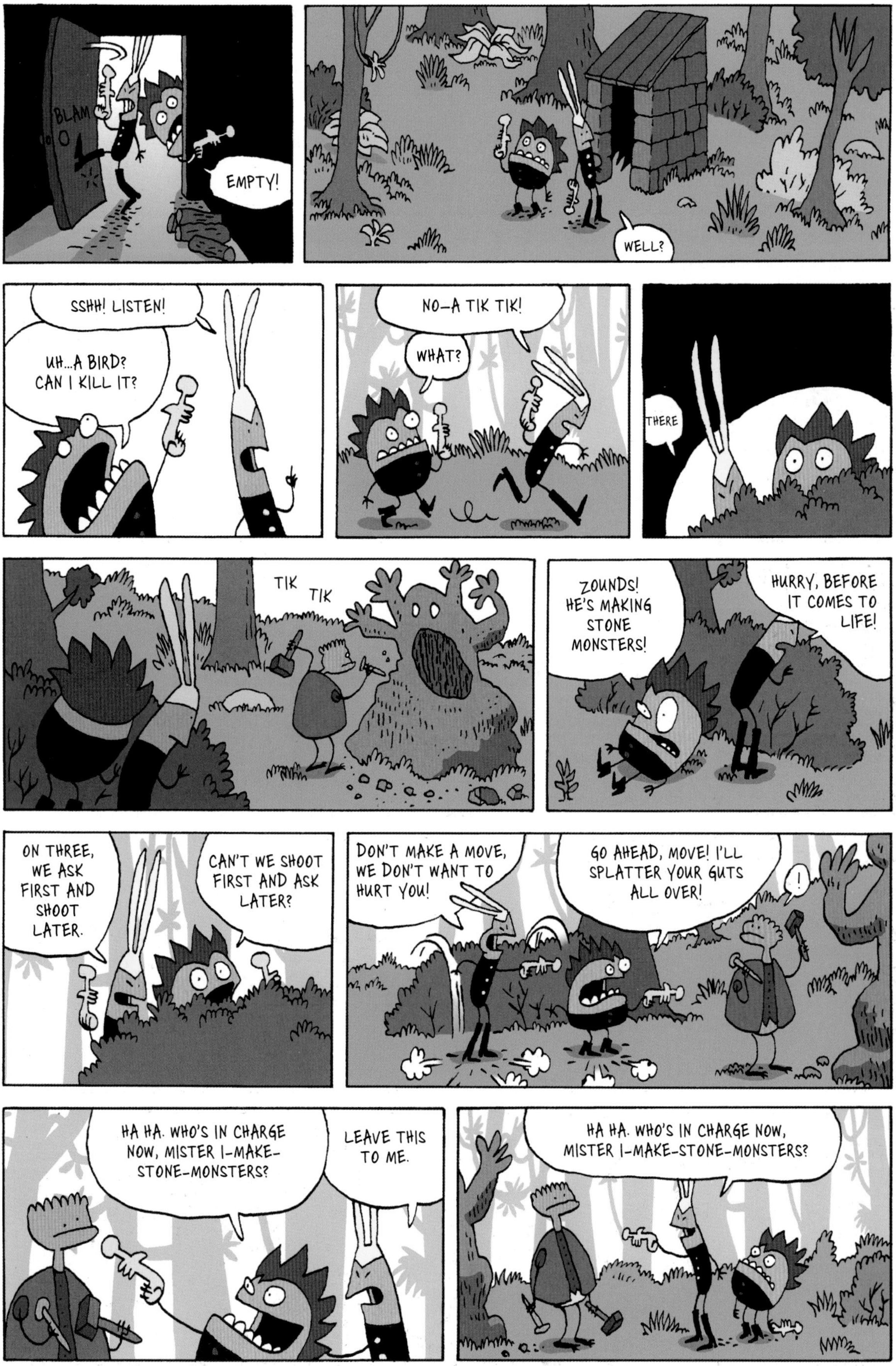
BLAM
EMPTY!
WELL?
SSHH! LISTEN!
UH...A BIRD? CAN I KILL IT?
NO—A TIK TIK!
WHAT?
THERE
TIK
TIK
ZOUNDS! HE'S MAKING STONE MONSTERS!
HURRY, BEFORE IT COMES TO LIFE!
ON THREE, WE ASK FIRST AND SHOOT LATER.
CAN'T WE SHOOT FIRST AND ASK LATER?
DON'T MAKE A MOVE, WE DON'T WANT TO HURT YOU!
GO AHEAD, MOVE! I'LL SPLATTER YOUR GUTS ALL OVER!
!
HA HA. WHO'S IN CHARGE NOW, MISTER I-MAKE-STONE-MONSTERS?
LEAVE THIS TO ME.
HA HA. WHO'S IN CHARGE NOW, MISTER I-MAKE-STONE-MONSTERS?

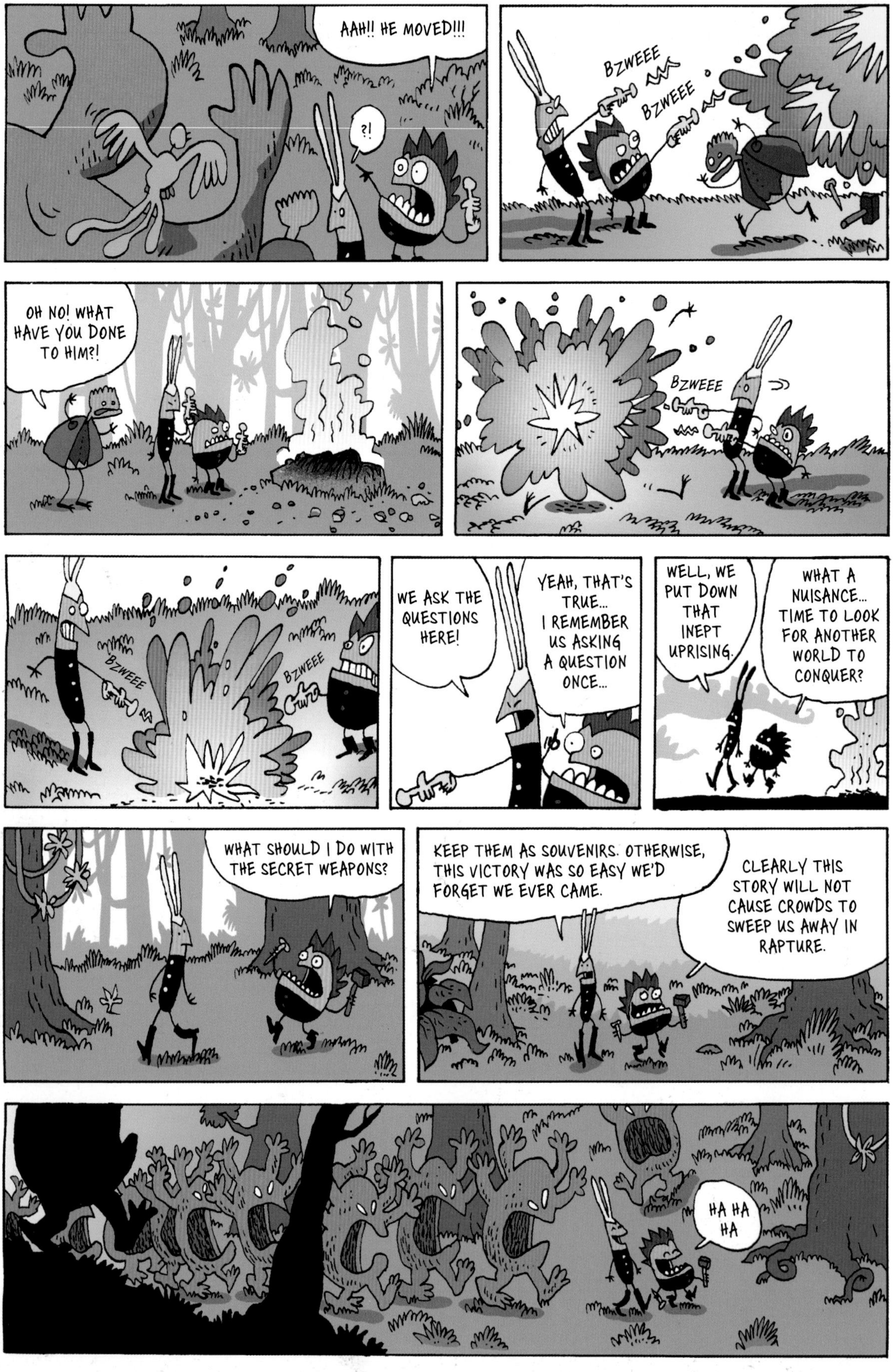
AAH!! HE MOVED!!!
?!
BZWEEE
BZWEEE
OH NO! WHAT HAVE YOU DONE TO HIM?!
BZWEEE
BZWEEE
BZWEEE
WE ASK THE QUESTIONS HERE!
YEAH, THAT'S TRUE... I REMEMBER US ASKING A QUESTION ONCE...
WELL, WE PUT DOWN THAT INEPT UPRISING.
WHAT A NUISANCE... TIME TO LOOK FOR ANOTHER WORLD TO CONQUER?
WHAT SHOULD I DO WITH THE SECRET WEAPONS?
KEEP THEM AS SOUVENIRS. OTHERWISE, THIS VICTORY WAS SO EASY WE'D FORGET WE EVER CAME.
CLEARLY THIS STORY WILL NOT CAUSE CROWDS TO SWEEP US AWAY IN RAPTURE.
HA HA HA

the Cosmonaut

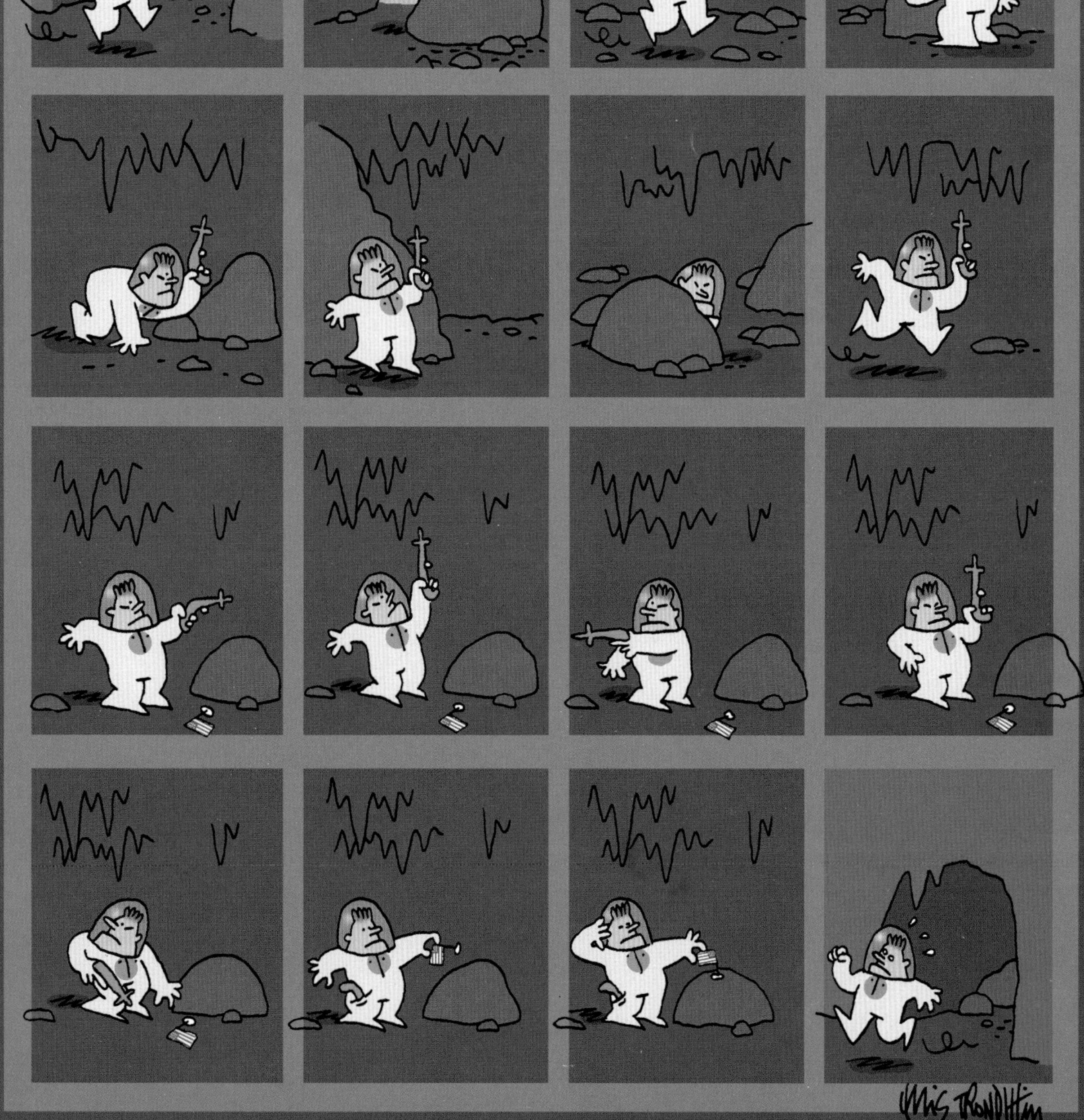

TRONDHEIM

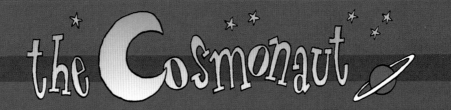

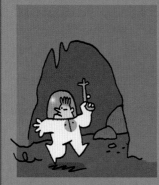

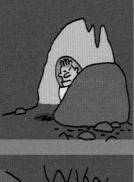

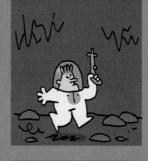

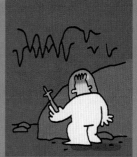

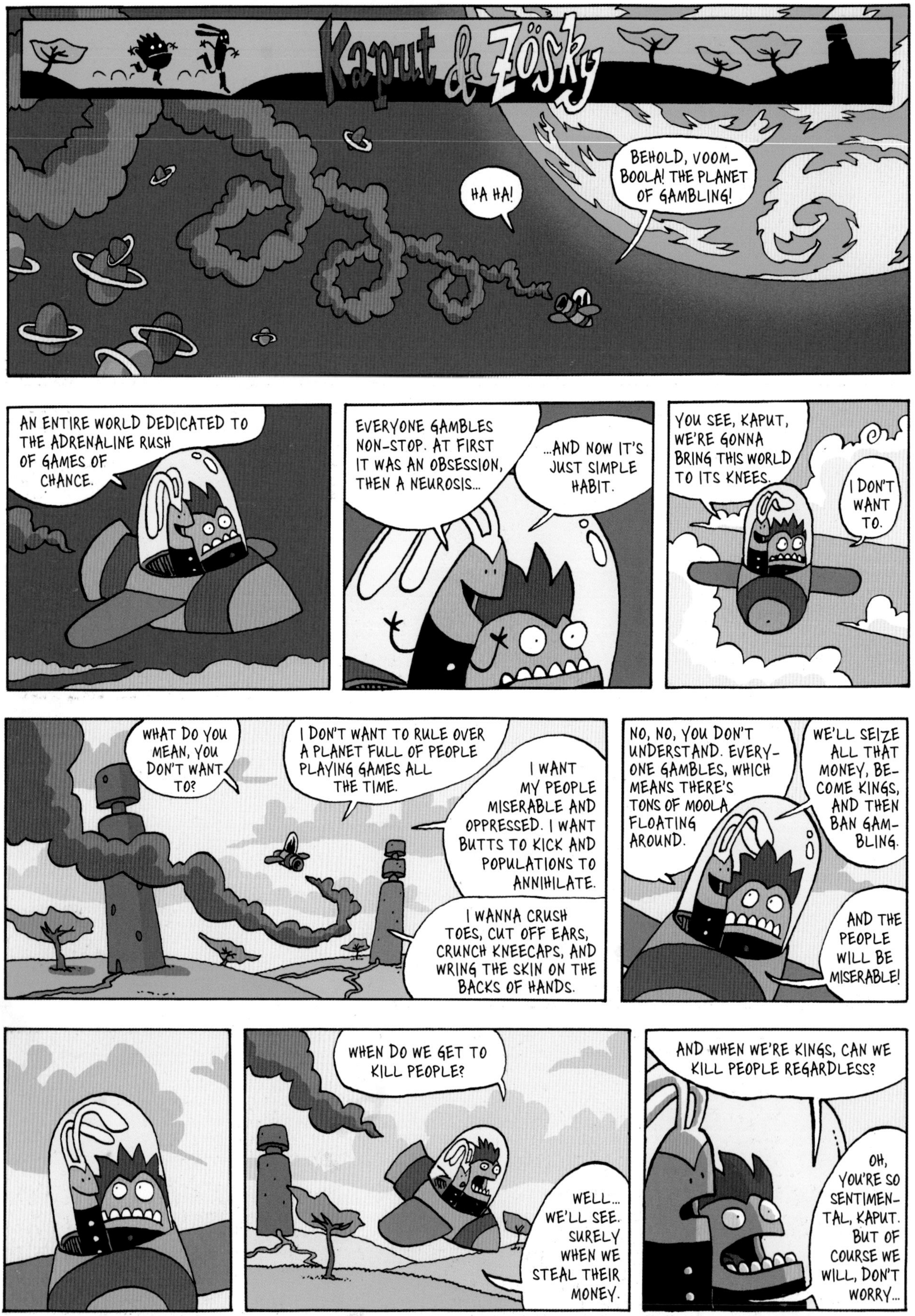
Kaput & Zösky
HA HA!
BEHOLD, VOOMBOOLA! THE PLANET OF GAMBLING!
AN ENTIRE WORLD DEDICATED TO THE ADRENALINE RUSH OF GAMES OF CHANCE.
EVERYONE GAMBLES NON-STOP. AT FIRST IT WAS AN OBSESSION, THEN A NEUROSIS...
...AND NOW IT'S JUST SIMPLE HABIT.
YOU SEE, KAPUT, WE'RE GONNA BRING THIS WORLD TO ITS KNEES.
I DON'T WANT TO.
WHAT DO YOU MEAN, YOU DON'T WANT TO?
I DON'T WANT TO RULE OVER A PLANET FULL OF PEOPLE PLAYING GAMES ALL THE TIME.
I WANT MY PEOPLE MISERABLE AND OPPRESSED. I WANT BUTTS TO KICK AND POPULATIONS TO ANNIHILATE.
I WANNA CRUSH TOES, CUT OFF EARS, CRUNCH KNEECAPS, AND WRING THE SKIN ON THE BACKS OF HANDS.
NO, NO, YOU DON'T UNDERSTAND. EVERYONE GAMBLES, WHICH MEANS THERE'S TONS OF MOOLA FLOATING AROUND.
WE'LL SEIZE ALL THAT MONEY, BECOME KINGS, AND THEN BAN GAMBLING.
AND THE PEOPLE WILL BE MISERABLE!
WHEN DO WE GET TO KILL PEOPLE?
WELL... WE'LL SEE. SURELY WHEN WE STEAL THEIR MONEY.
AND WHEN WE'RE KINGS, CAN WE KILL PEOPLE REGARDLESS?
OH, YOU'RE SO SENTIMENTAL, KAPUT. BUT OF COURSE WE WILL, DON'T WORRY...

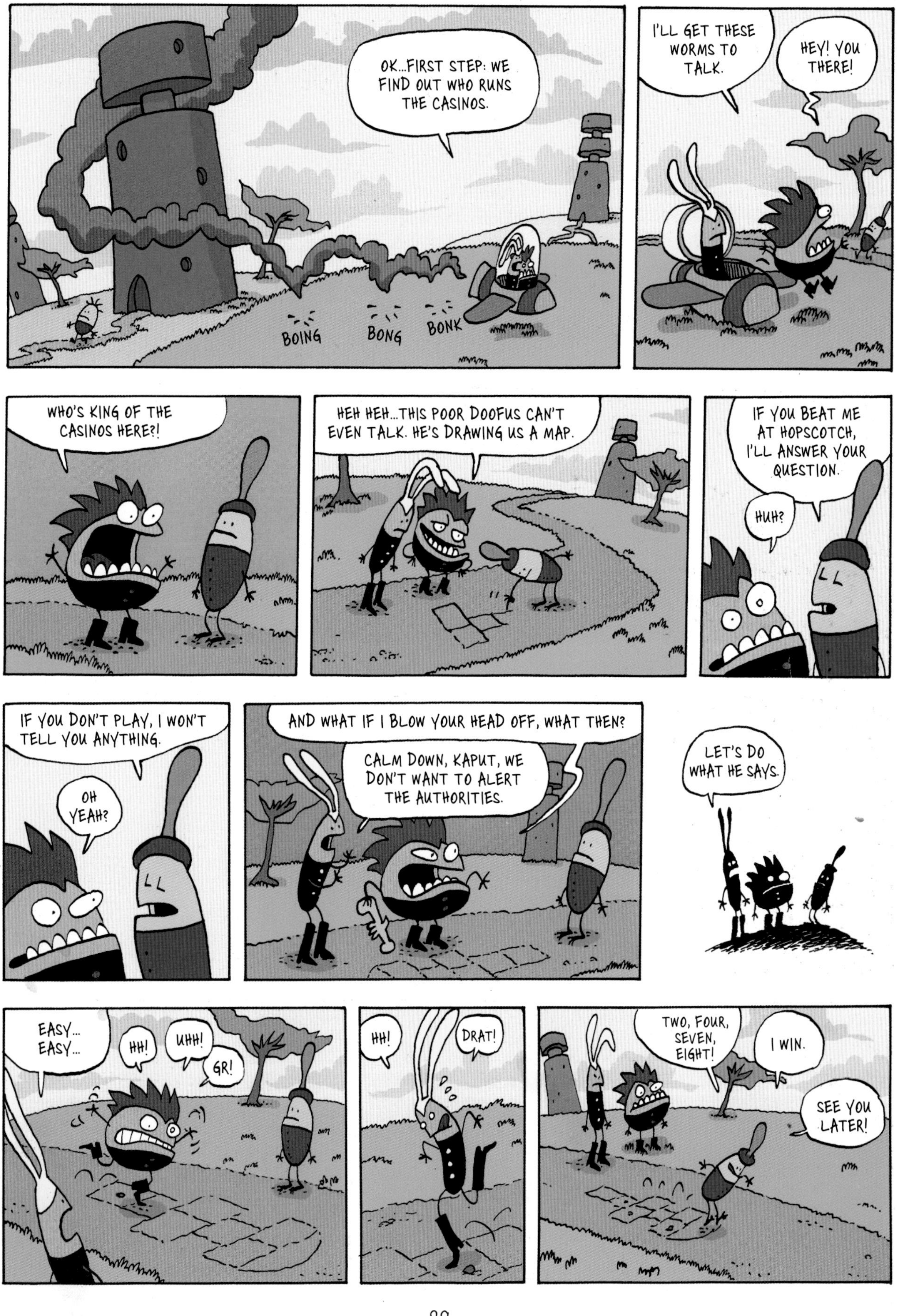
OK...FIRST STEP: WE FIND OUT WHO RUNS THE CASINOS.
BOING
BONG
BONK
I'LL GET THESE WORMS TO TALK.
HEY! YOU THERE!
WHO'S KING OF THE CASINOS HERE?!
HEH HEH...THIS POOR DOOFUS CAN'T EVEN TALK. HE'S DRAWING US A MAP.
IF YOU BEAT ME AT HOPSCOTCH, I'LL ANSWER YOUR QUESTION.
HUH?
IF YOU DON'T PLAY, I WON'T TELL YOU ANYTHING.
OH YEAH?
AND WHAT IF I BLOW YOUR HEAD OFF, WHAT THEN?
CALM DOWN, KAPUT, WE DON'T WANT TO ALERT THE AUTHORITIES.
LET'S DO WHAT HE SAYS.
EASY... EASY...
HH!
UHH!
GR!
HH!
DRAT!
TWO, FOUR, SEVEN, EIGHT!
I WIN.
SEE YOU LATER!

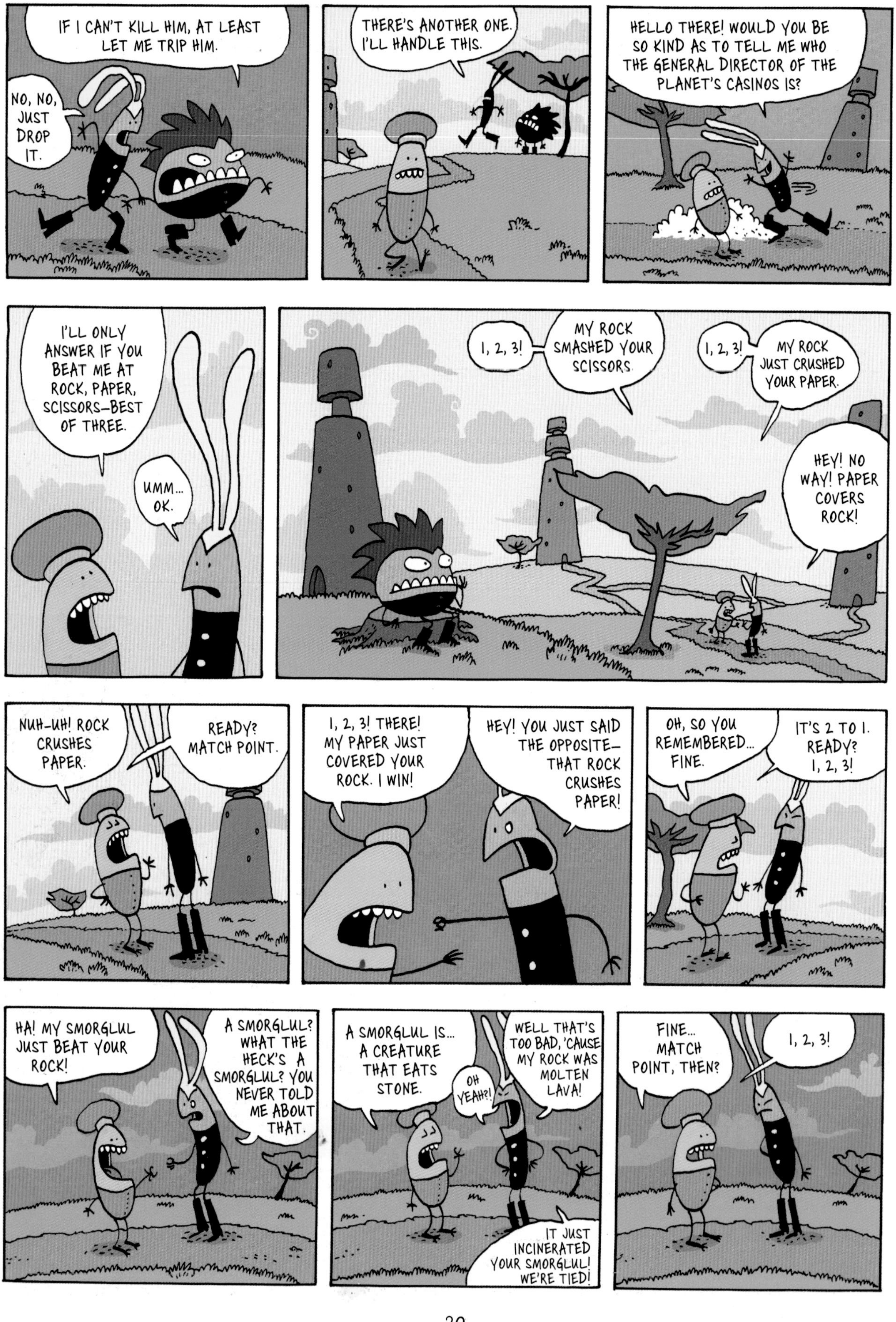

IF I CAN'T KILL HIM, AT LEAST LET ME TRIP HIM.
NO, NO, JUST DROP IT.
THERE'S ANOTHER ONE. I'LL HANDLE THIS.
HELLO THERE! WOULD YOU BE SO KIND AS TO TELL ME WHO THE GENERAL DIRECTOR OF THE PLANET'S CASINOS IS?
I'LL ONLY ANSWER IF YOU BEAT ME AT ROCK, PAPER, SCISSORS—BEST OF THREE.
UMM... OK.
1, 2, 3!
MY ROCK SMASHED YOUR SCISSORS.
1, 2, 3!
MY ROCK JUST CRUSHED YOUR PAPER.
HEY! NO WAY! PAPER COVERS ROCK!
NUH-UH! ROCK CRUSHES PAPER.
READY? MATCH POINT.
1, 2, 3! THERE! MY PAPER JUST COVERED YOUR ROCK. I WIN!
HEY! YOU JUST SAID THE OPPOSITE—THAT ROCK CRUSHES PAPER!
OH, SO YOU REMEMBERED... FINE.
IT'S 2 TO 1. READY? 1, 2, 3!
HA! MY SMORGLUL JUST BEAT YOUR ROCK!
A SMORGLUL? WHAT THE HECK'S A SMORGLUL? YOU NEVER TOLD ME ABOUT THAT.
A SMORGLUL IS... A CREATURE THAT EATS STONE.
OH YEAH?!
WELL THAT'S TOO BAD, 'CAUSE MY ROCK WAS MOLTEN LAVA!
IT JUST INCINERATED YOUR SMORGLUL! WE'RE TIED!
FINE... MATCH POINT, THEN?
1, 2, 3!

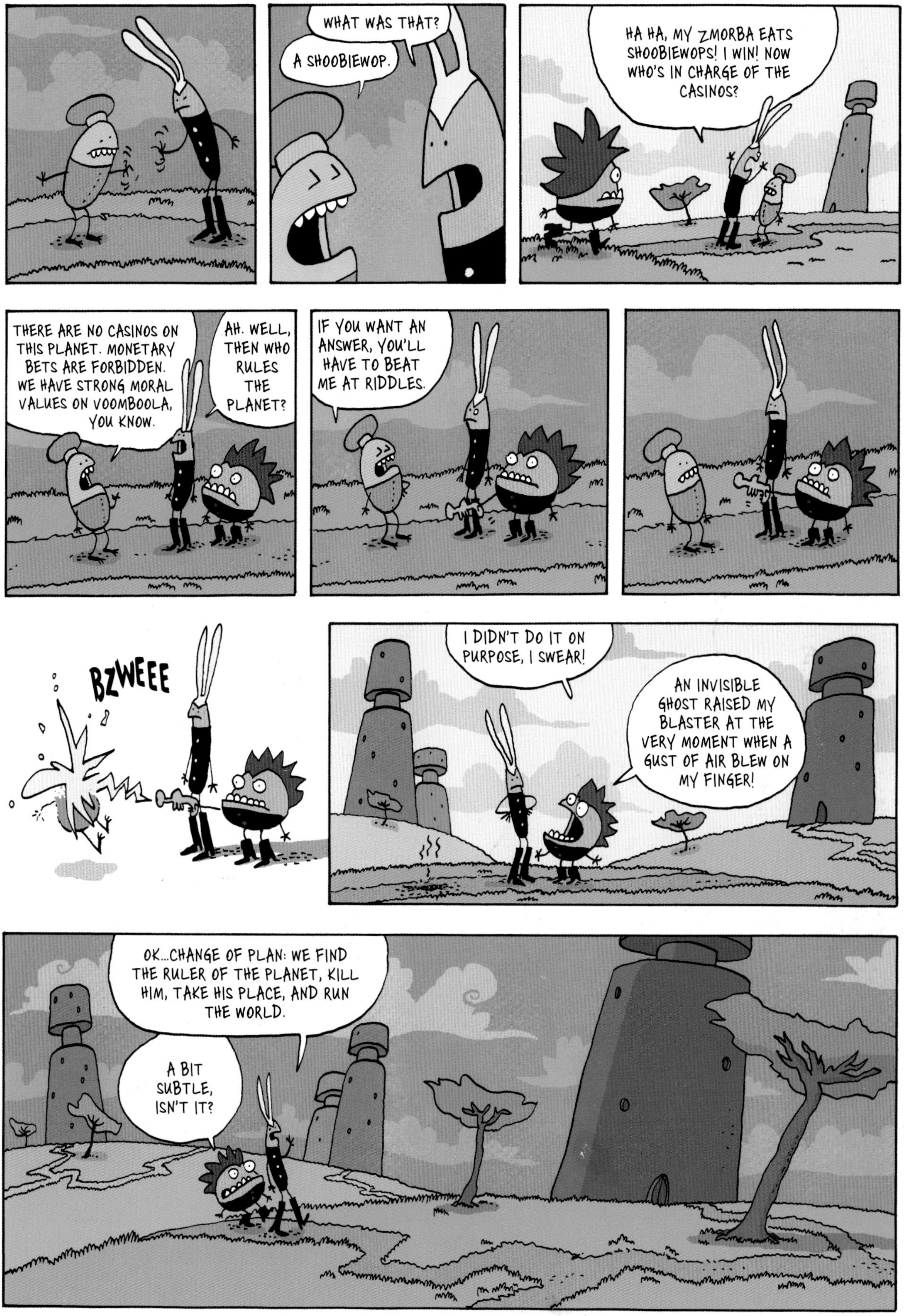
WHAT WAS THAT?
A SHOOBIEWOP.
HA HA, MY ZMORBA EATS SHOOBIEWOPS! I WIN! NOW WHO'S IN CHARGE OF THE CASINOS?
THERE ARE NO CASINOS ON THIS PLANET. MONETARY BETS ARE FORBIDDEN. WE HAVE STRONG MORAL VALUES ON VOOMBOOLA, YOU KNOW.
AH. WELL, THEN WHO RULES THE PLANET?
IF YOU WANT AN ANSWER, YOU'LL HAVE TO BEAT ME AT RIDDLES.
BZWEEE
I DIDN'T DO IT ON PURPOSE, I SWEAR!
AN INVISIBLE GHOST RAISED MY BLASTER AT THE VERY MOMENT WHEN A GUST OF AIR BLEW ON MY FINGER!
OK...CHANGE OF PLAN: WE FIND THE RULER OF THE PLANET, KILL HIM, TAKE HIS PLACE, AND RUN THE WORLD.
A BIT SUBTLE, ISN'T IT?

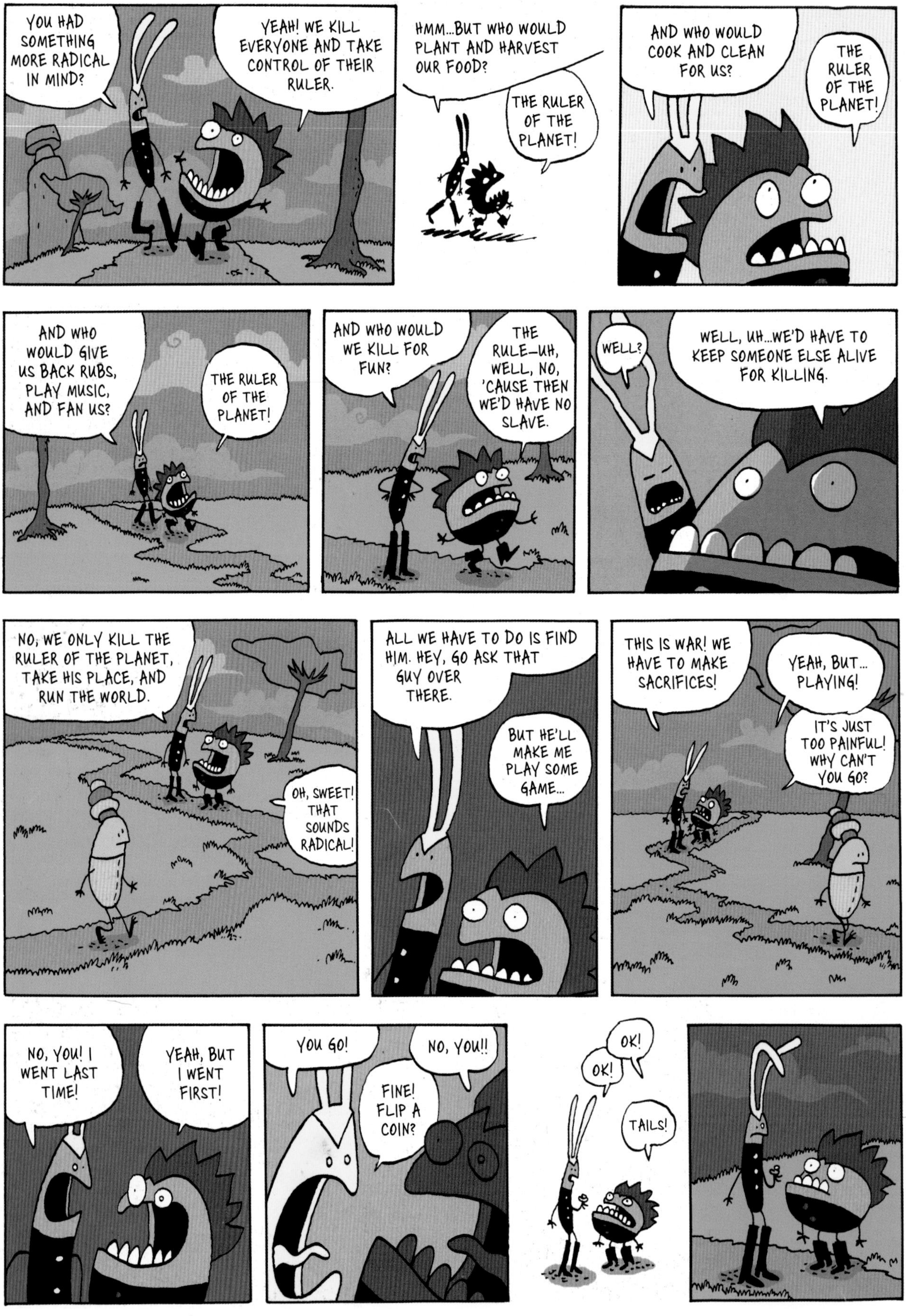
YOU HAD SOMETHING MORE RADICAL IN MIND?
YEAH! WE KILL EVERYONE AND TAKE CONTROL OF THEIR RULER.
HMM...BUT WHO WOULD PLANT AND HARVEST OUR FOOD?
THE RULER OF THE PLANET!
AND WHO WOULD COOK AND CLEAN FOR US?
THE RULER OF THE PLANET!
AND WHO WOULD GIVE US BACK RUBS, PLAY MUSIC, AND FAN US?
THE RULER OF THE PLANET!
AND WHO WOULD WE KILL FOR FUN?
THE RULE—UH, WELL, NO, 'CAUSE THEN WE'D HAVE NO SLAVE.
WELL?
WELL, UH...WE'D HAVE TO KEEP SOMEONE ELSE ALIVE FOR KILLING.
NO, WE ONLY KILL THE RULER OF THE PLANET, TAKE HIS PLACE, AND RUN THE WORLD.
OH, SWEET! THAT SOUNDS RADICAL!
ALL WE HAVE TO DO IS FIND HIM. HEY, GO ASK THAT GUY OVER THERE.
BUT HE'LL MAKE ME PLAY SOME GAME...
THIS IS WAR! WE HAVE TO MAKE SACRIFICES!
YEAH, BUT... PLAYING!
IT'S JUST TOO PAINFUL! WHY CAN'T YOU GO?
NO, YOU! I WENT LAST TIME!
YEAH, BUT I WENT FIRST!
YOU GO!
NO, YOU!!
FINE! FLIP A COIN?
OK!
OK!
TAILS!

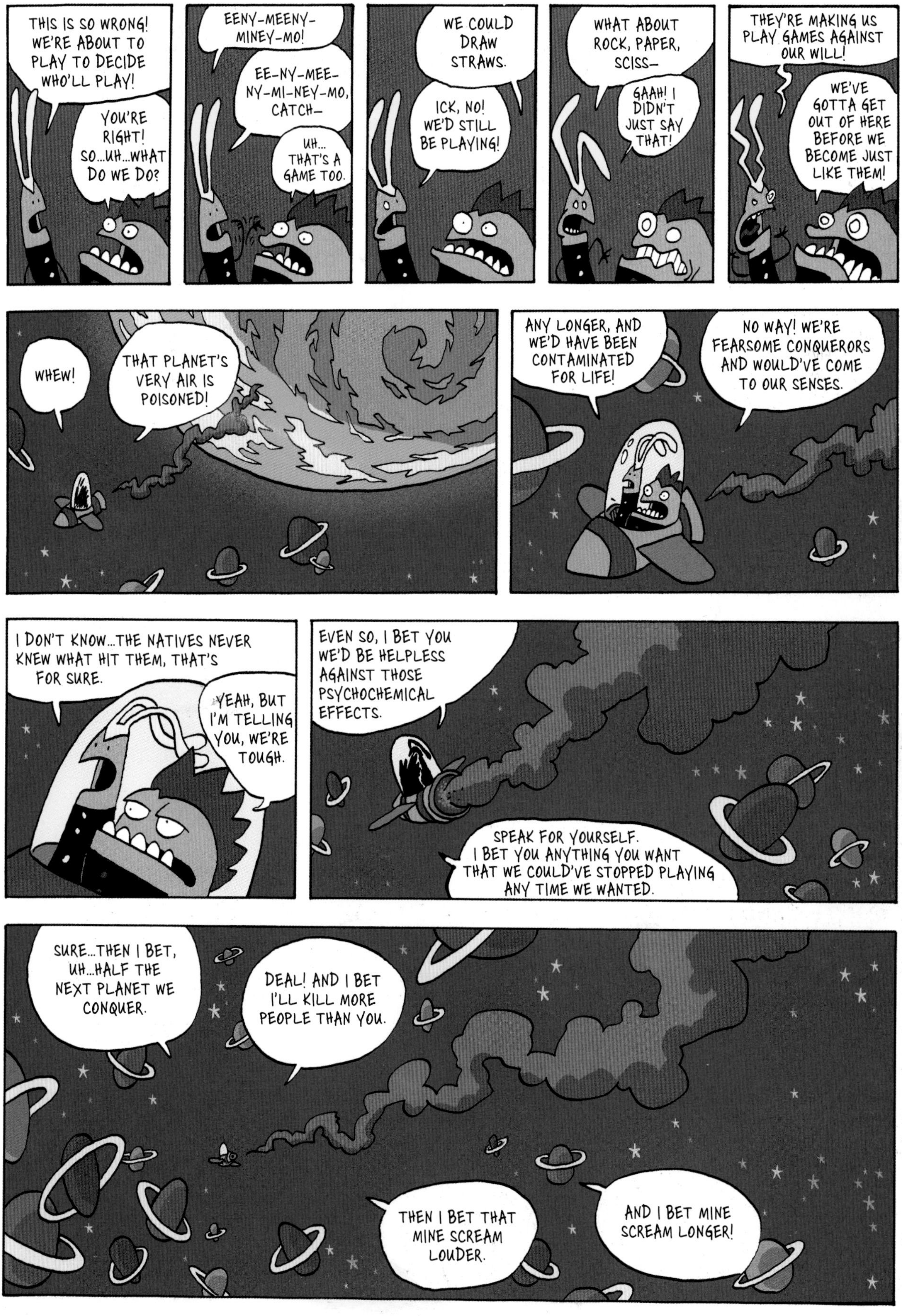
THIS IS SO WRONG! WE'RE ABOUT TO PLAY TO DECIDE WHO'LL PLAY!
YOU'RE RIGHT! SO...UH...WHAT DO WE DO?
EENY-MEENY-MINEY-MO!
EE-NY-MEE-NY-MI-NEY-MO, CATCH—
UH... THAT'S A GAME TOO.
WE COULD DRAW STRAWS.
ICK, NO! WE'D STILL BE PLAYING!
WHAT ABOUT ROCK, PAPER, SCISS—
GAAH! I DIDN'T JUST SAY THAT!
THEY'RE MAKING US PLAY GAMES AGAINST OUR WILL!
WE'VE GOTTA GET OUT OF HERE BEFORE WE BECOME JUST LIKE THEM!
WHEW!
THAT PLANET'S VERY AIR IS POISONED!
ANY LONGER, AND WE'D HAVE BEEN CONTAMINATED FOR LIFE!
NO WAY! WE'RE FEARSOME CONQUERORS AND WOULD'VE COME TO OUR SENSES.
I DON'T KNOW...THE NATIVES NEVER KNEW WHAT HIT THEM, THAT'S FOR SURE.
YEAH, BUT I'M TELLING YOU, WE'RE TOUGH.
EVEN SO, I BET YOU WE'D BE HELPLESS AGAINST THOSE PSYCHOCHEMICAL EFFECTS.
SPEAK FOR YOURSELF. I BET YOU ANYTHING YOU WANT THAT WE COULD'VE STOPPED PLAYING ANY TIME WE WANTED.
SURE...THEN I BET, UH...HALF THE NEXT PLANET WE CONQUER.
DEAL! AND I BET I'LL KILL MORE PEOPLE THAN YOU.
THEN I BET THAT MINE SCREAM LOUDER.
AND I BET MINE SCREAM LONGER!

the Cosmonaut

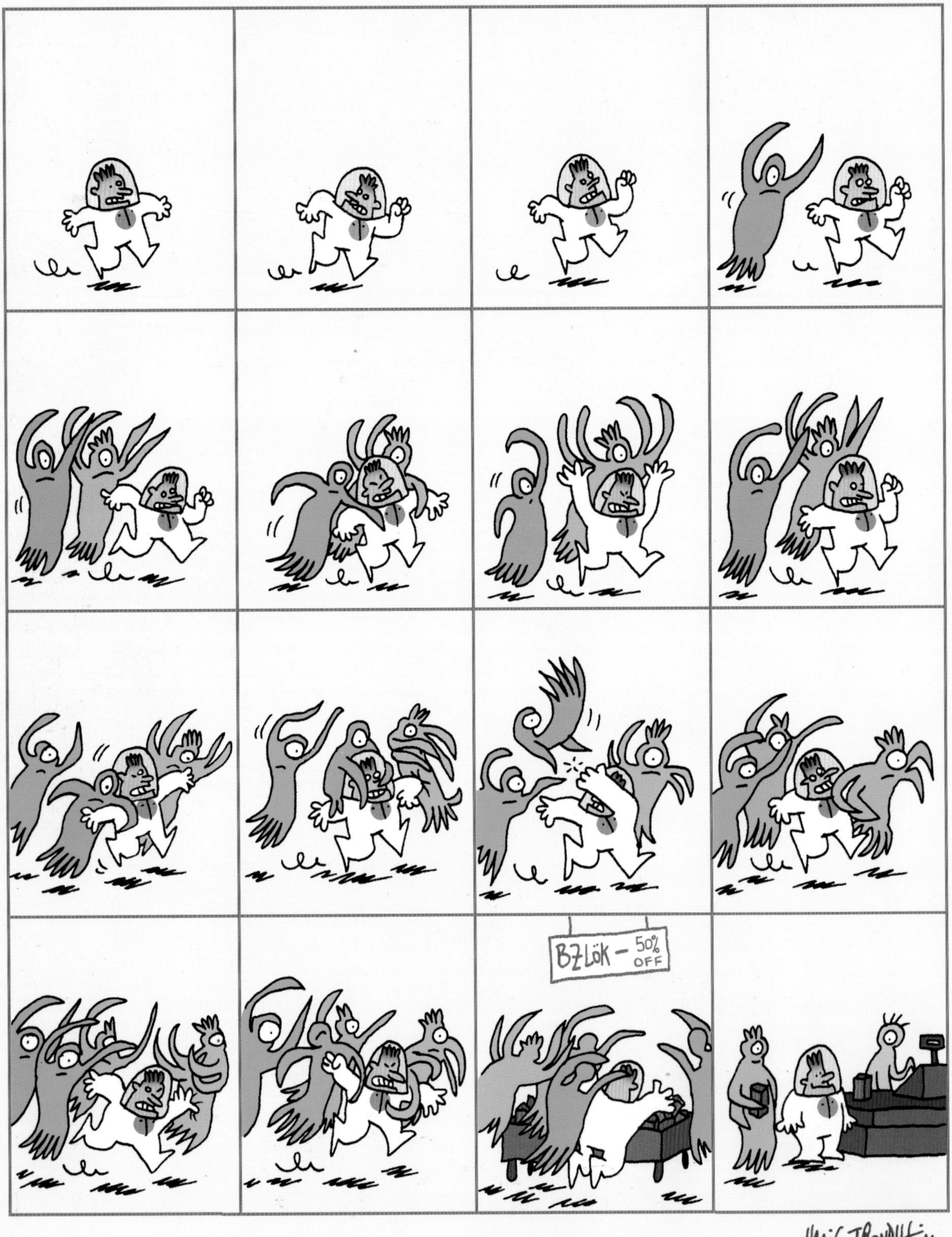
BZ LÖK – 50% OFF

Chris TRONDHEIM

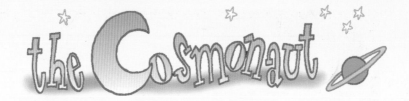

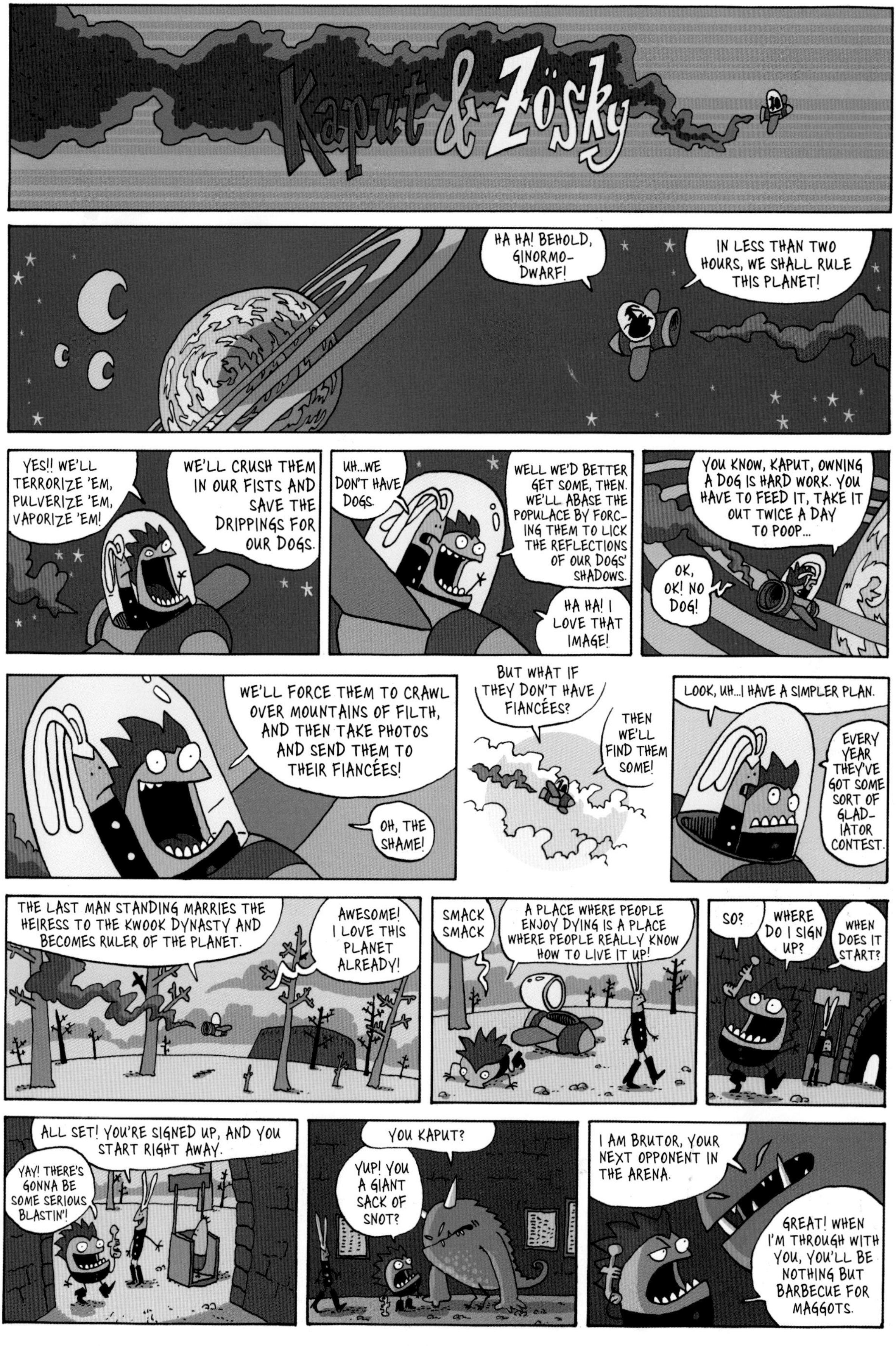

Kaput & Zösky
HA HA! BEHOLD, GINORMO-DWARF!
IN LESS THAN TWO HOURS, WE SHALL RULE THIS PLANET!
YES!! WE'LL TERRORIZE 'EM, PULVERIZE 'EM, VAPORIZE 'EM!
WE'LL CRUSH THEM IN OUR FISTS AND SAVE THE DRIPPINGS FOR OUR DOGS.
UH...WE DON'T HAVE DOGS.
WELL WE'D BETTER GET SOME, THEN. WE'LL ABASE THE POPULACE BY FORCING THEM TO LICK THE REFLECTIONS OF OUR DOGS' SHADOWS.
HA HA! I LOVE THAT IMAGE!
YOU KNOW, KAPUT, OWNING A DOG IS HARD WORK. YOU HAVE TO FEED IT, TAKE IT OUT TWICE A DAY TO POOP...
OK, OK! NO DOG!
WE'LL FORCE THEM TO CRAWL OVER MOUNTAINS OF FILTH, AND THEN TAKE PHOTOS AND SEND THEM TO THEIR FIANCÉES!
OH, THE SHAME!
BUT WHAT IF THEY DON'T HAVE FIANCÉES?
THEN WE'LL FIND THEM SOME!
LOOK, UH...I HAVE A SIMPLER PLAN.
EVERY YEAR THEY'VE GOT SOME SORT OF GLADIATOR CONTEST.
THE LAST MAN STANDING MARRIES THE HEIRESS TO THE KWOOK DYNASTY AND BECOMES RULER OF THE PLANET.
AWESOME! I LOVE THIS PLANET ALREADY!
SMACK SMACK
A PLACE WHERE PEOPLE ENJOY DYING IS A PLACE WHERE PEOPLE REALLY KNOW HOW TO LIVE IT UP!
SO?
WHERE DO I SIGN UP?
WHEN DOES IT START?
ALL SET! YOU'RE SIGNED UP, AND YOU START RIGHT AWAY.
YAY! THERE'S GONNA BE SOME SERIOUS BLASTIN'!
YOU KAPUT?
YUP! YOU A GIANT SACK OF SNOT?
I AM BRUTOR, YOUR NEXT OPPONENT IN THE ARENA.
GREAT! WHEN I'M THROUGH WITH YOU, YOU'LL BE NOTHING BUT BARBECUE FOR MAGGOTS.

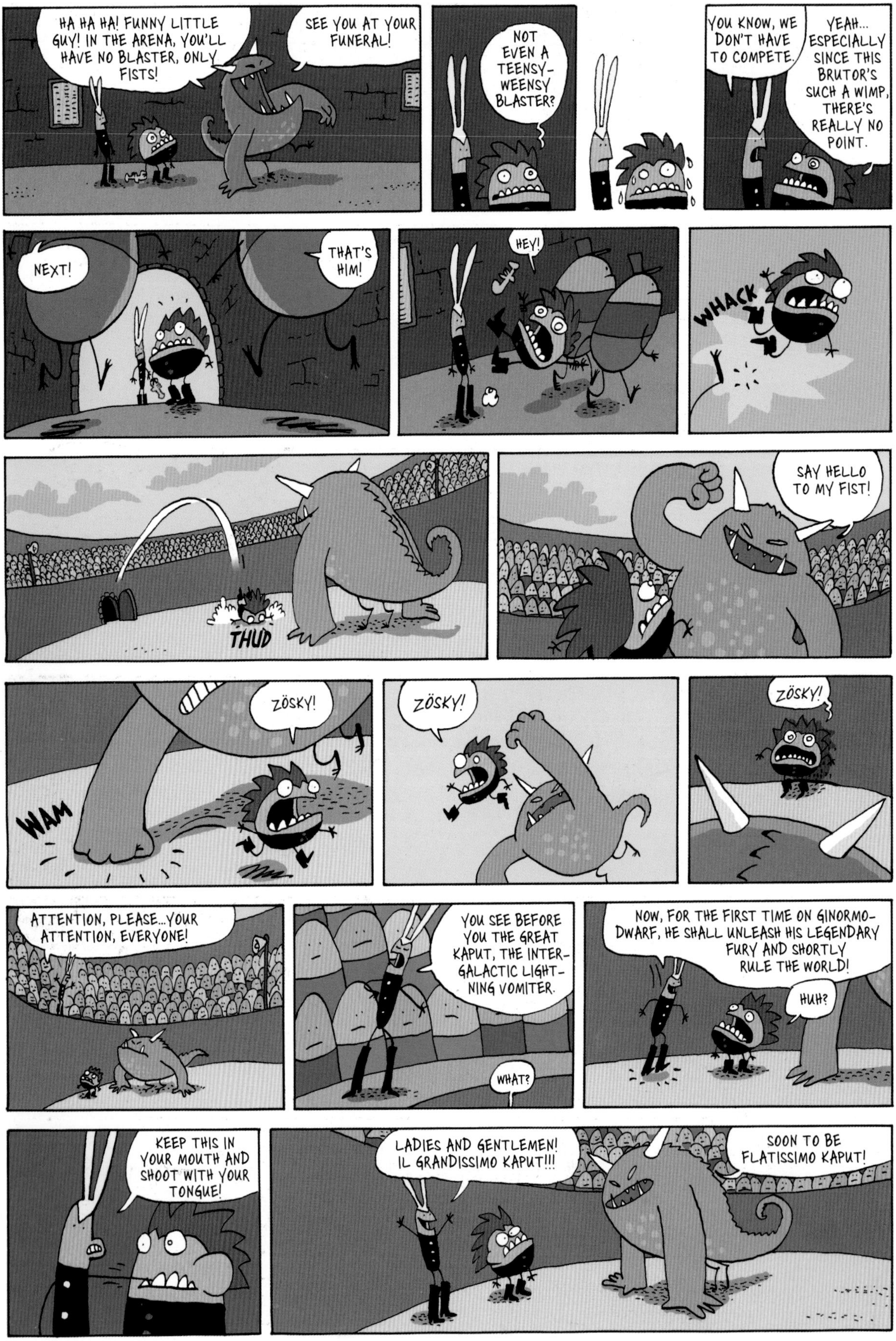
HA HA HA! FUNNY LITTLE GUY! IN THE ARENA, YOU'LL HAVE NO BLASTER, ONLY FISTS!
SEE YOU AT YOUR FUNERAL!
NOT EVEN A TEENSY-WEENSY BLASTER?
YOU KNOW, WE DON'T HAVE TO COMPETE.
YEAH... ESPECIALLY SINCE THIS BRUTOR'S SUCH A WIMP, THERE'S REALLY NO POINT.
NEXT!
THAT'S HIM!
HEY!
WHACK
THUD
SAY HELLO TO MY FIST!
ZÖSKY!
WAM
ZÖSKY!
ZÖSKY!
ATTENTION, PLEASE...YOUR ATTENTION, EVERYONE!
YOU SEE BEFORE YOU THE GREAT KAPUT, THE INTER-GALACTIC LIGHT-NING VOMITER.
WHAT?
NOW, FOR THE FIRST TIME ON GINORMO-DWARF, HE SHALL UNLEASH HIS LEGENDARY FURY AND SHORTLY RULE THE WORLD!
HUH?
KEEP THIS IN YOUR MOUTH AND SHOOT WITH YOUR TONGUE!
LADIES AND GENTLEMEN! IL GRANDISSIMO KAPUT!!!
SOON TO BE FLATISSIMO KAPUT!

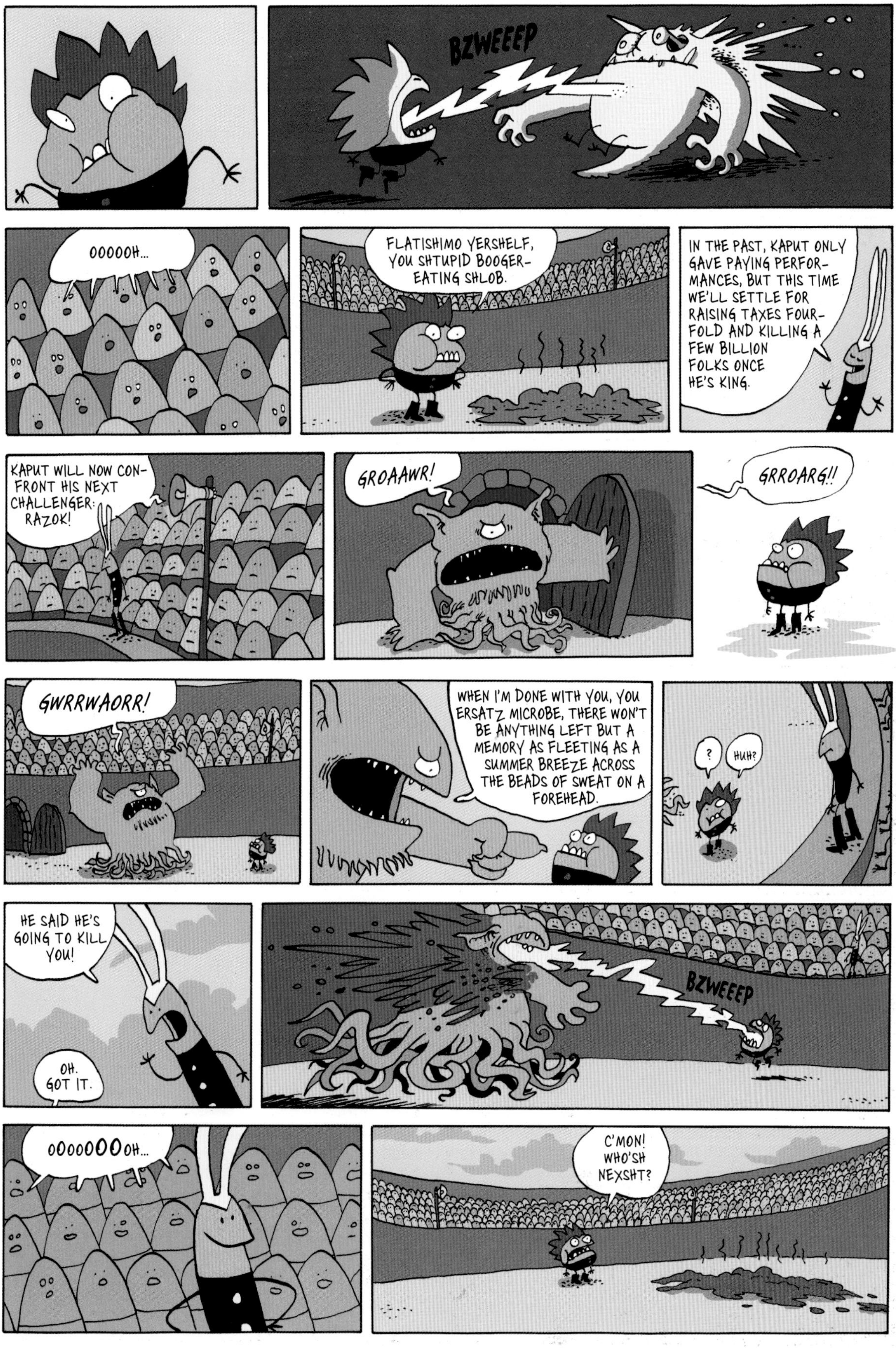

BZWEEEP
OOOOOH...
FLATISHIMO YERSHELF, YOU SHTUPID BOOGER-EATING SHLOB.
IN THE PAST, KAPUT ONLY GAVE PAYING PERFORMANCES, BUT THIS TIME WE'LL SETTLE FOR RAISING TAXES FOURFOLD AND KILLING A FEW BILLION FOLKS ONCE HE'S KING.
KAPUT WILL NOW CONFRONT HIS NEXT CHALLENGER: RAZOK!
GROAAWR!
GRROARG!!
GWRRWAORR!
WHEN I'M DONE WITH YOU, YOU ERSATZ MICROBE, THERE WON'T BE ANYTHING LEFT BUT A MEMORY AS FLEETING AS A SUMMER BREEZE ACROSS THE BEADS OF SWEAT ON A FOREHEAD.
?
HUH?
HE SAID HE'S GOING TO KILL YOU!
OH. GOT IT.
BZWEEEP
OOOOOOOOH...
C'MON! WHO'SH NEXSHT?

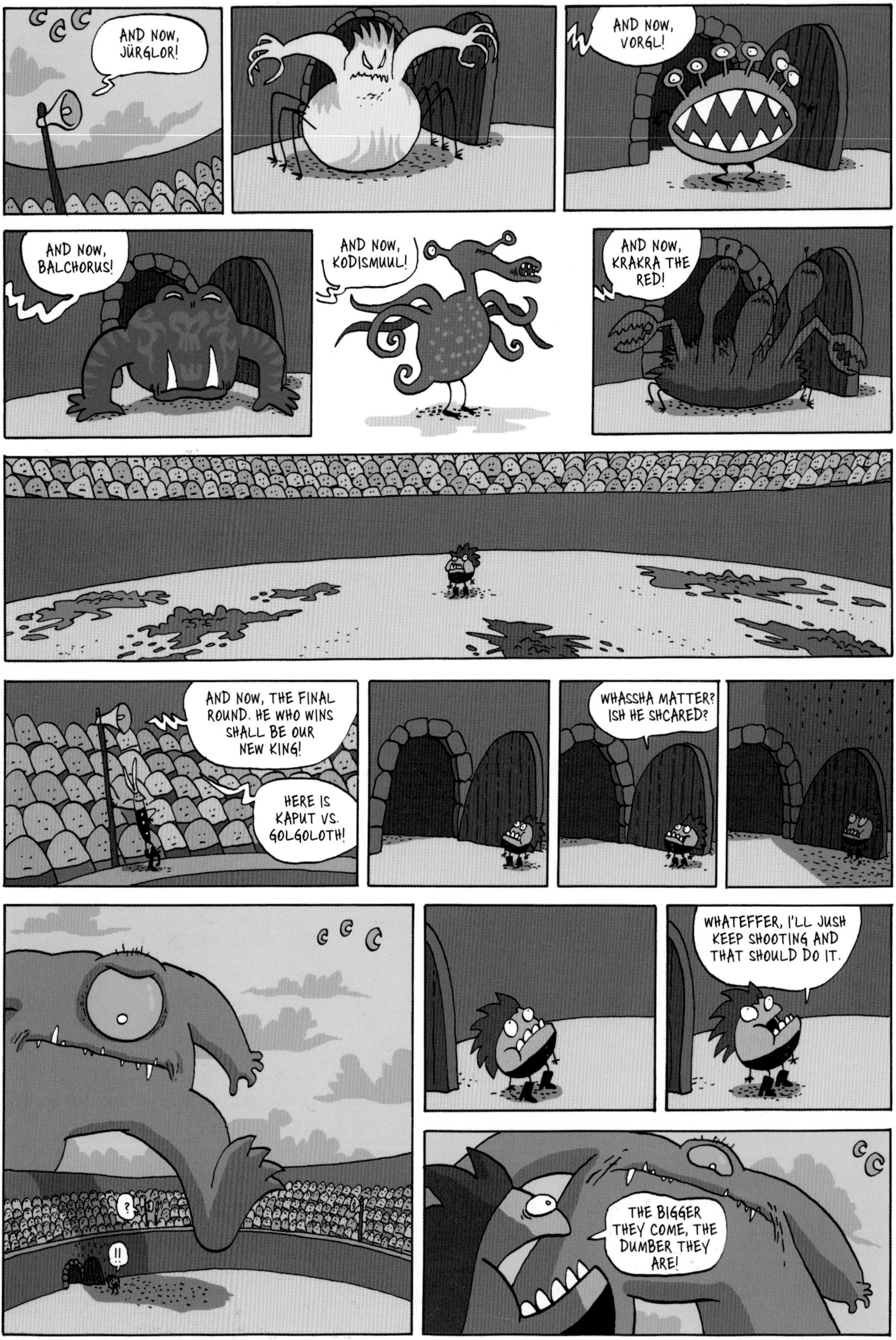

AND NOW, JÜRGLOR!
AND NOW, VORGL!
AND NOW, BALCHORUS!
AND NOW, KODISMUUL!
AND NOW, KRAKRA THE RED!
AND NOW, THE FINAL ROUND. HE WHO WINS SHALL BE OUR NEW KING!
HERE IS KAPUT VS. GOLGOLOTH!
WHASSHA MATTER? ISH HE SHCARED?
?
!!
WHATEFFER, I'LL JUSH KEEP SHOOTING AND THAT SHOULD DO IT.
THE BIGGER THEY COME, THE DUMBER THEY ARE!

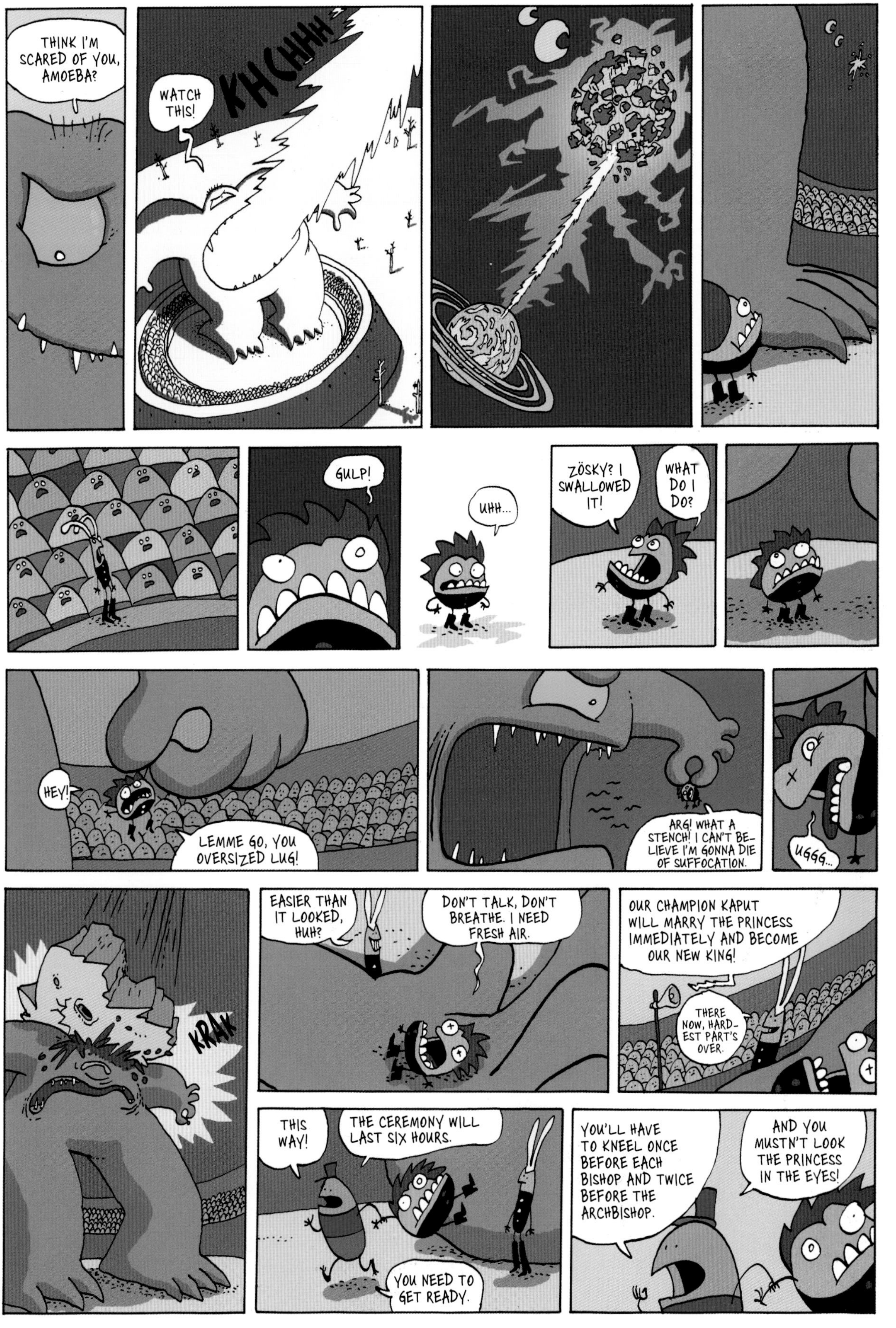
THINK I'M SCARED OF YOU, AMOEBA?
WATCH THIS!
KHCHHH
GULP!
UHH...
ZÖSKY? I SWALLOWED IT!
WHAT DO I DO?
HEY!
LEMME GO, YOU OVERSIZED LUG!
ARG! WHAT A STENCH! I CAN'T BE-LIEVE I'M GONNA DIE OF SUFFOCATION.
UGGG...
KRAK
EASIER THAN IT LOOKED, HUH?
DON'T TALK, DON'T BREATHE. I NEED FRESH AIR.
OUR CHAMPION KAPUT WILL MARRY THE PRINCESS IMMEDIATELY AND BECOME OUR NEW KING!
THERE NOW, HARD-EST PART'S OVER.
THIS WAY!
THE CEREMONY WILL LAST SIX HOURS.
YOU NEED TO GET READY.
YOU'LL HAVE TO KNEEL ONCE BEFORE EACH BISHOP AND TWICE BEFORE THE ARCHBISHOP.
AND YOU MUSTN'T LOOK THE PRINCESS IN THE EYES!

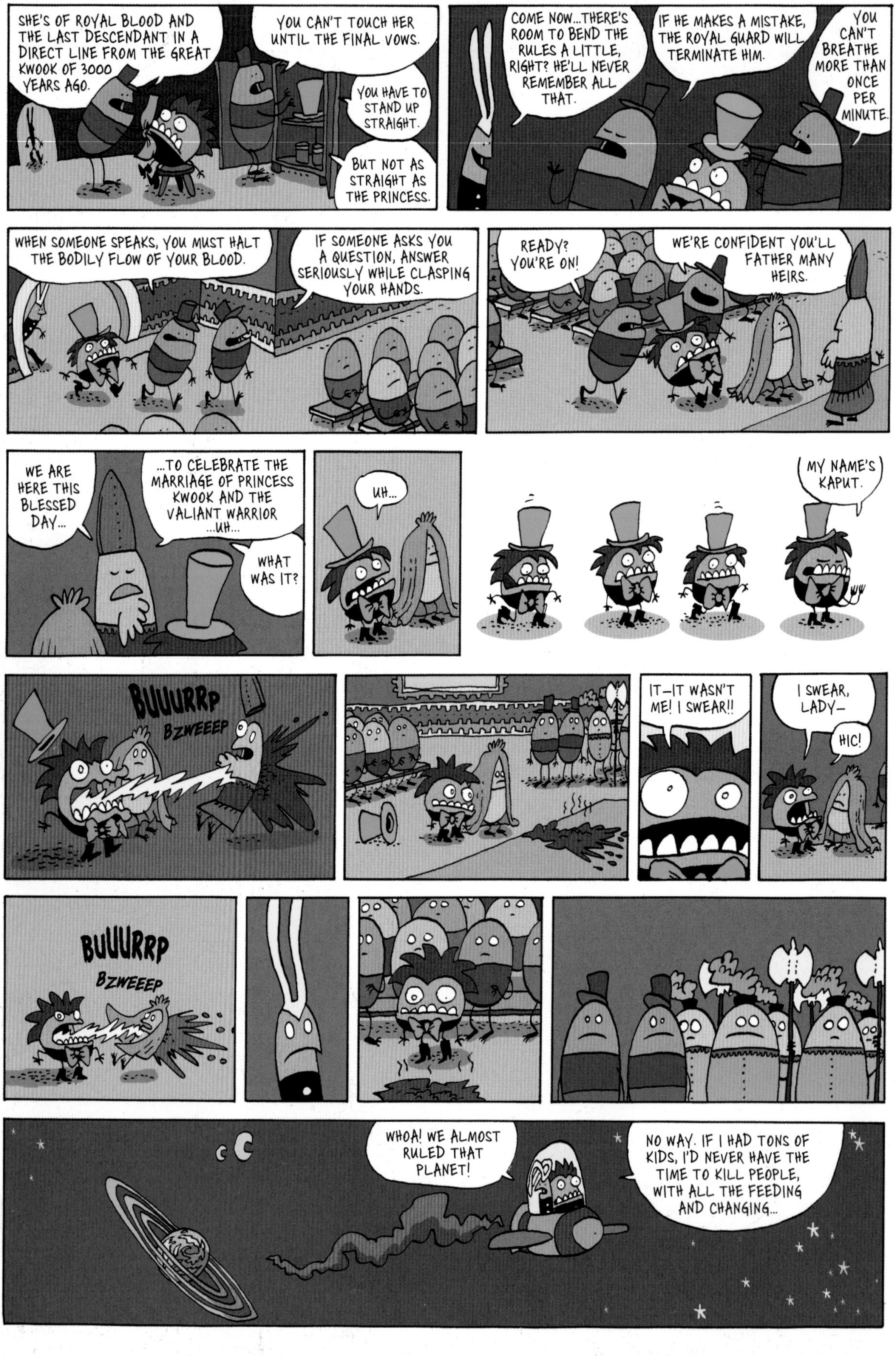
SHE'S OF ROYAL BLOOD AND THE LAST DESCENDANT IN A DIRECT LINE FROM THE GREAT KWOOK OF 3000 YEARS AGO.
YOU CAN'T TOUCH HER UNTIL THE FINAL VOWS.
YOU HAVE TO STAND UP STRAIGHT.
BUT NOT AS STRAIGHT AS THE PRINCESS.
COME NOW...THERE'S ROOM TO BEND THE RULES A LITTLE, RIGHT? HE'LL NEVER REMEMBER ALL THAT.
IF HE MAKES A MISTAKE, THE ROYAL GUARD WILL TERMINATE HIM.
YOU CAN'T BREATHE MORE THAN ONCE PER MINUTE.
WHEN SOMEONE SPEAKS, YOU MUST HALT THE BODILY FLOW OF YOUR BLOOD.
IF SOMEONE ASKS YOU A QUESTION, ANSWER SERIOUSLY WHILE CLASPING YOUR HANDS.
READY? YOU'RE ON!
WE'RE CONFIDENT YOU'LL FATHER MANY HEIRS.
WE ARE HERE THIS BLESSED DAY...
...TO CELEBRATE THE MARRIAGE OF PRINCESS KWOOK AND THE VALIANT WARRIOR ...UH...
WHAT WAS IT?
UH...
MY NAME'S KAPUT.
BUUURRP
BZWEEEP
IT—IT WASN'T ME! I SWEAR!!
I SWEAR, LADY—
HIC!
BUUURRP
BZWEEEP
WHOA! WE ALMOST RULED THAT PLANET!
NO WAY. IF I HAD TONS OF KIDS, I'D NEVER HAVE THE TIME TO KILL PEOPLE, WITH ALL THE FEEDING AND CHANGING...

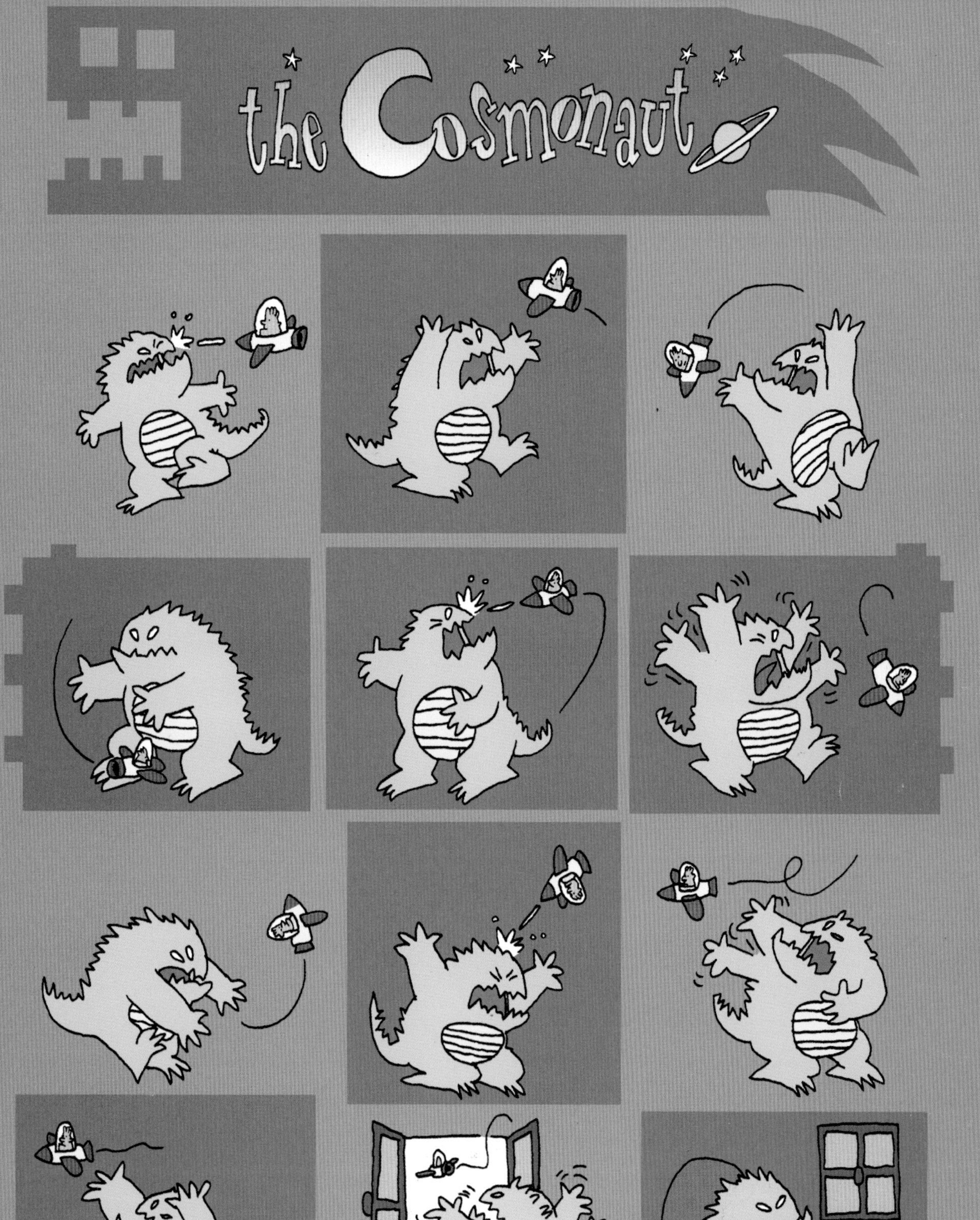
the Cosmonaut
Lewis Trondheim

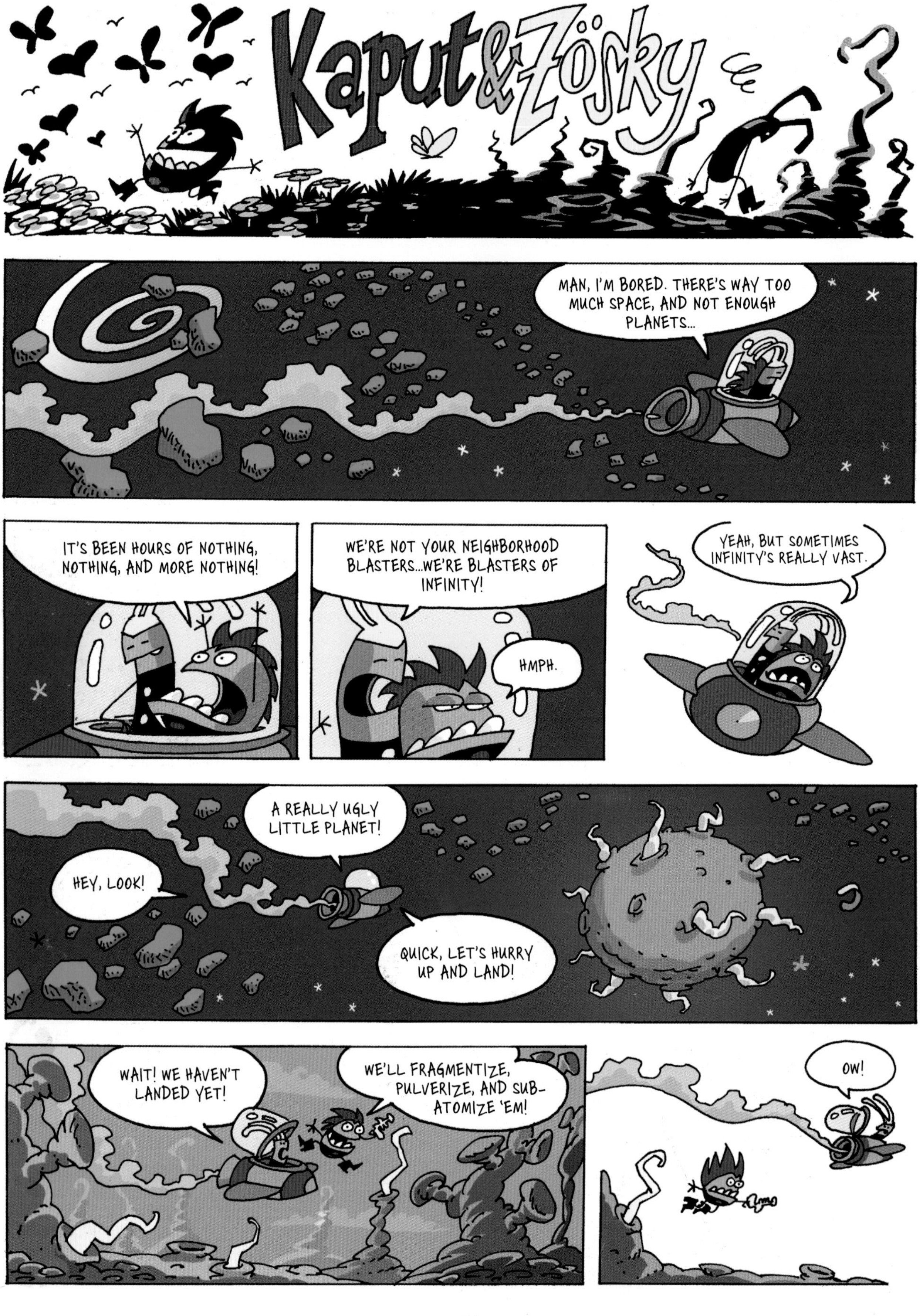
Kaput & Zösky
MAN, I'M BORED. THERE'S WAY TOO MUCH SPACE, AND NOT ENOUGH PLANETS...
IT'S BEEN HOURS OF NOTHING, NOTHING, AND MORE NOTHING!
WE'RE NOT YOUR NEIGHBORHOOD BLASTERS...WE'RE BLASTERS OF INFINITY!
HMPH.
YEAH, BUT SOMETIMES INFINITY'S REALLY VAST.
HEY, LOOK!
A REALLY UGLY LITTLE PLANET!
QUICK, LET'S HURRY UP AND LAND!
WAIT! WE HAVEN'T LANDED YET!
WE'LL FRAGMENTIZE, PULVERIZE, AND SUB-ATOMIZE 'EM!
OW!

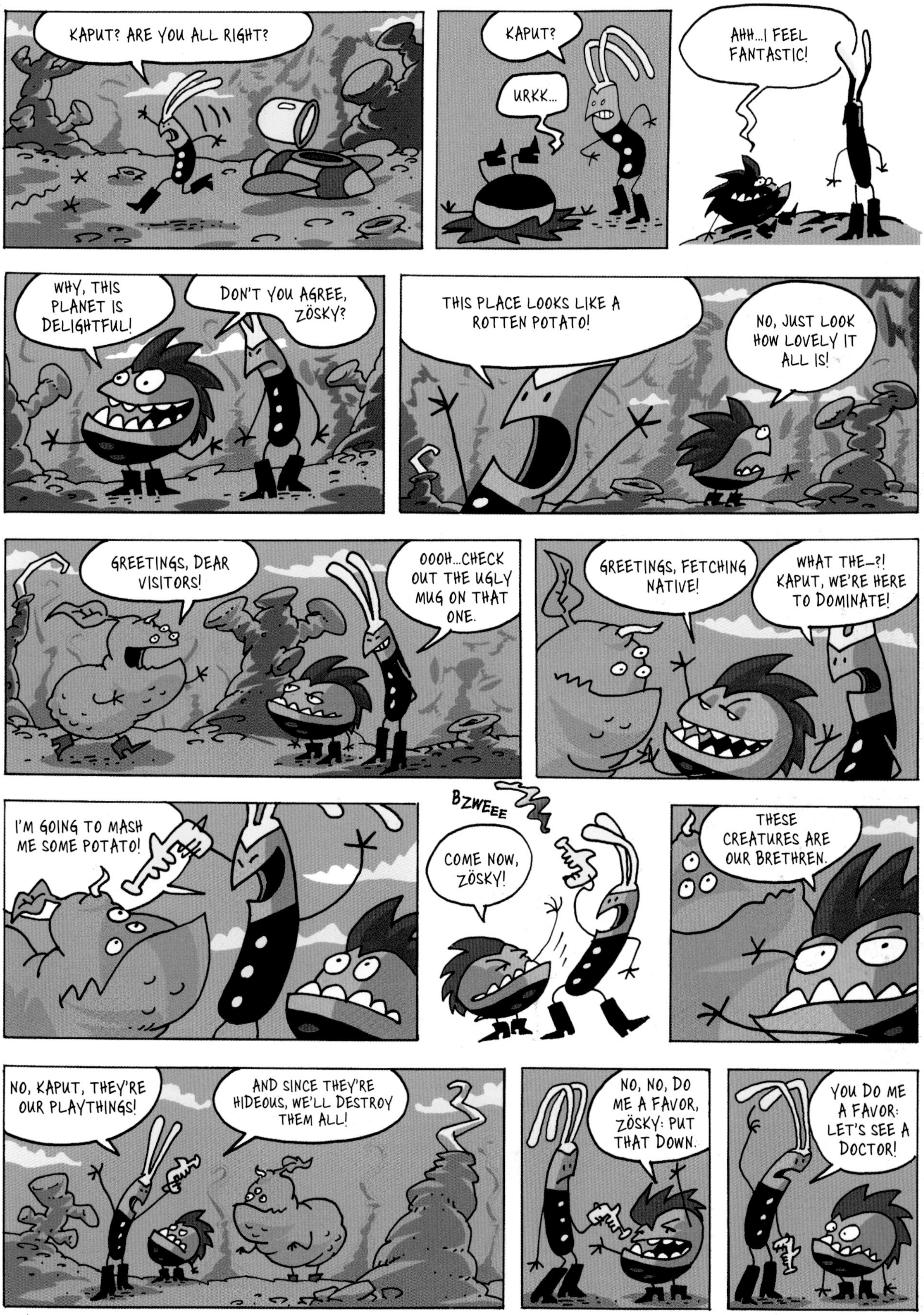
KAPUT? ARE YOU ALL RIGHT?
KAPUT?
URKK...
AHH...I FEEL FANTASTIC!
WHY, THIS PLANET IS DELIGHTFUL!
DON'T YOU AGREE, ZÖSKY?
THIS PLACE LOOKS LIKE A ROTTEN POTATO!
NO, JUST LOOK HOW LOVELY IT ALL IS!
GREETINGS, DEAR VISITORS!
OOOH...CHECK OUT THE UGLY MUG ON THAT ONE.
GREETINGS, FETCHING NATIVE!
WHAT THE—?! KAPUT, WE'RE HERE TO DOMINATE!
I'M GOING TO MASH ME SOME POTATO!
BZWEEE
COME NOW, ZÖSKY!
THESE CREATURES ARE OUR BRETHREN.
NO, KAPUT, THEY'RE OUR PLAYTHINGS!
AND SINCE THEY'RE HIDEOUS, WE'LL DESTROY THEM ALL!
NO, NO, DO ME A FAVOR, ZÖSKY: PUT THAT DOWN.
YOU DO ME A FAVOR: LET'S SEE A DOCTOR!

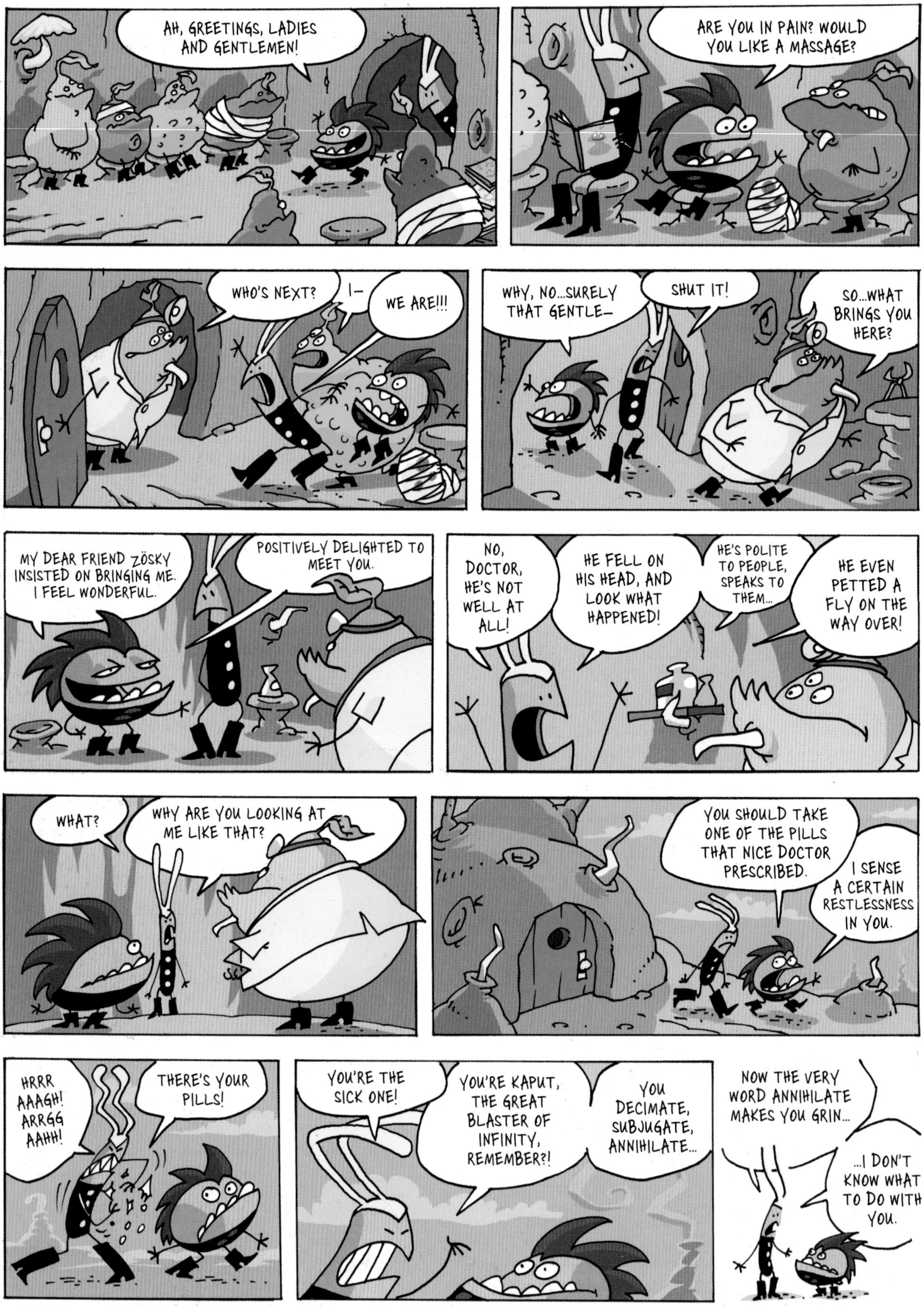
AH, GREETINGS, LADIES AND GENTLEMEN!
ARE YOU IN PAIN? WOULD YOU LIKE A MASSAGE?
WHO'S NEXT?
I—
WE ARE!!!
WHY, NO...SURELY THAT GENTLE—
SHUT IT!
SO...WHAT BRINGS YOU HERE?
MY DEAR FRIEND ZÖSKY INSISTED ON BRINGING ME. I FEEL WONDERFUL.
POSITIVELY DELIGHTED TO MEET YOU.
NO, DOCTOR, HE'S NOT WELL AT ALL!
HE FELL ON HIS HEAD, AND LOOK WHAT HAPPENED!
HE'S POLITE TO PEOPLE, SPEAKS TO THEM...
HE EVEN PETTED A FLY ON THE WAY OVER!
WHAT?
WHY ARE YOU LOOKING AT ME LIKE THAT?
YOU SHOULD TAKE ONE OF THE PILLS THAT NICE DOCTOR PRESCRIBED.
I SENSE A CERTAIN RESTLESSNESS IN YOU.
HRRR AAAGH! ARRGG AAHH!
THERE'S YOUR PILLS!
YOU'RE THE SICK ONE!
YOU'RE KAPUT, THE GREAT BLASTER OF INFINITY, REMEMBER?!
YOU DECIMATE, SUBJUGATE, ANNIHILATE...
NOW THE VERY WORD ANNIHILATE MAKES YOU GRIN...
...I DON'T KNOW WHAT TO DO WITH YOU.

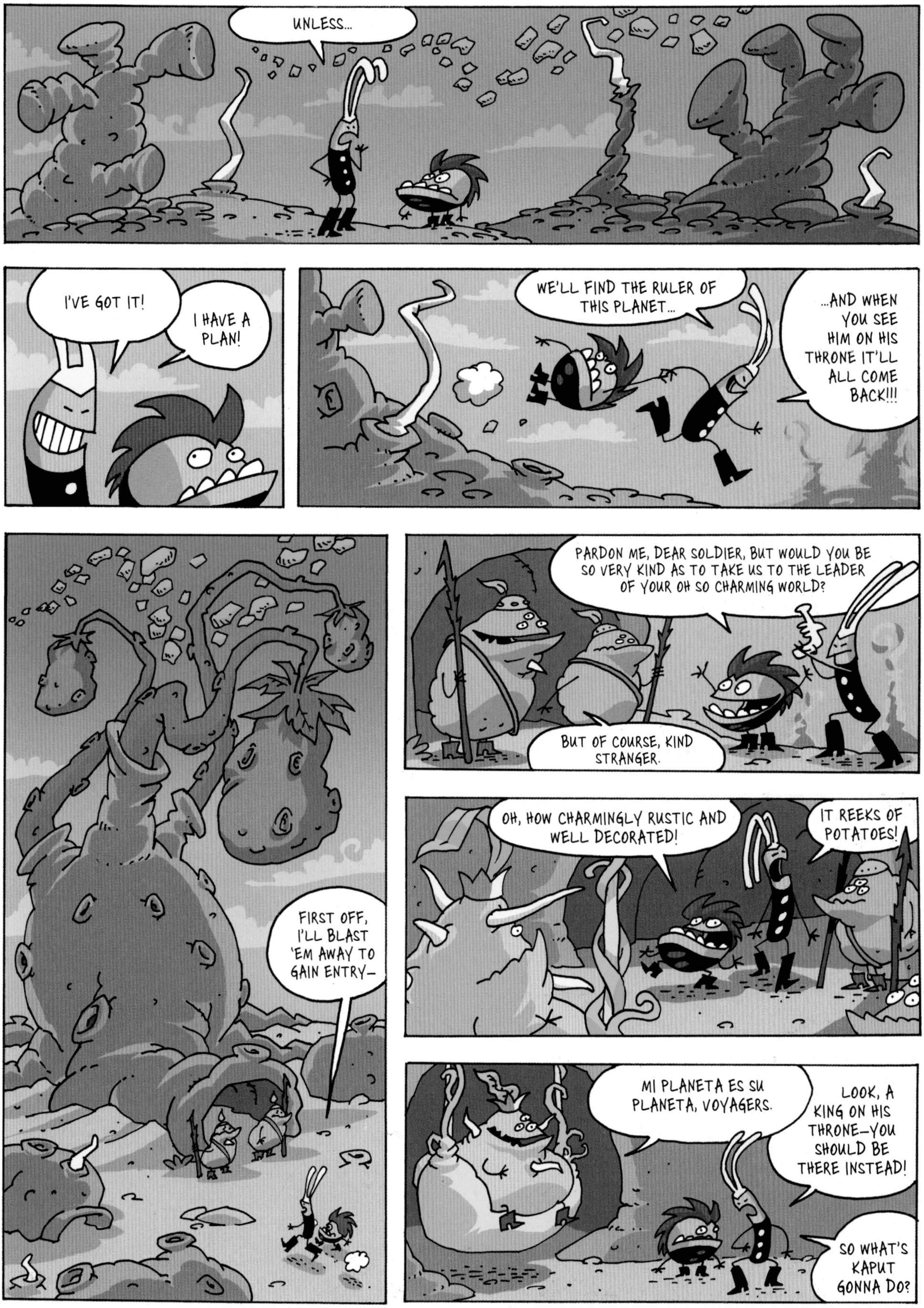
UNLESS...
I'VE GOT IT!
I HAVE A PLAN!
WE'LL FIND THE RULER OF THIS PLANET...
...AND WHEN YOU SEE HIM ON HIS THRONE IT'LL ALL COME BACK!!!
FIRST OFF, I'LL BLAST 'EM AWAY TO GAIN ENTRY—
PARDON ME, DEAR SOLDIER, BUT WOULD YOU BE SO VERY KIND AS TO TAKE US TO THE LEADER OF YOUR OH SO CHARMING WORLD?
BUT OF COURSE, KIND STRANGER.
OH, HOW CHARMINGLY RUSTIC AND WELL DECORATED!
IT REEKS OF POTATOES!
MI PLANETA ES SU PLANETA, VOYAGERS.
LOOK, A KING ON HIS THRONE—YOU SHOULD BE THERE INSTEAD!
SO WHAT'S KAPUT GONNA DO?

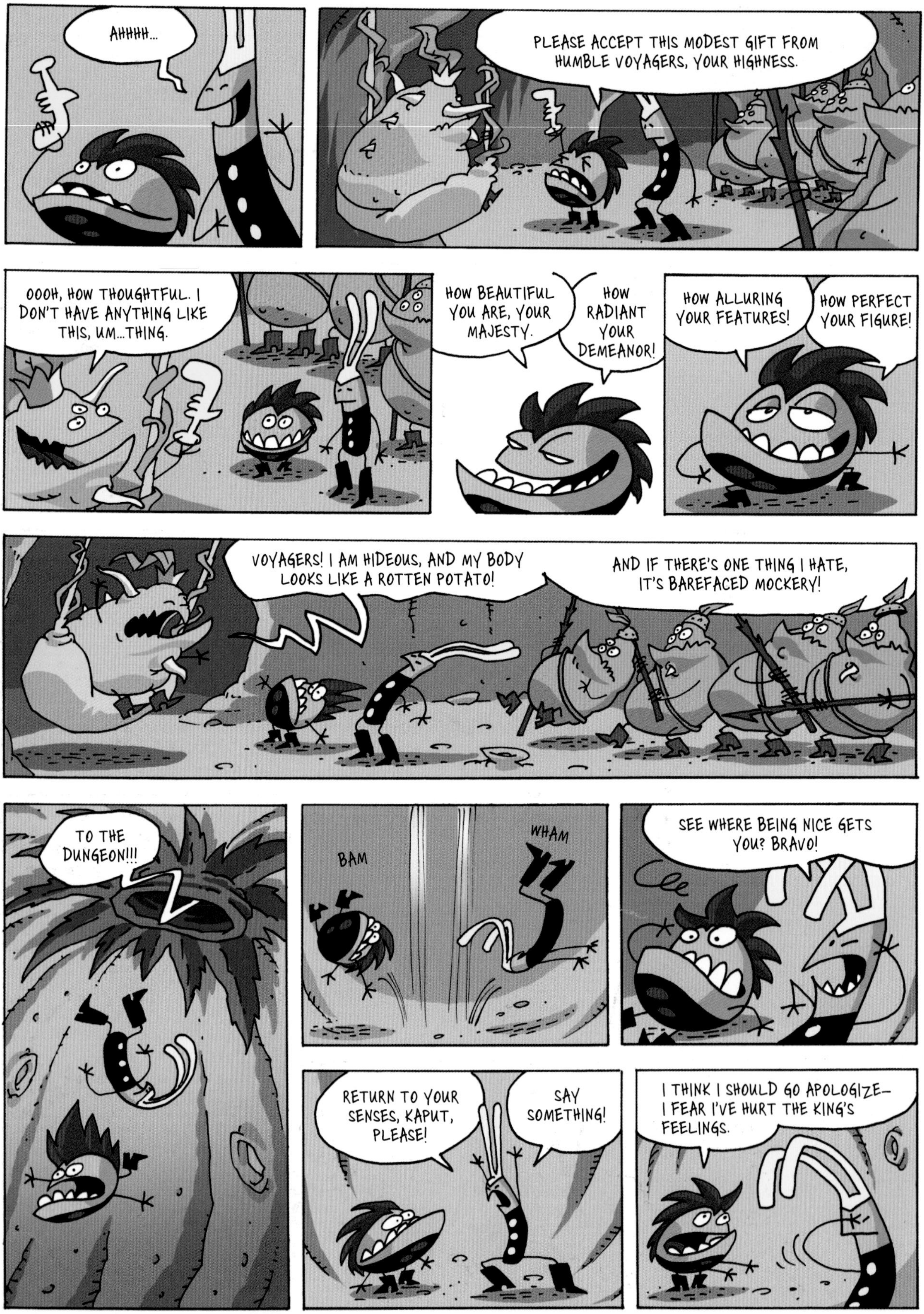
AHHHH...
PLEASE ACCEPT THIS MODEST GIFT FROM HUMBLE VOYAGERS, YOUR HIGHNESS.
OOOH, HOW THOUGHTFUL. I DON'T HAVE ANYTHING LIKE THIS, UM...THING.
HOW BEAUTIFUL YOU ARE, YOUR MAJESTY.
HOW RADIANT YOUR DEMEANOR!
HOW ALLURING YOUR FEATURES!
HOW PERFECT YOUR FIGURE!
VOYAGERS! I AM HIDEOUS, AND MY BODY LOOKS LIKE A ROTTEN POTATO!
AND IF THERE'S ONE THING I HATE, IT'S BAREFACED MOCKERY!
TO THE DUNGEON!!!
BAM
WHAM
SEE WHERE BEING NICE GETS YOU? BRAVO!
RETURN TO YOUR SENSES, KAPUT, PLEASE!
SAY SOMETHING!
I THINK I SHOULD GO APOLOGIZE— I FEAR I'VE HURT THE KING'S FEELINGS.

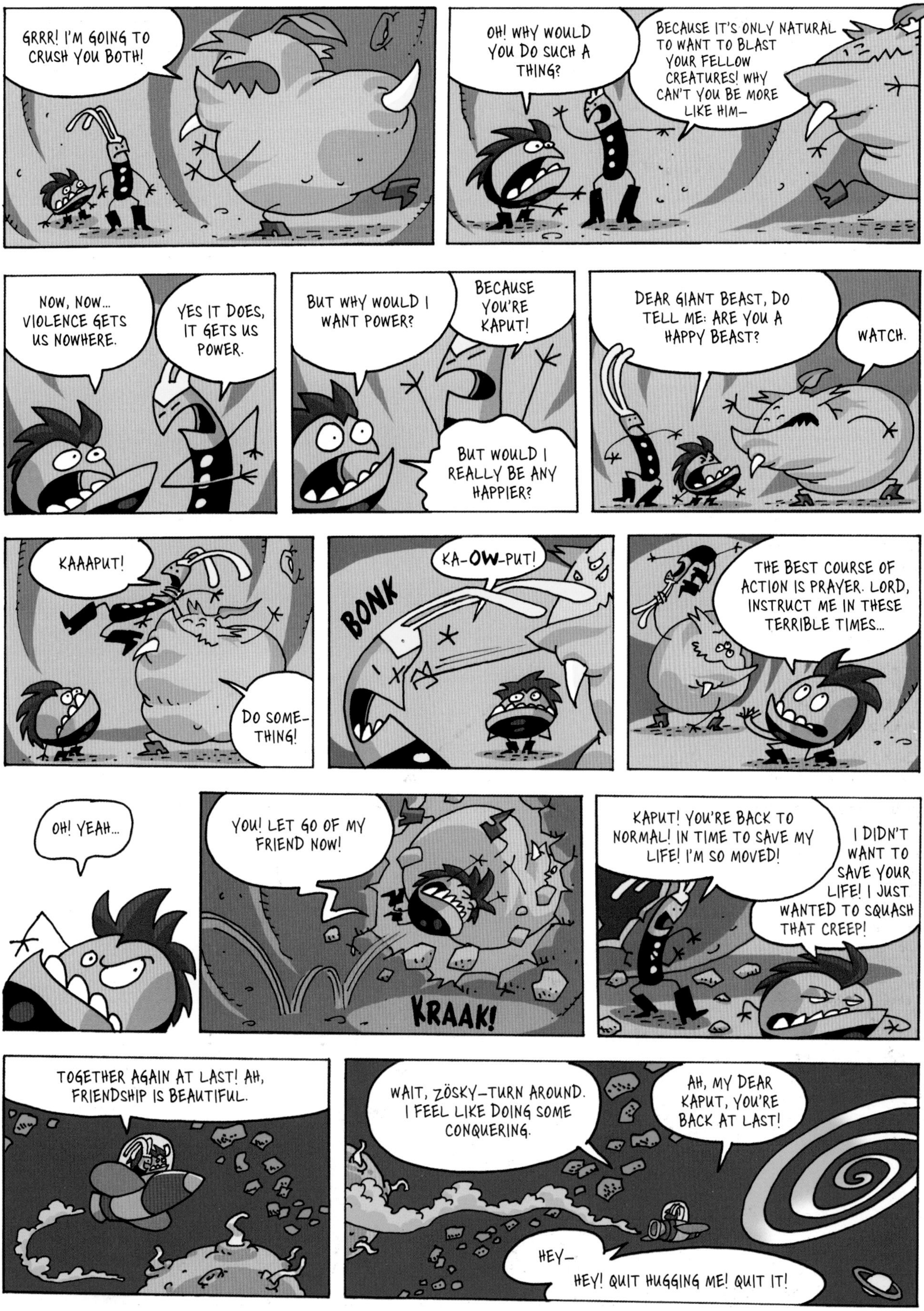
GRRR! I'M GOING TO CRUSH YOU BOTH!
OH! WHY WOULD YOU DO SUCH A THING?
BECAUSE IT'S ONLY NATURAL TO WANT TO BLAST YOUR FELLOW CREATURES! WHY CAN'T YOU BE MORE LIKE HIM–
NOW, NOW... VIOLENCE GETS US NOWHERE.
YES IT DOES, IT GETS US POWER.
BUT WHY WOULD I WANT POWER?
BECAUSE YOU'RE KAPUT!
BUT WOULD I REALLY BE ANY HAPPIER?
DEAR GIANT BEAST, DO TELL ME: ARE YOU A HAPPY BEAST?
WATCH.
KAAAPUT!
DO SOME-THING!
KA-OW-PUT!
BONK
THE BEST COURSE OF ACTION IS PRAYER. LORD, INSTRUCT ME IN THESE TERRIBLE TIMES...
OH! YEAH...
YOU! LET GO OF MY FRIEND NOW!
KRAAK!
KAPUT! YOU'RE BACK TO NORMAL! IN TIME TO SAVE MY LIFE! I'M SO MOVED!
I DIDN'T WANT TO SAVE YOUR LIFE! I JUST WANTED TO SQUASH THAT CREEP!
TOGETHER AGAIN AT LAST! AH, FRIENDSHIP IS BEAUTIFUL.
WAIT, ZÖSKY–TURN AROUND. I FEEL LIKE DOING SOME CONQUERING.
AH, MY DEAR KAPUT, YOU'RE BACK AT LAST!
HEY–
HEY! QUIT HUGGING ME! QUIT IT!

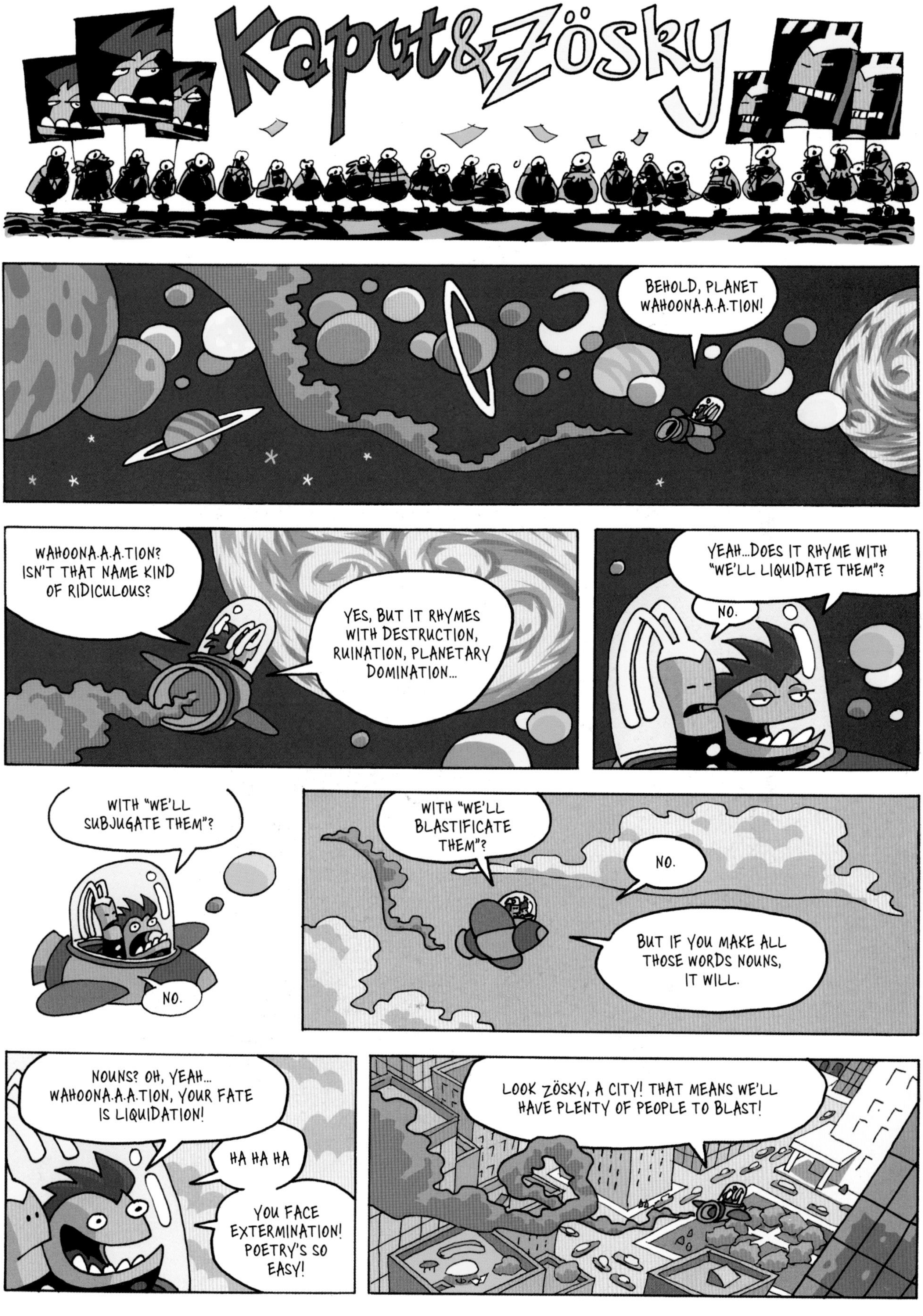
Kaput & Zösky
BEHOLD, PLANET WAHOONA.A.A.TION!
WAHOONA.A.A.TION? ISN'T THAT NAME KIND OF RIDICULOUS?
YES, BUT IT RHYMES WITH DESTRUCTION, RUINATION, PLANETARY DOMINATION...
YEAH...DOES IT RHYME WITH "WE'LL LIQUIDATE THEM"?
NO.
WITH "WE'LL SUBJUGATE THEM"?
NO.
WITH "WE'LL BLASTIFICATE THEM"?
NO.
BUT IF YOU MAKE ALL THOSE WORDS NOUNS, IT WILL.
NOUNS? OH, YEAH... WAHOONA.A.A.TION, YOUR FATE IS LIQUIDATION!
HA HA HA
YOU FACE EXTERMINATION! POETRY'S SO EASY!
LOOK ZÖSKY, A CITY! THAT MEANS WE'LL HAVE PLENTY OF PEOPLE TO BLAST!

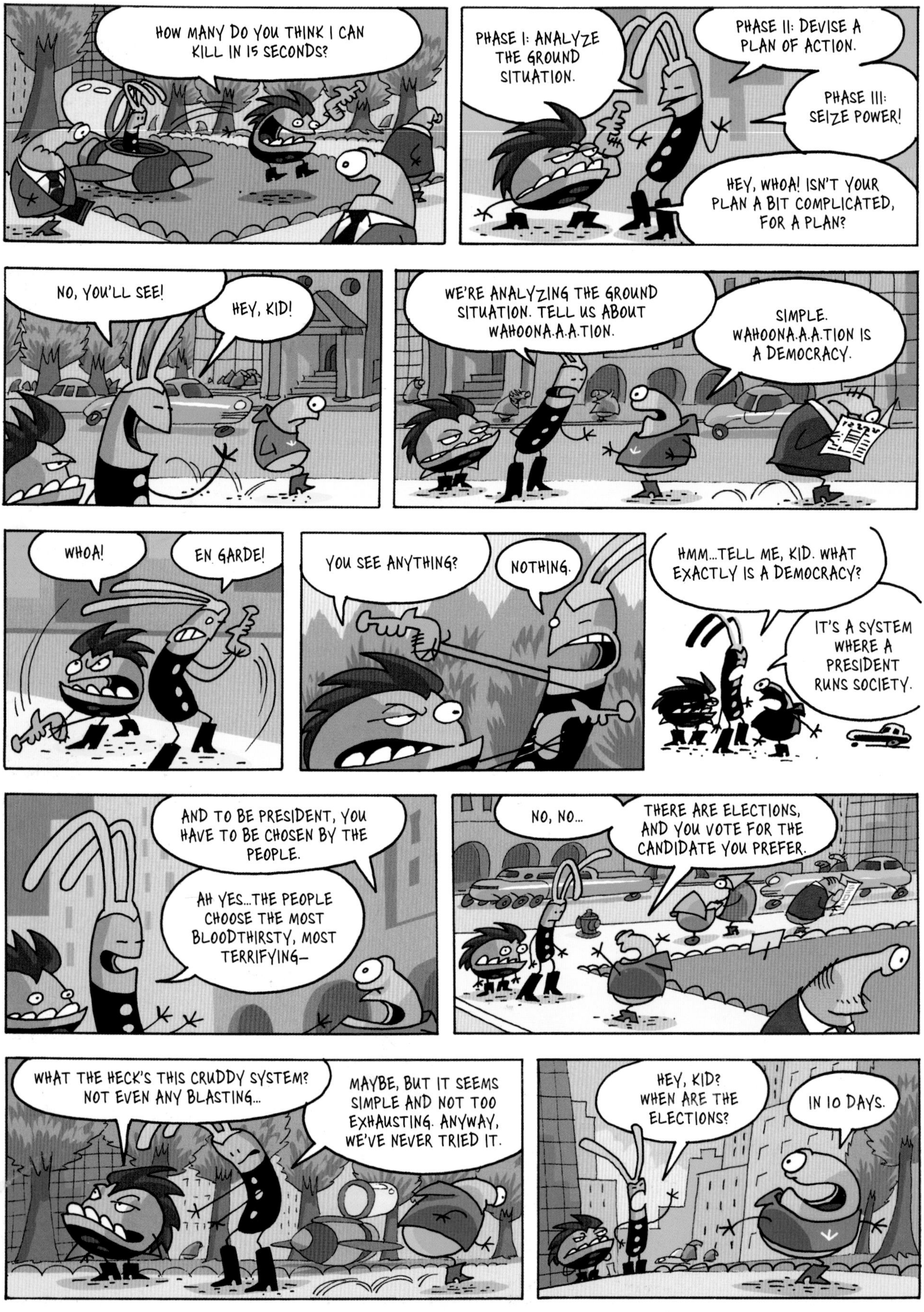
HOW MANY DO YOU THINK I CAN KILL IN 15 SECONDS?
PHASE I: ANALYZE THE GROUND SITUATION.
PHASE II: DEVISE A PLAN OF ACTION.
PHASE III: SEIZE POWER!
HEY, WHOA! ISN'T YOUR PLAN A BIT COMPLICATED, FOR A PLAN?
NO, YOU'LL SEE!
HEY, KID!
WE'RE ANALYZING THE GROUND SITUATION. TELL US ABOUT WAHOONA.A.A.TION.
SIMPLE. WAHOONA.A.A.TION IS A DEMOCRACY.
WHOA!
EN GARDE!
YOU SEE ANYTHING?
NOTHING.
HMM...TELL ME, KID. WHAT EXACTLY IS A DEMOCRACY?
IT'S A SYSTEM WHERE A PRESIDENT RUNS SOCIETY.
AND TO BE PRESIDENT, YOU HAVE TO BE CHOSEN BY THE PEOPLE.
AH YES...THE PEOPLE CHOOSE THE MOST BLOODTHIRSTY, MOST TERRIFYING—
NO, NO...
THERE ARE ELECTIONS, AND YOU VOTE FOR THE CANDIDATE YOU PREFER.
WHAT THE HECK'S THIS CRUDDY SYSTEM? NOT EVEN ANY BLASTING...
MAYBE, BUT IT SEEMS SIMPLE AND NOT TOO EXHAUSTING. ANYWAY, WE'VE NEVER TRIED IT.
HEY, KID? WHEN ARE THE ELECTIONS?
IN 10 DAYS.

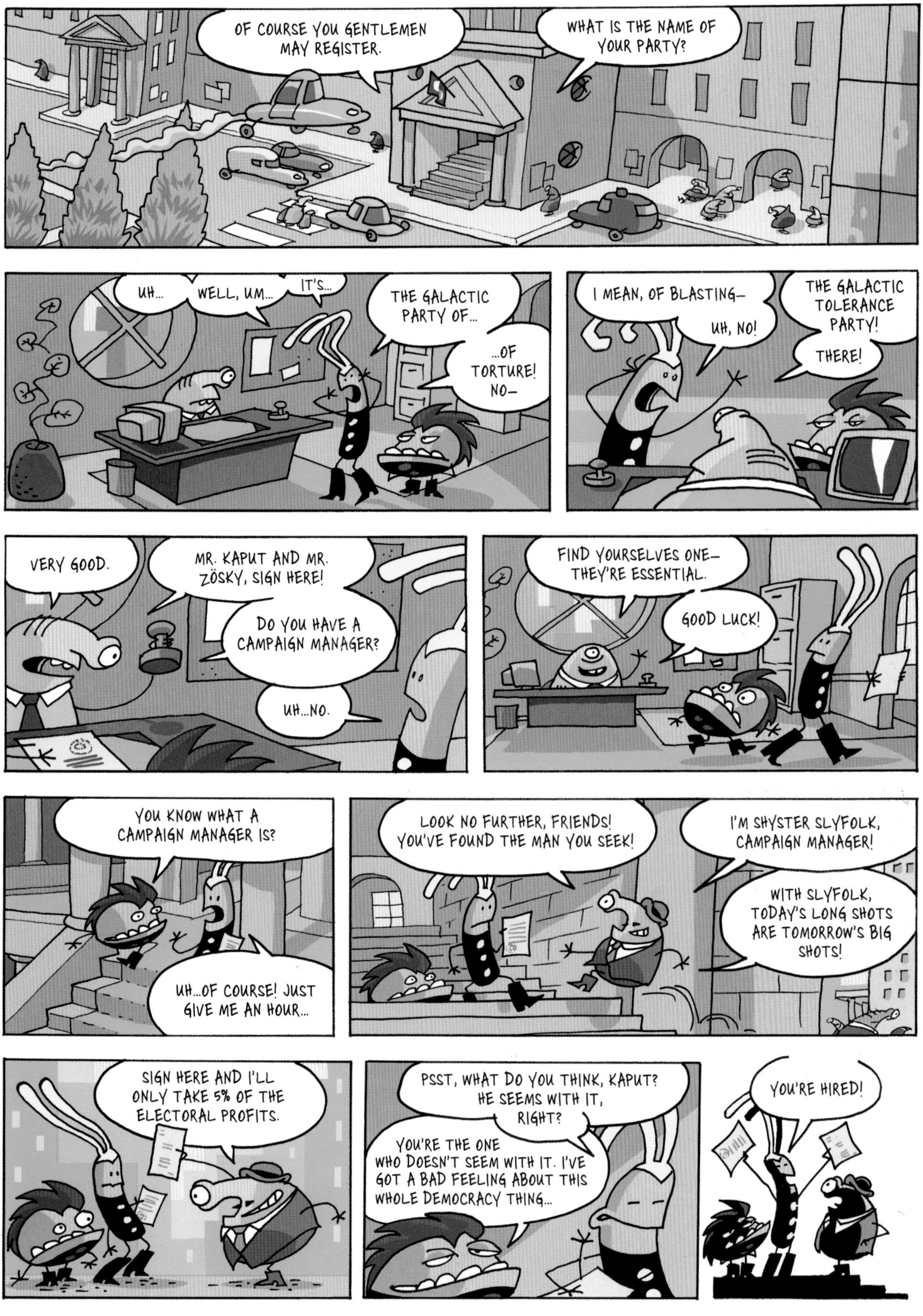

OF COURSE YOU GENTLEMEN MAY REGISTER.
WHAT IS THE NAME OF YOUR PARTY?
UH...
WELL, UM...
IT'S...
THE GALACTIC PARTY OF...
...OF TORTURE! NO—
I MEAN, OF BLASTING—
UH, NO!
THE GALACTIC TOLERANCE PARTY!
THERE!
VERY GOOD.
MR. KAPUT AND MR. ZÖSKY, SIGN HERE!
DO YOU HAVE A CAMPAIGN MANAGER?
UH...NO.
FIND YOURSELVES ONE— THEY'RE ESSENTIAL.
GOOD LUCK!
YOU KNOW WHAT A CAMPAIGN MANAGER IS?
UH...OF COURSE! JUST GIVE ME AN HOUR...
LOOK NO FURTHER, FRIENDS! YOU'VE FOUND THE MAN YOU SEEK!
I'M SHYSTER SLYFOLK, CAMPAIGN MANAGER!
WITH SLYFOLK, TODAY'S LONG SHOTS ARE TOMORROW'S BIG SHOTS!
SIGN HERE AND I'LL ONLY TAKE 5% OF THE ELECTORAL PROFITS.
PSST, WHAT DO YOU THINK, KAPUT? HE SEEMS WITH IT, RIGHT?
YOU'RE THE ONE WHO DOESN'T SEEM WITH IT. I'VE GOT A BAD FEELING ABOUT THIS WHOLE DEMOCRACY THING...
YOU'RE HIRED!

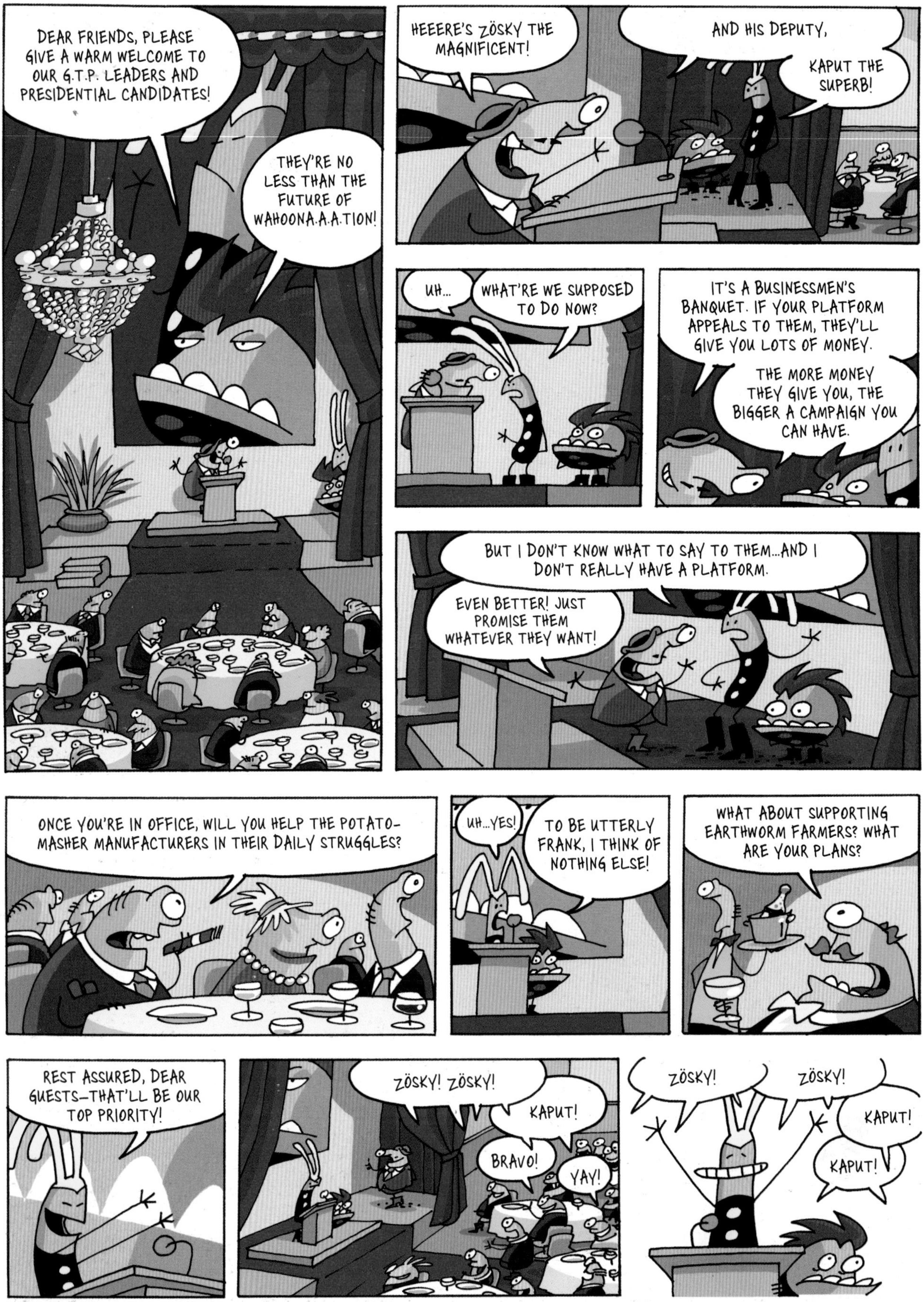

DEAR FRIENDS, PLEASE GIVE A WARM WELCOME TO OUR G.T.P. LEADERS AND PRESIDENTIAL CANDIDATES!
THEY'RE NO LESS THAN THE FUTURE OF WAHOONA.A.A.TION!
HEEERE'S ZÖSKY THE MAGNIFICENT!
AND HIS DEPUTY,
KAPUT THE SUPERB!
UH...
WHAT'RE WE SUPPOSED TO DO NOW?
IT'S A BUSINESSMEN'S BANQUET. IF YOUR PLATFORM APPEALS TO THEM, THEY'LL GIVE YOU LOTS OF MONEY.
THE MORE MONEY THEY GIVE YOU, THE BIGGER A CAMPAIGN YOU CAN HAVE.
BUT I DON'T KNOW WHAT TO SAY TO THEM...AND I DON'T REALLY HAVE A PLATFORM.
EVEN BETTER! JUST PROMISE THEM WHATEVER THEY WANT!
ONCE YOU'RE IN OFFICE, WILL YOU HELP THE POTATO-MASHER MANUFACTURERS IN THEIR DAILY STRUGGLES?
UH...YES!
TO BE UTTERLY FRANK, I THINK OF NOTHING ELSE!
WHAT ABOUT SUPPORTING EARTHWORM FARMERS? WHAT ARE YOUR PLANS?
REST ASSURED, DEAR GUESTS—THAT'LL BE OUR TOP PRIORITY!
ZÖSKY! ZÖSKY!
KAPUT!
BRAVO!
YAY!
ZÖSKY!
ZÖSKY!
KAPUT!
KAPUT!

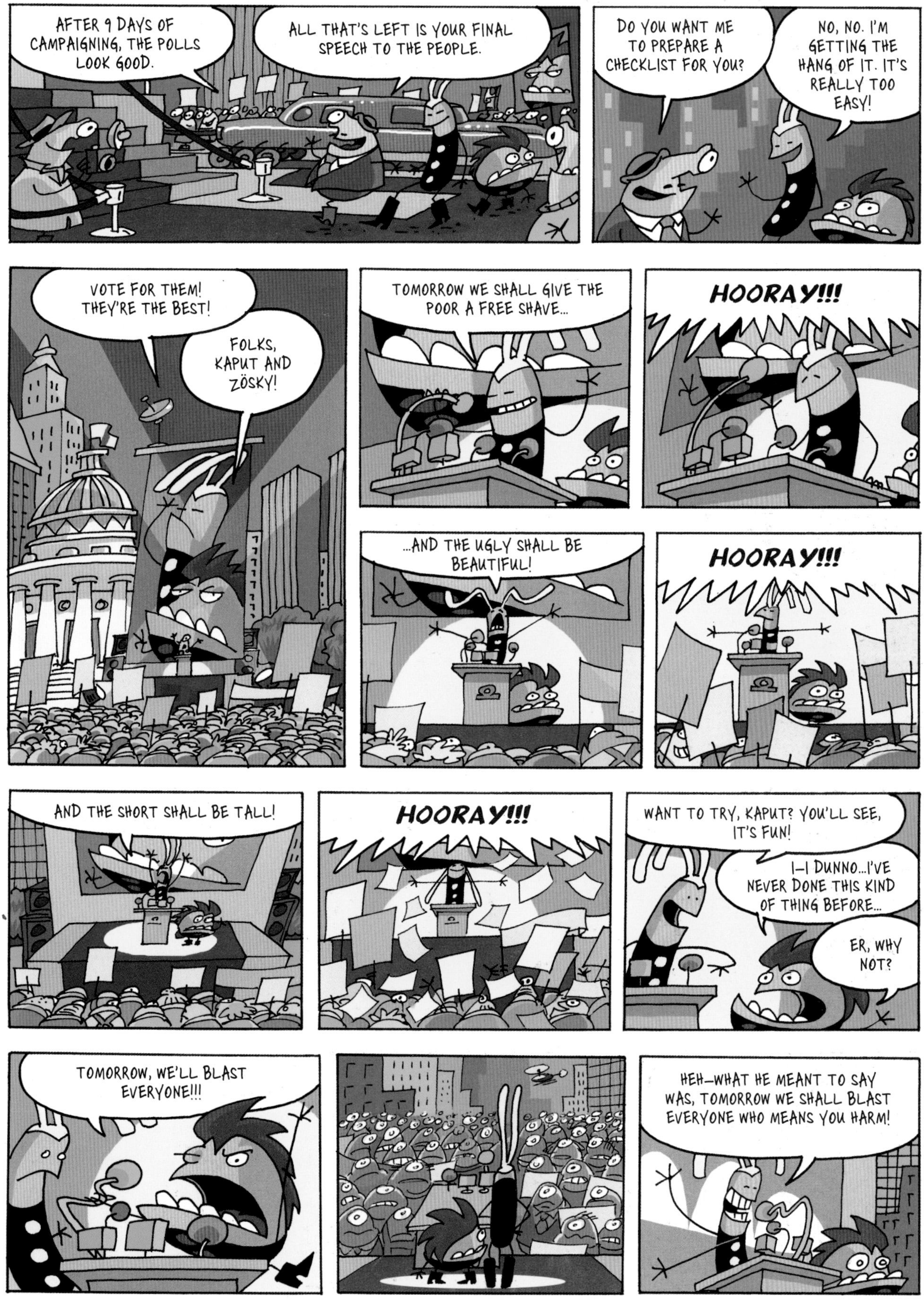
AFTER 9 DAYS OF CAMPAIGNING, THE POLLS LOOK GOOD.
ALL THAT'S LEFT IS YOUR FINAL SPEECH TO THE PEOPLE.
DO YOU WANT ME TO PREPARE A CHECKLIST FOR YOU?
NO, NO. I'M GETTING THE HANG OF IT. IT'S REALLY TOO EASY!
VOTE FOR THEM! THEY'RE THE BEST!
FOLKS, KAPUT AND ZÖSKY!
TOMORROW WE SHALL GIVE THE POOR A FREE SHAVE...
HOORAY!!!
...AND THE UGLY SHALL BE BEAUTIFUL!
HOORAY!!!
AND THE SHORT SHALL BE TALL!
HOORAY!!!
WANT TO TRY, KAPUT? YOU'LL SEE, IT'S FUN!
I—I DUNNO...I'VE NEVER DONE THIS KIND OF THING BEFORE...
ER, WHY NOT?
TOMORROW, WE'LL BLAST EVERYONE!!!
HEH—WHAT HE MEANT TO SAY WAS, TOMORROW WE SHALL BLAST EVERYONE WHO MEANS YOU HARM!

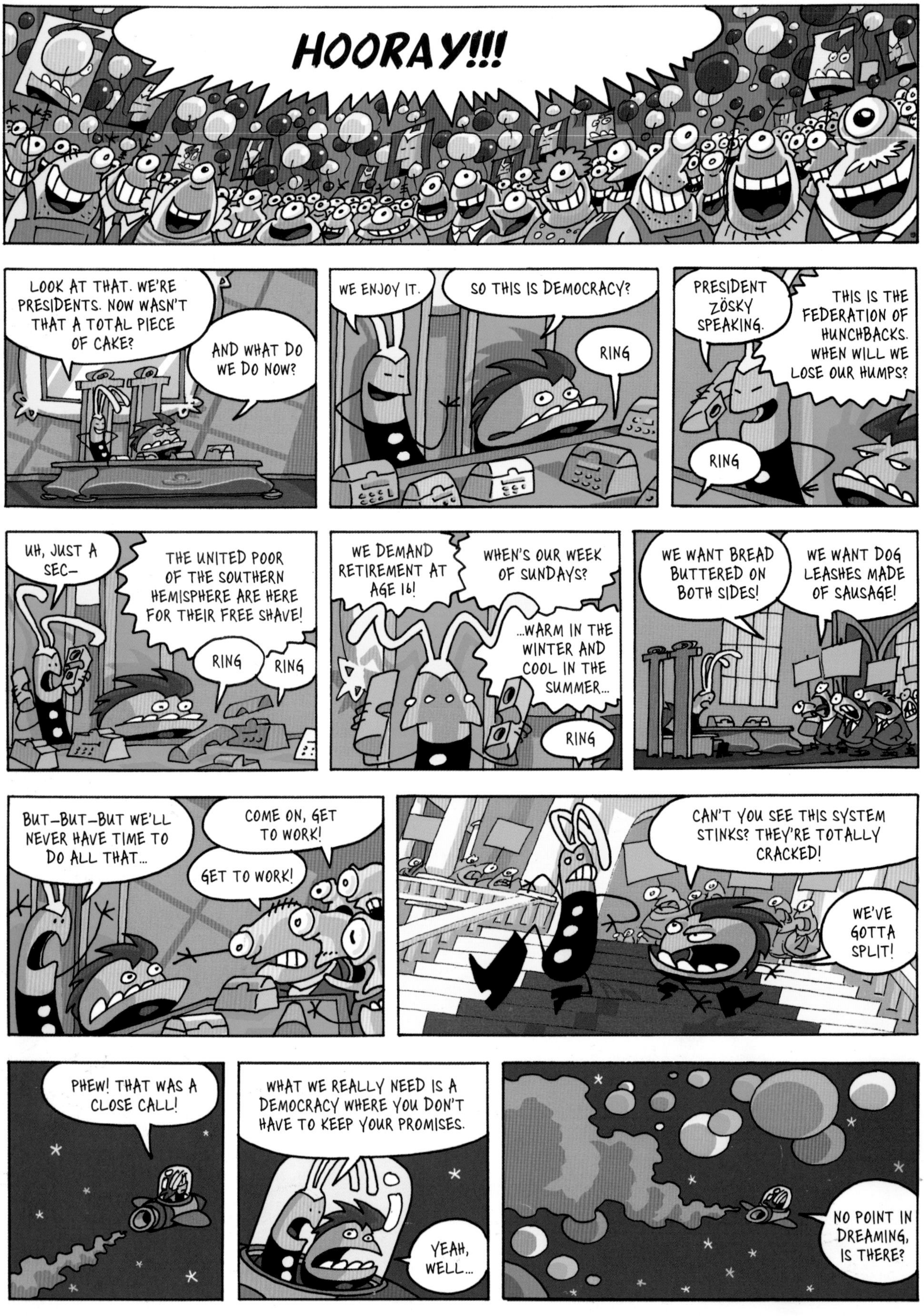
HOORAY!!!
LOOK AT THAT. WE'RE PRESIDENTS. NOW WASN'T THAT A TOTAL PIECE OF CAKE?
AND WHAT DO WE DO NOW?
WE ENJOY IT.
SO THIS IS DEMOCRACY?
RING
PRESIDENT ZÖSKY SPEAKING.
THIS IS THE FEDERATION OF HUNCHBACKS. WHEN WILL WE LOSE OUR HUMPS?
RING
UH, JUST A SEC—
THE UNITED POOR OF THE SOUTHERN HEMISPHERE ARE HERE FOR THEIR FREE SHAVE!
RING
RING
WE DEMAND RETIREMENT AT AGE 16!
WHEN'S OUR WEEK OF SUNDAYS?
...WARM IN THE WINTER AND COOL IN THE SUMMER...
RING
WE WANT BREAD BUTTERED ON BOTH SIDES!
WE WANT DOG LEASHES MADE OF SAUSAGE!
BUT—BUT—BUT WE'LL NEVER HAVE TIME TO DO ALL THAT...
COME ON, GET TO WORK!
GET TO WORK!
CAN'T YOU SEE THIS SYSTEM STINKS? THEY'RE TOTALLY CRACKED!
WE'VE GOTTA SPLIT!
PHEW! THAT WAS A CLOSE CALL!
WHAT WE REALLY NEED IS A DEMOCRACY WHERE YOU DON'T HAVE TO KEEP YOUR PROMISES.
YEAH, WELL...
NO POINT IN DREAMING, IS THERE?

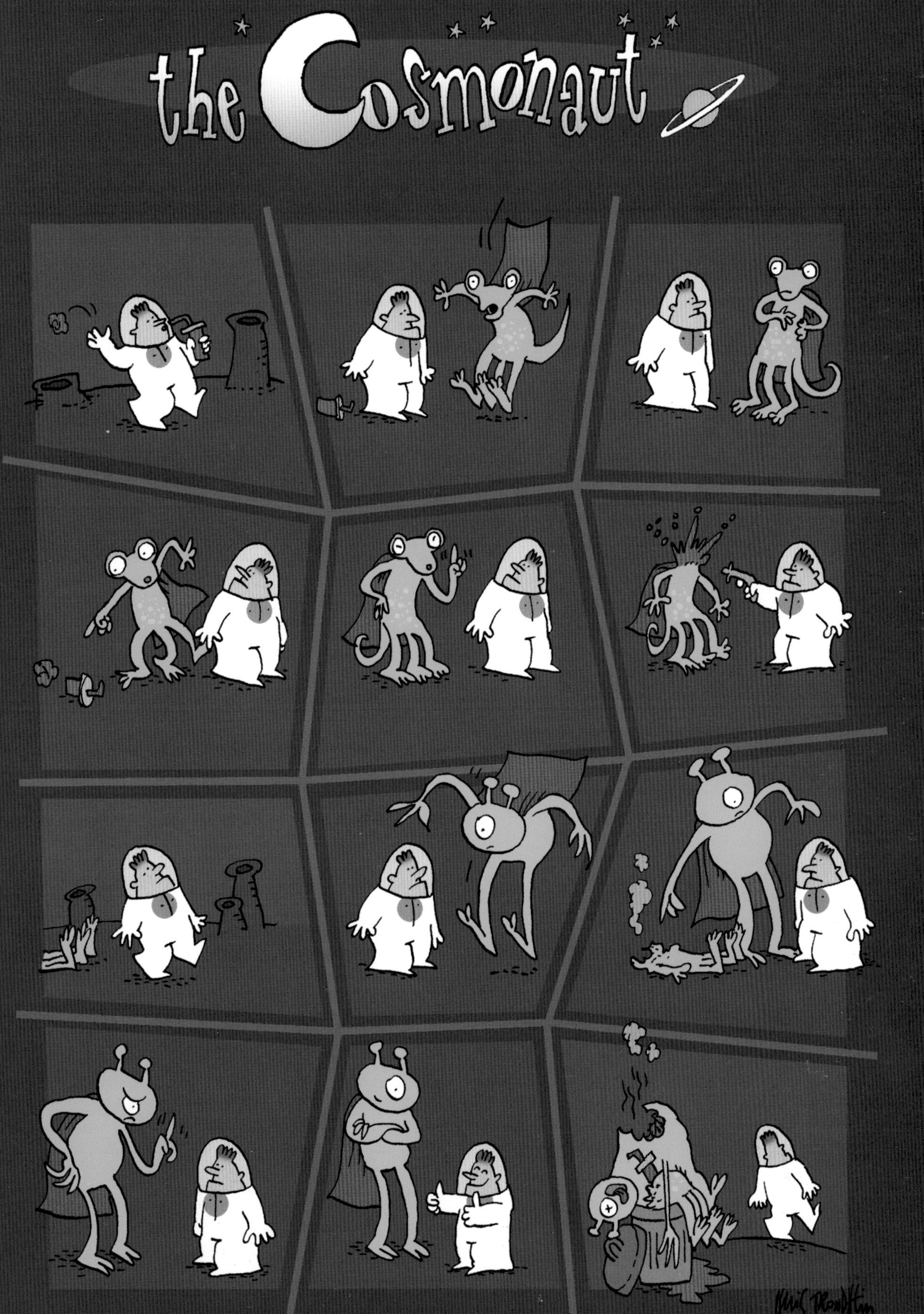
the Cosmonaut

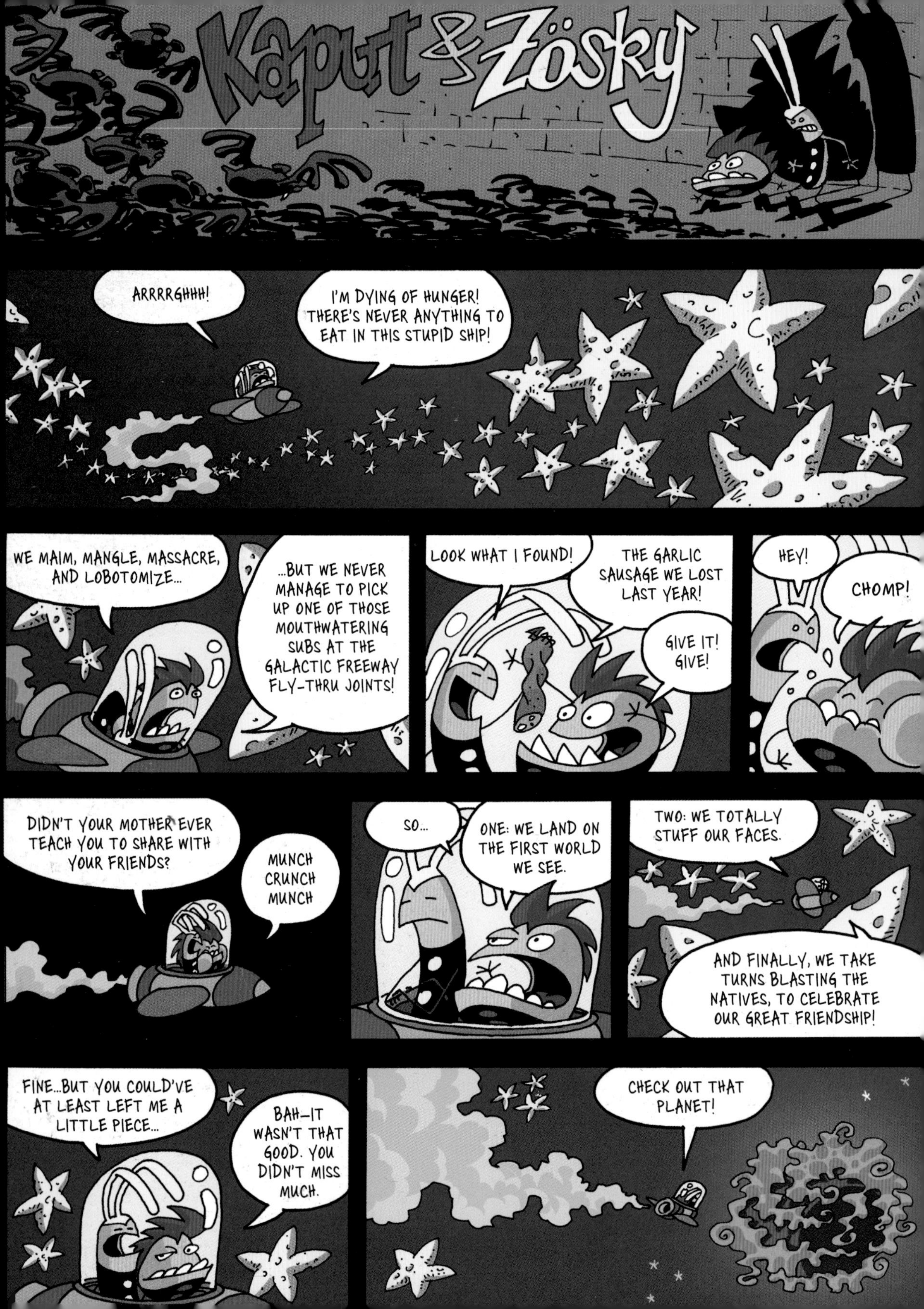
Kaput & Zösky
ARRRRGHHH!
I'M DYING OF HUNGER! THERE'S NEVER ANYTHING TO EAT IN THIS STUPID SHIP!
WE MAIM, MANGLE, MASSACRE, AND LOBOTOMIZE...
...BUT WE NEVER MANAGE TO PICK UP ONE OF THOSE MOUTHWATERING SUBS AT THE GALACTIC FREEWAY FLY-THRU JOINTS!
LOOK WHAT I FOUND!
THE GARLIC SAUSAGE WE LOST LAST YEAR!
GIVE IT! GIVE!
HEY!
CHOMP!
DIDN'T YOUR MOTHER EVER TEACH YOU TO SHARE WITH YOUR FRIENDS?
MUNCH CRUNCH MUNCH
SO...
ONE: WE LAND ON THE FIRST WORLD WE SEE.
TWO: WE TOTALLY STUFF OUR FACES.
AND FINALLY, WE TAKE TURNS BLASTING THE NATIVES, TO CELEBRATE OUR GREAT FRIENDSHIP!
FINE...BUT YOU COULD'VE AT LEAST LEFT ME A LITTLE PIECE...
BAH—IT WASN'T THAT GOOD. YOU DIDN'T MISS MUCH.
CHECK OUT THAT PLANET!

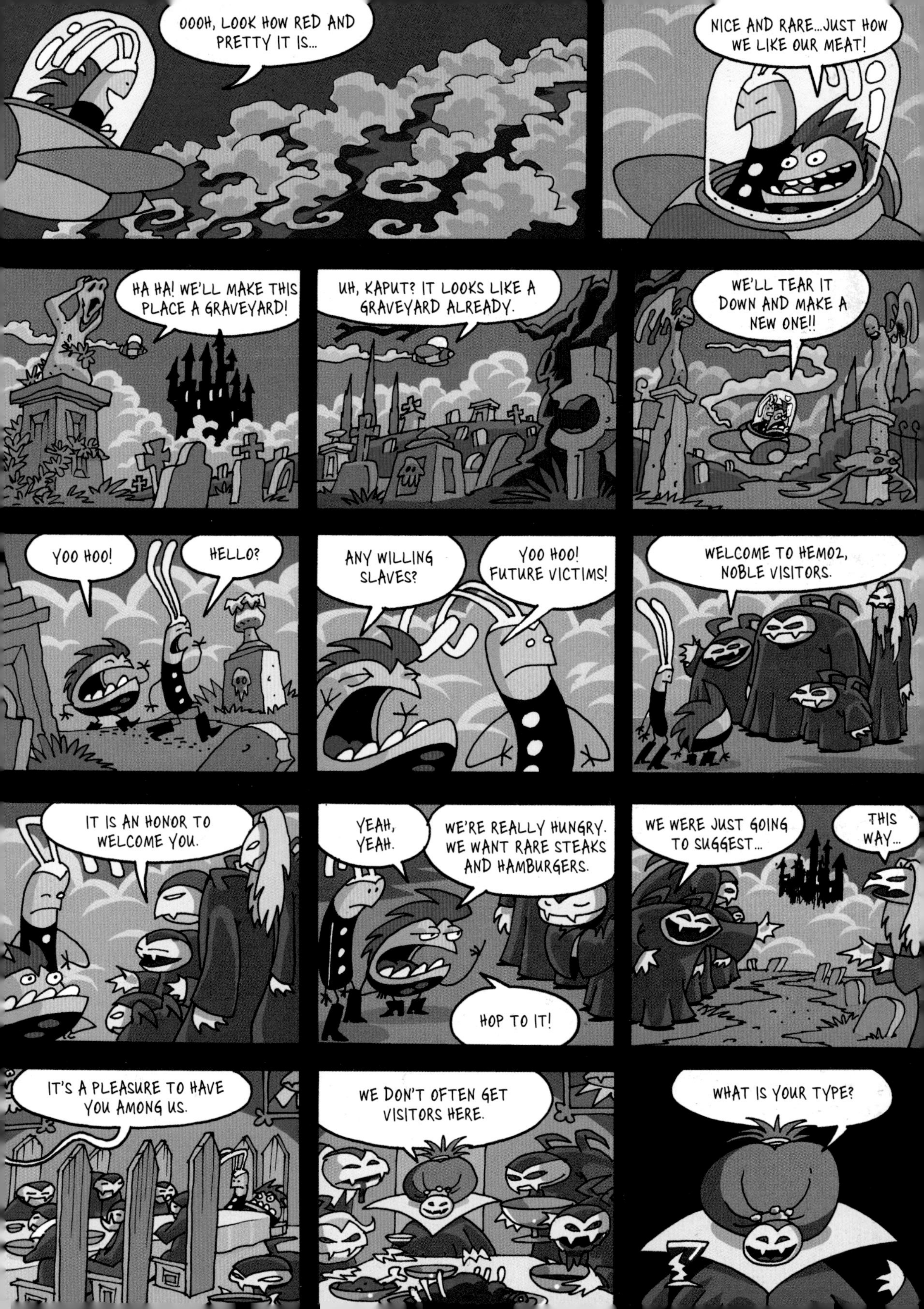
OOOH, LOOK HOW RED AND PRETTY IT IS...
NICE AND RARE...JUST HOW WE LIKE OUR MEAT!
HA HA! WE'LL MAKE THIS PLACE A GRAVEYARD!
UH, KAPUT? IT LOOKS LIKE A GRAVEYARD ALREADY.
WE'LL TEAR IT DOWN AND MAKE A NEW ONE!!
YOO HOO!
HELLO?
ANY WILLING SLAVES?
YOO HOO! FUTURE VICTIMS!
WELCOME TO HEMO2, NOBLE VISITORS.
IT IS AN HONOR TO WELCOME YOU.
YEAH, YEAH.
WE'RE REALLY HUNGRY. WE WANT RARE STEAKS AND HAMBURGERS.
HOP TO IT!
WE WERE JUST GOING TO SUGGEST...
THIS WAY...
IT'S A PLEASURE TO HAVE YOU AMONG US.
WE DON'T OFTEN GET VISITORS HERE.
WHAT IS YOUR TYPE?

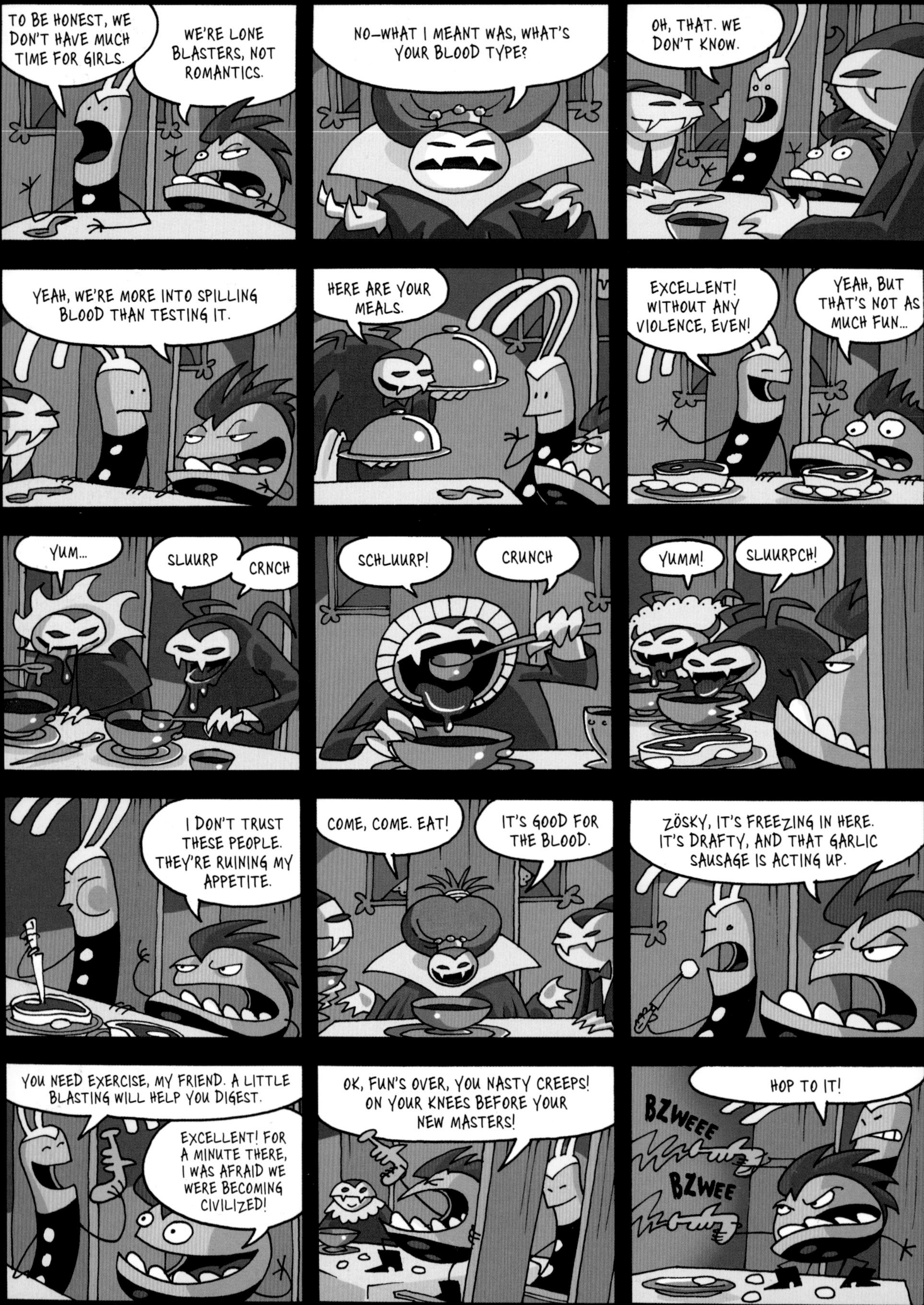
TO BE HONEST, WE DON'T HAVE MUCH TIME FOR GIRLS.
WE'RE LONE BLASTERS, NOT ROMANTICS.
NO—WHAT I MEANT WAS, WHAT'S YOUR BLOOD TYPE?
OH, THAT. WE DON'T KNOW.
YEAH, WE'RE MORE INTO SPILLING BLOOD THAN TESTING IT.
HERE ARE YOUR MEALS.
EXCELLENT! WITHOUT ANY VIOLENCE, EVEN!
YEAH, BUT THAT'S NOT AS MUCH FUN...
YUM...
SLUURP
CRNCH
SCHLUURP!
CRUNCH
YUMM!
SLUURPCH!
I DON'T TRUST THESE PEOPLE. THEY'RE RUINING MY APPETITE.
COME, COME. EAT!
IT'S GOOD FOR THE BLOOD.
ZÖSKY, IT'S FREEZING IN HERE. IT'S DRAFTY, AND THAT GARLIC SAUSAGE IS ACTING UP.
YOU NEED EXERCISE, MY FRIEND. A LITTLE BLASTING WILL HELP YOU DIGEST.
EXCELLENT! FOR A MINUTE THERE, I WAS AFRAID WE WERE BECOMING CIVILIZED!
OK, FUN'S OVER, YOU NASTY CREEPS! ON YOUR KNEES BEFORE YOUR NEW MASTERS!
HOP TO IT!
BZWEEE
BZWEE

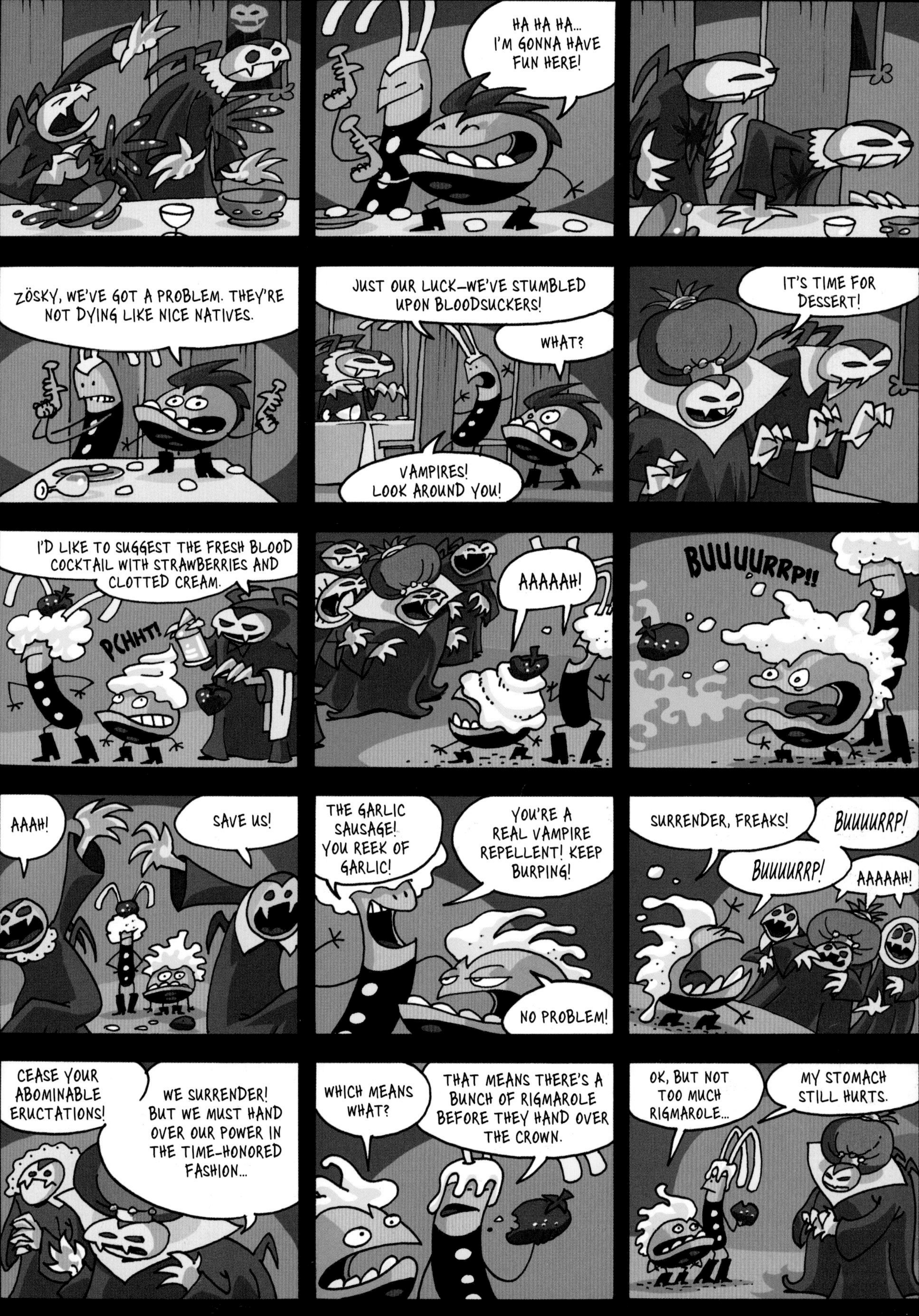
HA HA HA...
I'M GONNA HAVE FUN HERE!
ZÖSKY, WE'VE GOT A PROBLEM. THEY'RE NOT DYING LIKE NICE NATIVES.
JUST OUR LUCK—WE'VE STUMBLED UPON BLOODSUCKERS!
WHAT?
VAMPIRES! LOOK AROUND YOU!
IT'S TIME FOR DESSERT!
I'D LIKE TO SUGGEST THE FRESH BLOOD COCKTAIL WITH STRAWBERRIES AND CLOTTED CREAM.
PCHHT!
AAAAAH!
BUUUURRP!!
AAAH!
SAVE US!
THE GARLIC SAUSAGE! YOU REEK OF GARLIC!
YOU'RE A REAL VAMPIRE REPELLENT! KEEP BURPING!
NO PROBLEM!
SURRENDER, FREAKS!
BUUUURRP!
BUUUURRP!
AAAAAH!
CEASE YOUR ABOMINABLE ERUCTATIONS!
WE SURRENDER! BUT WE MUST HAND OVER OUR POWER IN THE TIME-HONORED FASHION...
WHICH MEANS WHAT?
THAT MEANS THERE'S A BUNCH OF RIGMAROLE BEFORE THEY HAND OVER THE CROWN.
OK, BUT NOT TOO MUCH RIGMAROLE...
MY STOMACH STILL HURTS.

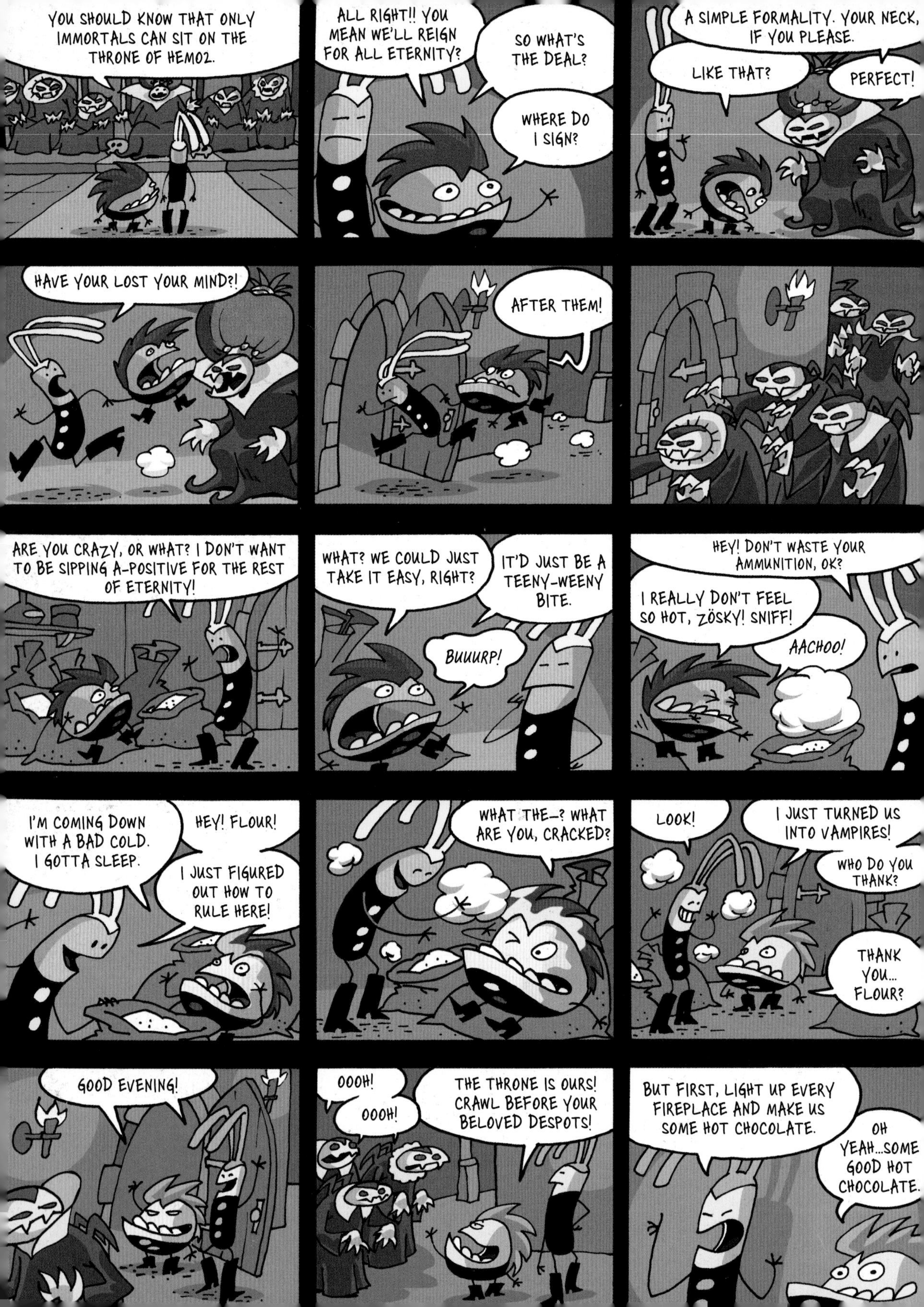
YOU SHOULD KNOW THAT ONLY IMMORTALS CAN SIT ON THE THRONE OF HEMOZ.
ALL RIGHT!! YOU MEAN WE'LL REIGN FOR ALL ETERNITY?
SO WHAT'S THE DEAL?
WHERE DO I SIGN?
A SIMPLE FORMALITY. YOUR NECK, IF YOU PLEASE.
LIKE THAT?
PERFECT!
HAVE YOUR LOST YOUR MIND?!
AFTER THEM!
ARE YOU CRAZY, OR WHAT? I DON'T WANT TO BE SIPPING A-POSITIVE FOR THE REST OF ETERNITY!
WHAT? WE COULD JUST TAKE IT EASY, RIGHT?
IT'D JUST BE A TEENY-WEENY BITE.
BUUURP!
HEY! DON'T WASTE YOUR AMMUNITION, OK?
I REALLY DON'T FEEL SO HOT, ZÖSKY! SNIFF!
AACHOO!
I'M COMING DOWN WITH A BAD COLD. I GOTTA SLEEP.
HEY! FLOUR!
I JUST FIGURED OUT HOW TO RULE HERE!
WHAT THE—? WHAT ARE YOU, CRACKED?
LOOK!
I JUST TURNED US INTO VAMPIRES!
WHO DO YOU THANK?
THANK YOU... FLOUR?
GOOD EVENING!
OOOH!
OOOH!
THE THRONE IS OURS! CRAWL BEFORE YOUR BELOVED DESPOTS!
BUT FIRST, LIGHT UP EVERY FIREPLACE AND MAKE US SOME HOT CHOCOLATE.
OH YEAH...SOME GOOD HOT CHOCOLATE.

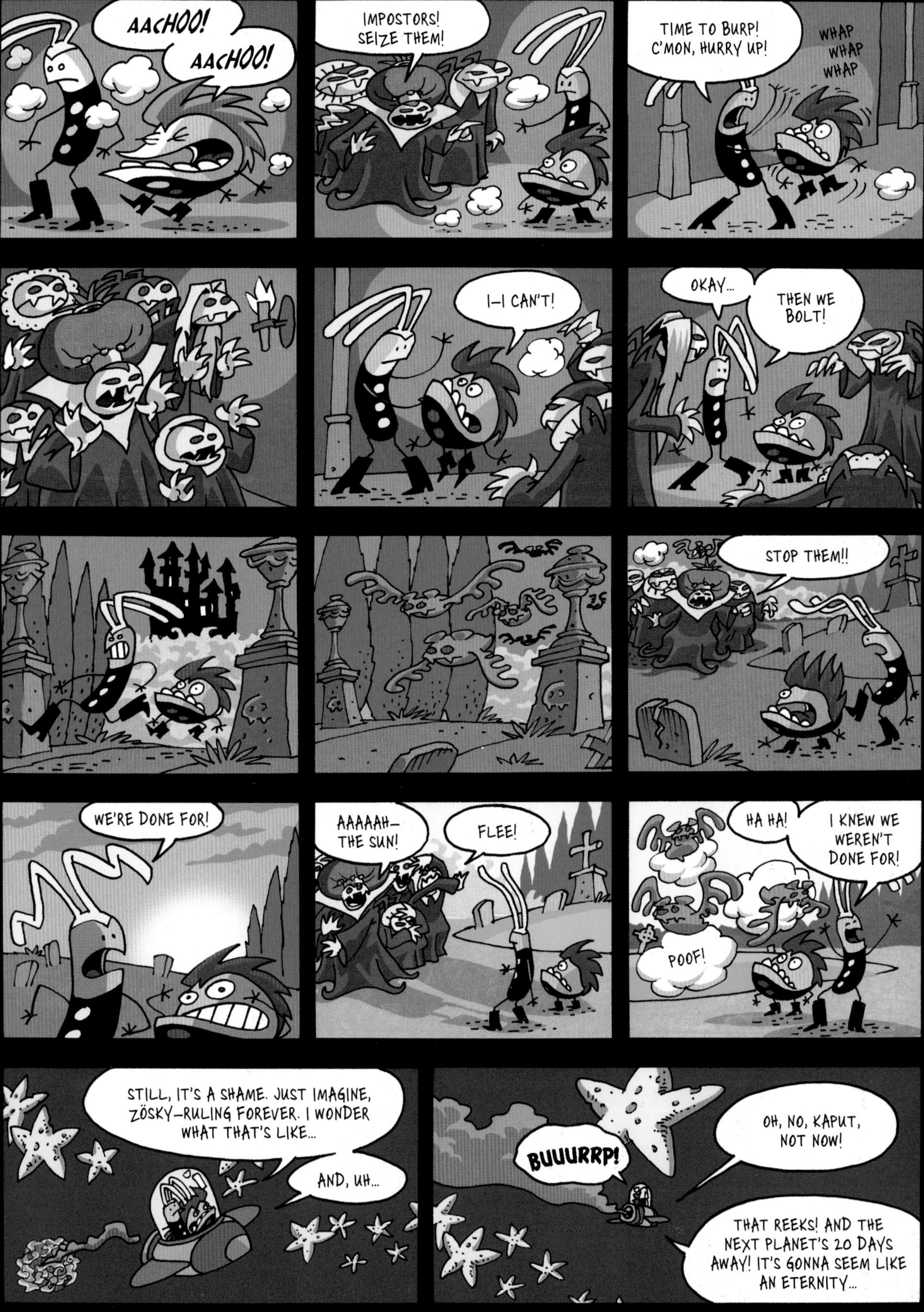
AACHOO!
AACHOO!
IMPOSTORS! SEIZE THEM!
TIME TO BURP! C'MON, HURRY UP!
WHAP WHAP WHAP
I–I CAN'T!
OKAY...
THEN WE BOLT!
STOP THEM!!
WE'RE DONE FOR!
AAAAAH– THE SUN!
FLEE!
HA HA!
I KNEW WE WEREN'T DONE FOR!
POOF!
STILL, IT'S A SHAME. JUST IMAGINE, ZÖSKY–RULING FOREVER. I WONDER WHAT THAT'S LIKE...
AND, UH...
BUUURRP!
OH, NO, KAPUT, NOT NOW!
THAT REEKS! AND THE NEXT PLANET'S 20 DAYS AWAY! IT'S GONNA SEEM LIKE AN ETERNITY...

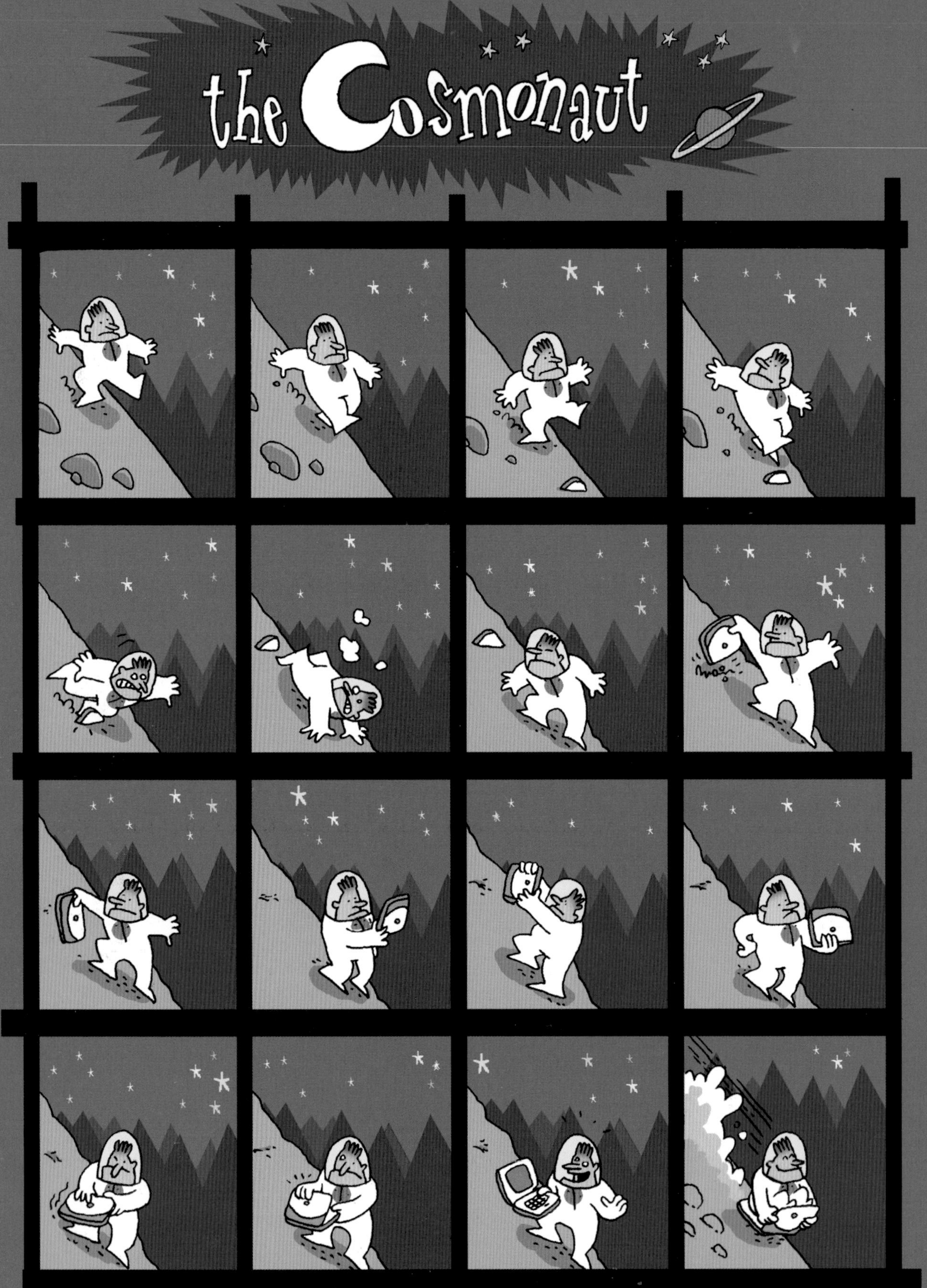
the Cosmonaut

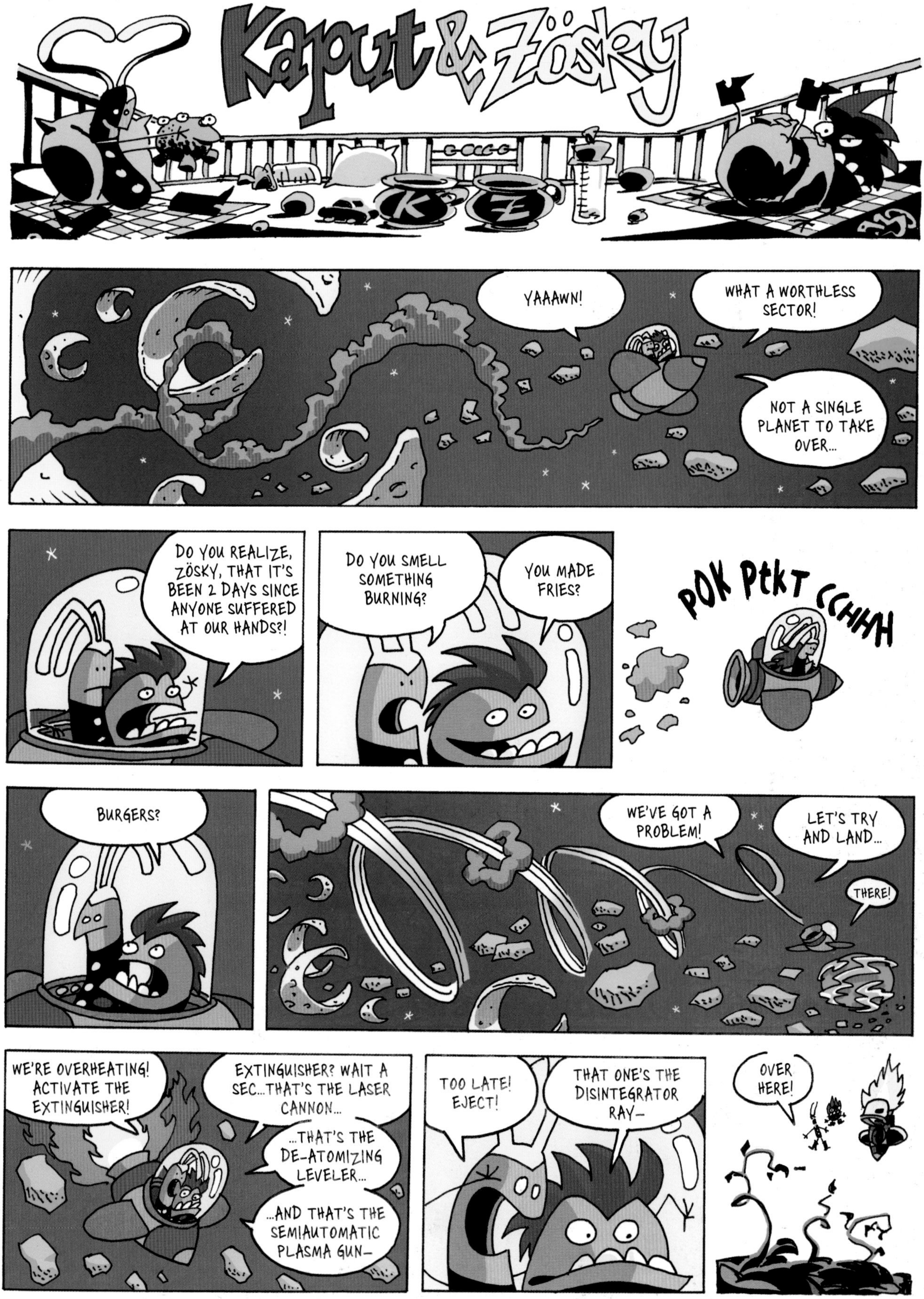

Kaput & Zösky
YAAAWN!
WHAT A WORTHLESS SECTOR!
NOT A SINGLE PLANET TO TAKE OVER...
DO YOU REALIZE, ZÖSKY, THAT IT'S BEEN 2 DAYS SINCE ANYONE SUFFERED AT OUR HANDS?!
DO YOU SMELL SOMETHING BURNING?
YOU MADE FRIES?
POK PtKT CCHHH
BURGERS?
WE'VE GOT A PROBLEM!
LET'S TRY AND LAND...
THERE!
WE'RE OVERHEATING! ACTIVATE THE EXTINGUISHER!
EXTINGUISHER? WAIT A SEC...THAT'S THE LASER CANNON...
...THAT'S THE DE-ATOMIZING LEVELER...
...AND THAT'S THE SEMIAUTOMATIC PLASMA GUN—
TOO LATE! EJECT!
THAT ONE'S THE DISINTEGRATOR RAY—
OVER HERE!

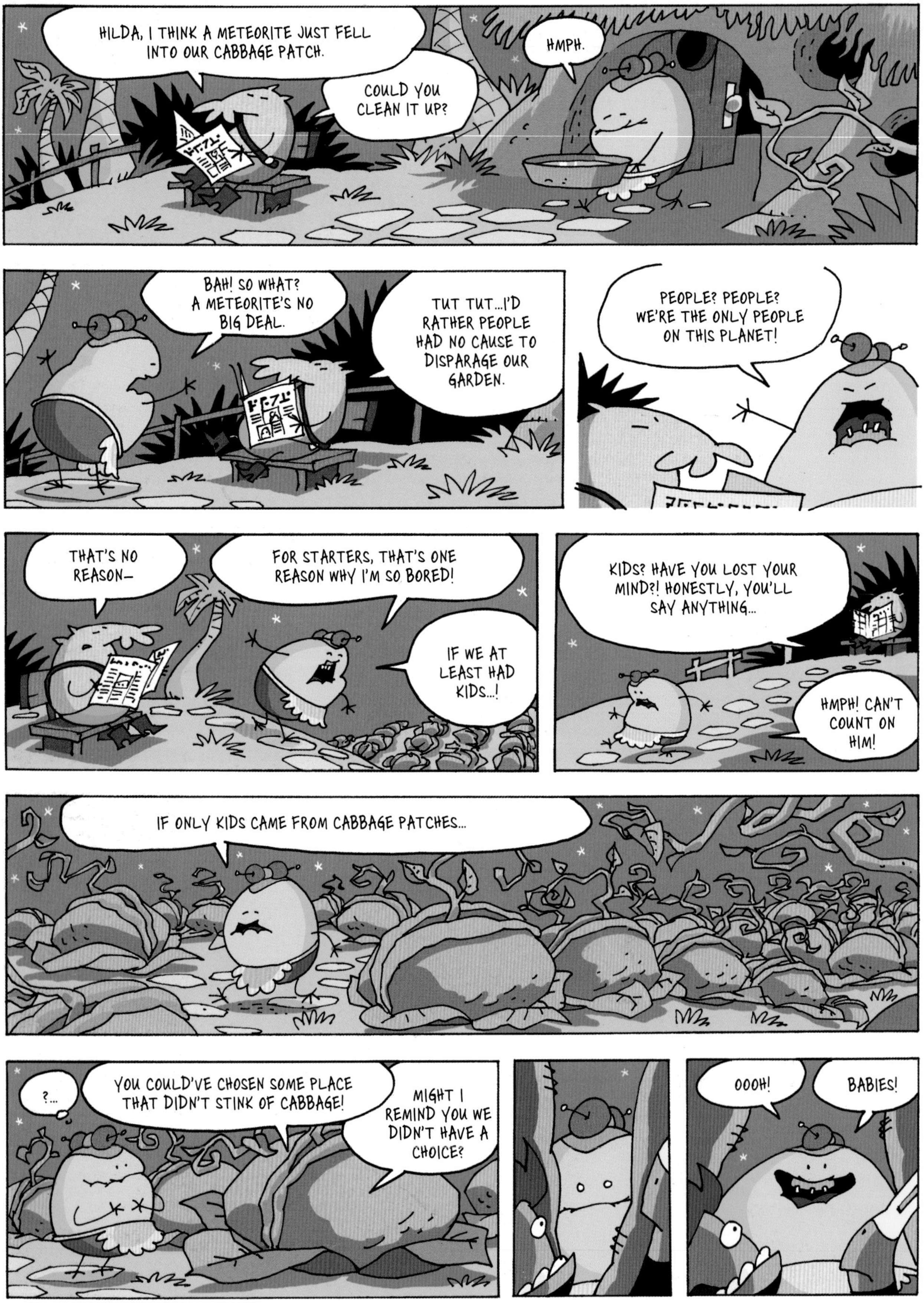
HILDA, I THINK A METEORITE JUST FELL INTO OUR CABBAGE PATCH.
COULD YOU CLEAN IT UP?
HMPH.
BAH! SO WHAT? A METEORITE'S NO BIG DEAL.
TUT TUT...I'D RATHER PEOPLE HAD NO CAUSE TO DISPARAGE OUR GARDEN.
PEOPLE? PEOPLE? WE'RE THE ONLY PEOPLE ON THIS PLANET!
THAT'S NO REASON—
FOR STARTERS, THAT'S ONE REASON WHY I'M SO BORED!
IF WE AT LEAST HAD KIDS...!
KIDS? HAVE YOU LOST YOUR MIND?! HONESTLY, YOU'LL SAY ANYTHING...
HMPH! CAN'T COUNT ON HIM!
IF ONLY KIDS CAME FROM CABBAGE PATCHES...
?...
YOU COULD'VE CHOSEN SOME PLACE THAT DIDN'T STINK OF CABBAGE!
MIGHT I REMIND YOU WE DIDN'T HAVE A CHOICE?
OOOH!
BABIES!

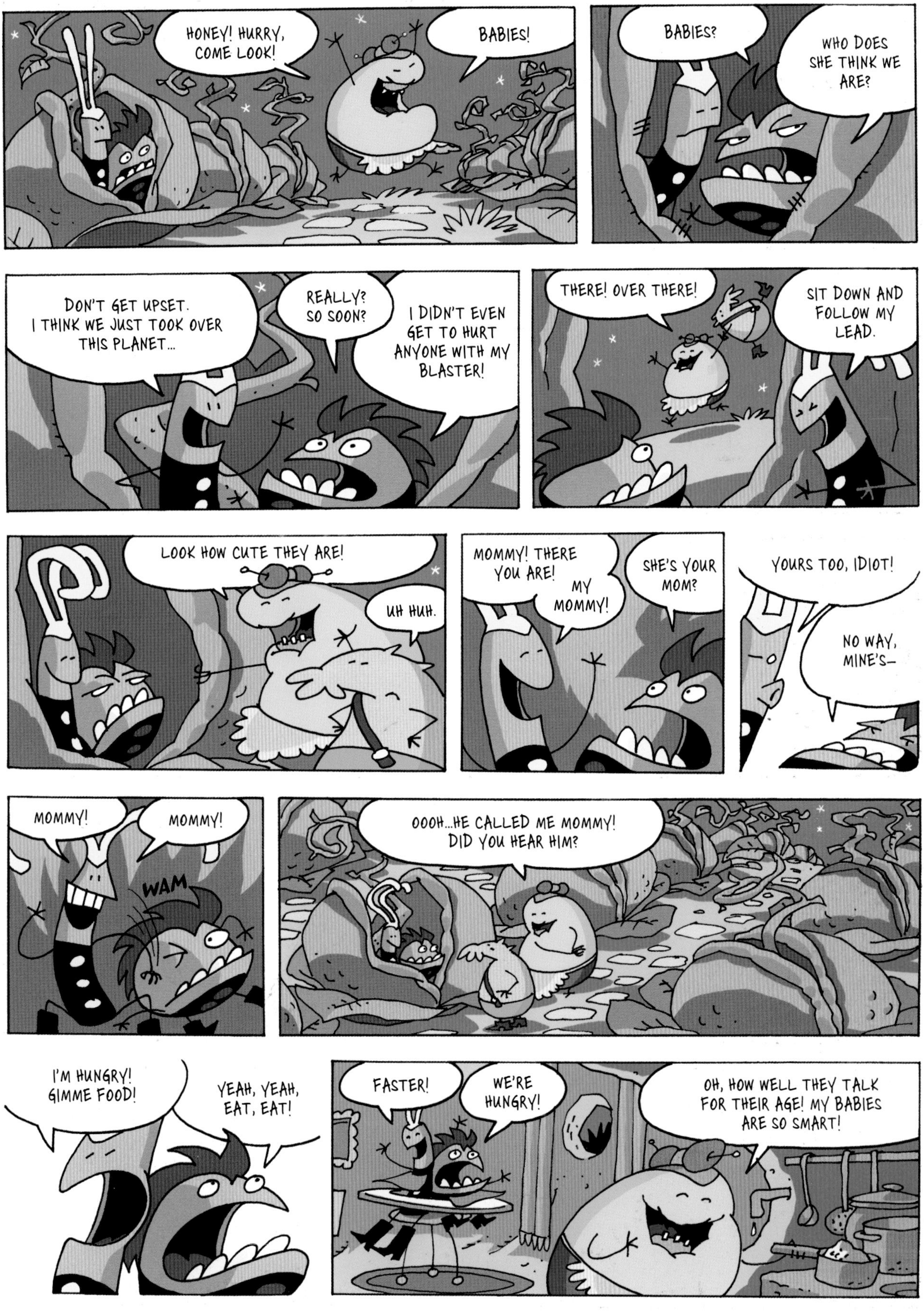
HONEY! HURRY, COME LOOK!
BABIES!
BABIES?
WHO DOES SHE THINK WE ARE?
DON'T GET UPSET. I THINK WE JUST TOOK OVER THIS PLANET...
REALLY? SO SOON?
I DIDN'T EVEN GET TO HURT ANYONE WITH MY BLASTER!
THERE! OVER THERE!
SIT DOWN AND FOLLOW MY LEAD.
LOOK HOW CUTE THEY ARE!
UH HUH.
MOMMY! THERE YOU ARE!
MY MOMMY!
SHE'S YOUR MOM?
YOURS TOO, IDIOT!
NO WAY, MINE'S—
MOMMY!
MOMMY!
WAM
OOOH...HE CALLED ME MOMMY! DID YOU HEAR HIM?
I'M HUNGRY! GIMME FOOD!
YEAH, YEAH, EAT, EAT!
FASTER!
WE'RE HUNGRY!
OH, HOW WELL THEY TALK FOR THEIR AGE! MY BABIES ARE SO SMART!

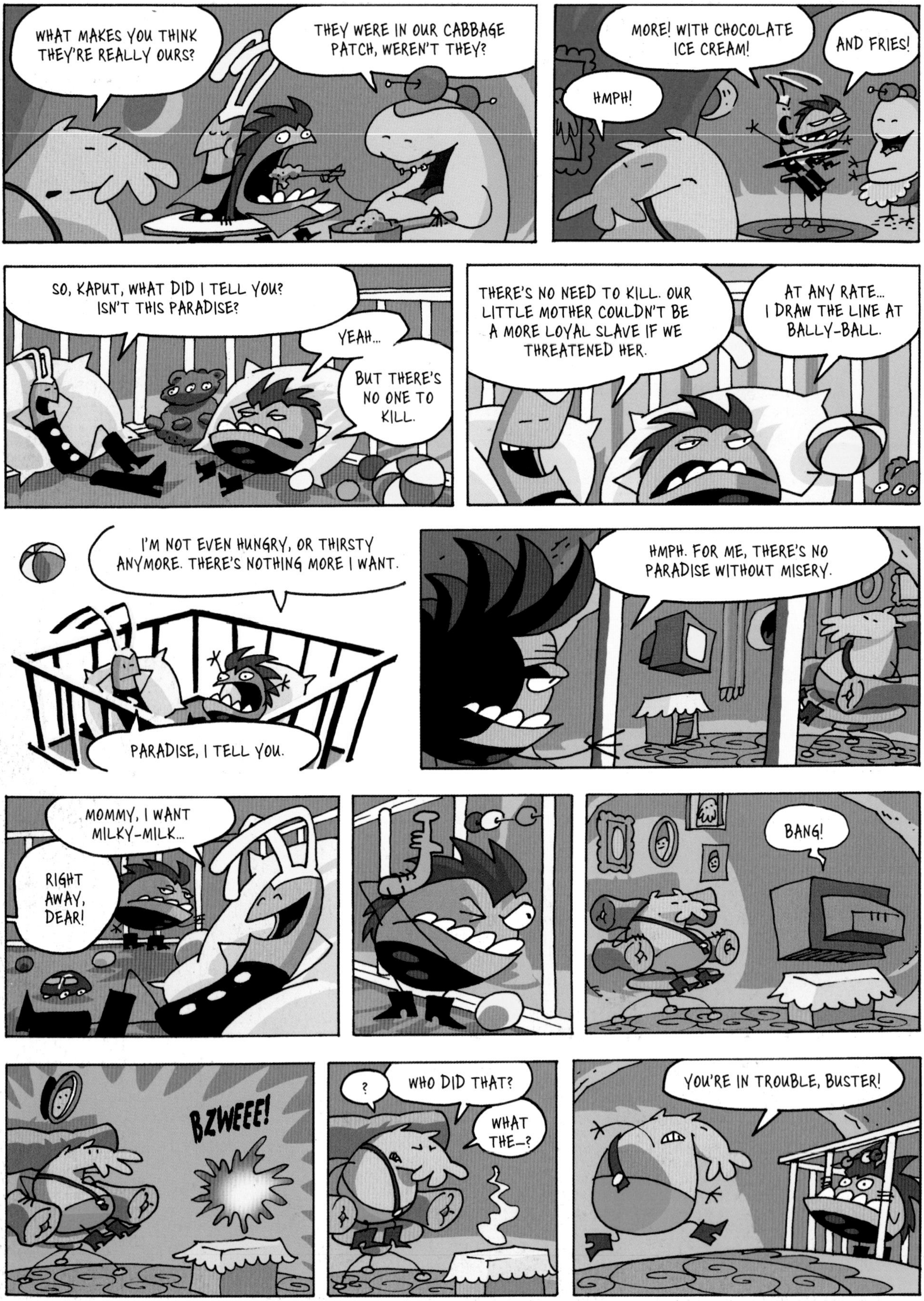
WHAT MAKES YOU THINK THEY'RE REALLY OURS?
THEY WERE IN OUR CABBAGE PATCH, WEREN'T THEY?
HMPH!
MORE! WITH CHOCOLATE ICE CREAM!
AND FRIES!
SO, KAPUT, WHAT DID I TELL YOU? ISN'T THIS PARADISE?
YEAH...
BUT THERE'S NO ONE TO KILL.
THERE'S NO NEED TO KILL. OUR LITTLE MOTHER COULDN'T BE A MORE LOYAL SLAVE IF WE THREATENED HER.
AT ANY RATE... I DRAW THE LINE AT BALLY-BALL.
I'M NOT EVEN HUNGRY, OR THIRSTY ANYMORE. THERE'S NOTHING MORE I WANT.
PARADISE, I TELL YOU.
HMPH. FOR ME, THERE'S NO PARADISE WITHOUT MISERY.
MOMMY, I WANT MILKY-MILK...
RIGHT AWAY, DEAR!
BANG!
BZWEEE!
?
WHO DID THAT?
WHAT THE–?
YOU'RE IN TROUBLE, BUSTER!

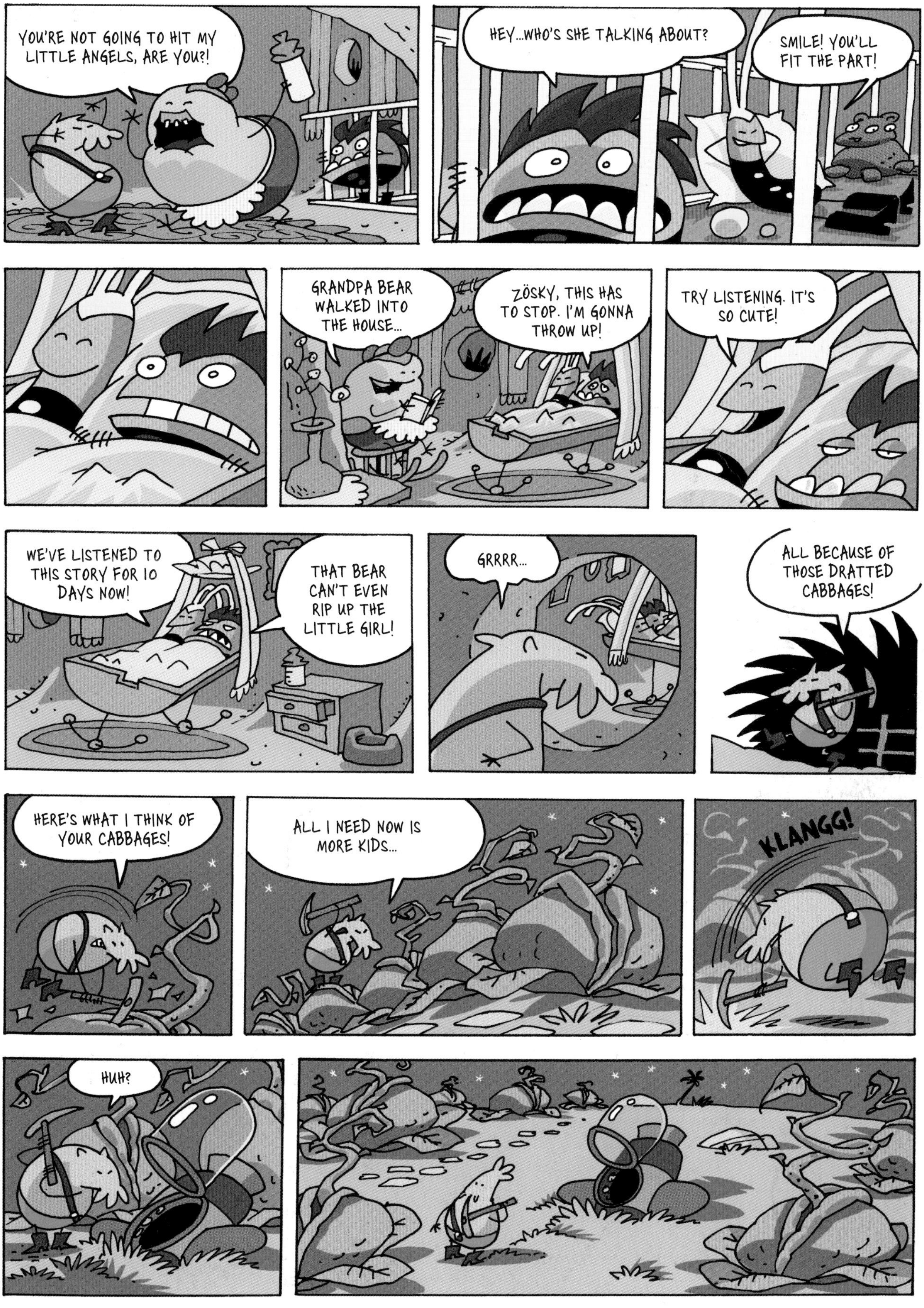
YOU'RE NOT GOING TO HIT MY LITTLE ANGELS, ARE YOU?!
HEY...WHO'S SHE TALKING ABOUT?
SMILE! YOU'LL FIT THE PART!
GRANDPA BEAR WALKED INTO THE HOUSE...
ZÖSKY, THIS HAS TO STOP. I'M GONNA THROW UP!
TRY LISTENING. IT'S SO CUTE!
WE'VE LISTENED TO THIS STORY FOR 10 DAYS NOW!
THAT BEAR CAN'T EVEN RIP UP THE LITTLE GIRL!
GRRRR...
ALL BECAUSE OF THOSE DRATTED CABBAGES!
HERE'S WHAT I THINK OF YOUR CABBAGES!
ALL I NEED NOW IS MORE KIDS...
KLANGG!
HUH?

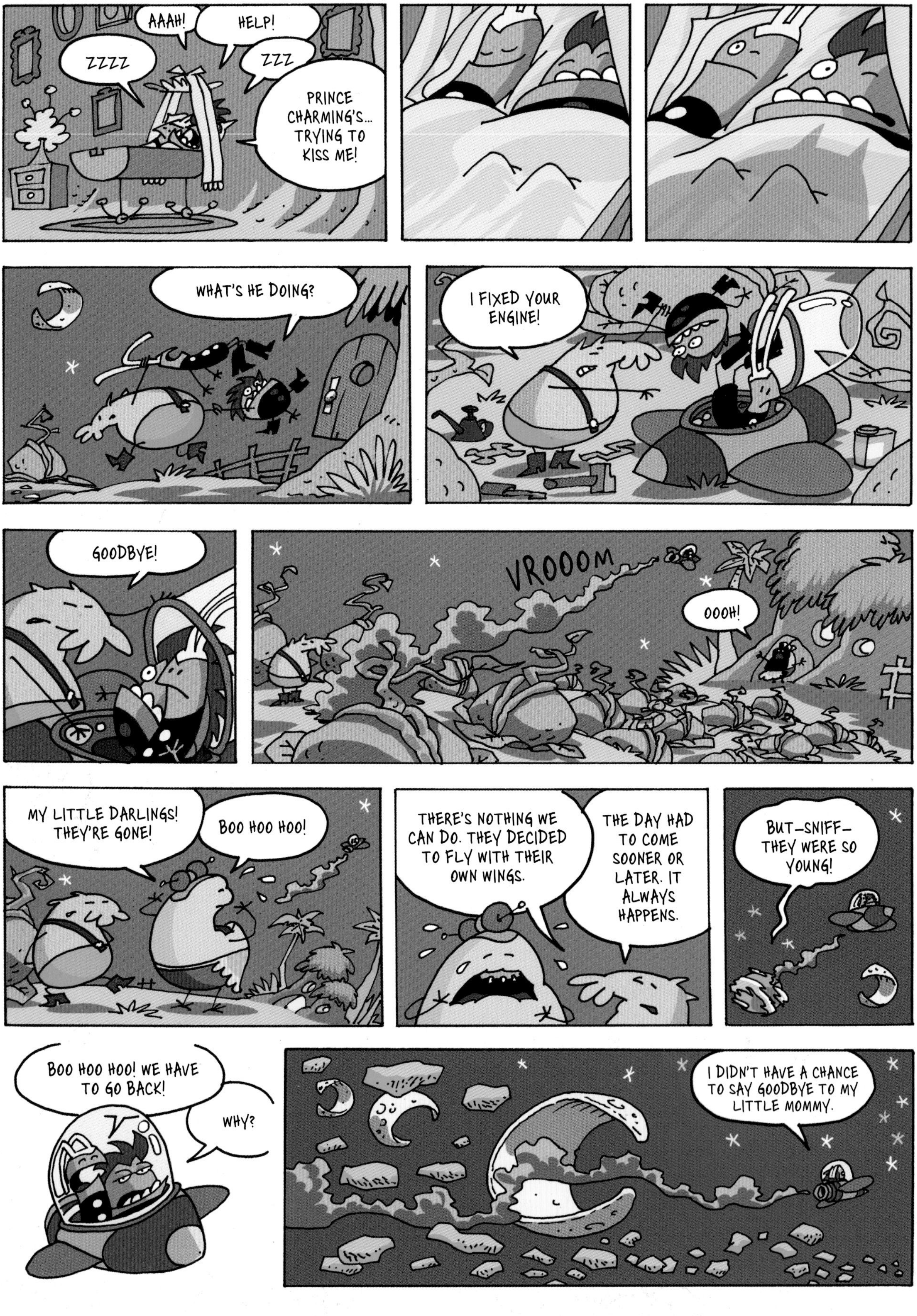
AAAH!
HELP!
ZZZZ
ZZZ
PRINCE CHARMING'S... TRYING TO KISS ME!
WHAT'S HE DOING?
I FIXED YOUR ENGINE!
GOODBYE!
VROOOM
OOOH!
MY LITTLE DARLINGS! THEY'RE GONE!
BOO HOO HOO!
THERE'S NOTHING WE CAN DO. THEY DECIDED TO FLY WITH THEIR OWN WINGS.
THE DAY HAD TO COME SOONER OR LATER. IT ALWAYS HAPPENS.
BUT–SNIFF–THEY WERE SO YOUNG!
BOO HOO HOO! WE HAVE TO GO BACK!
WHY?
I DIDN'T HAVE A CHANCE TO SAY GOODBYE TO MY LITTLE MOMMY.

the Cosmonaut

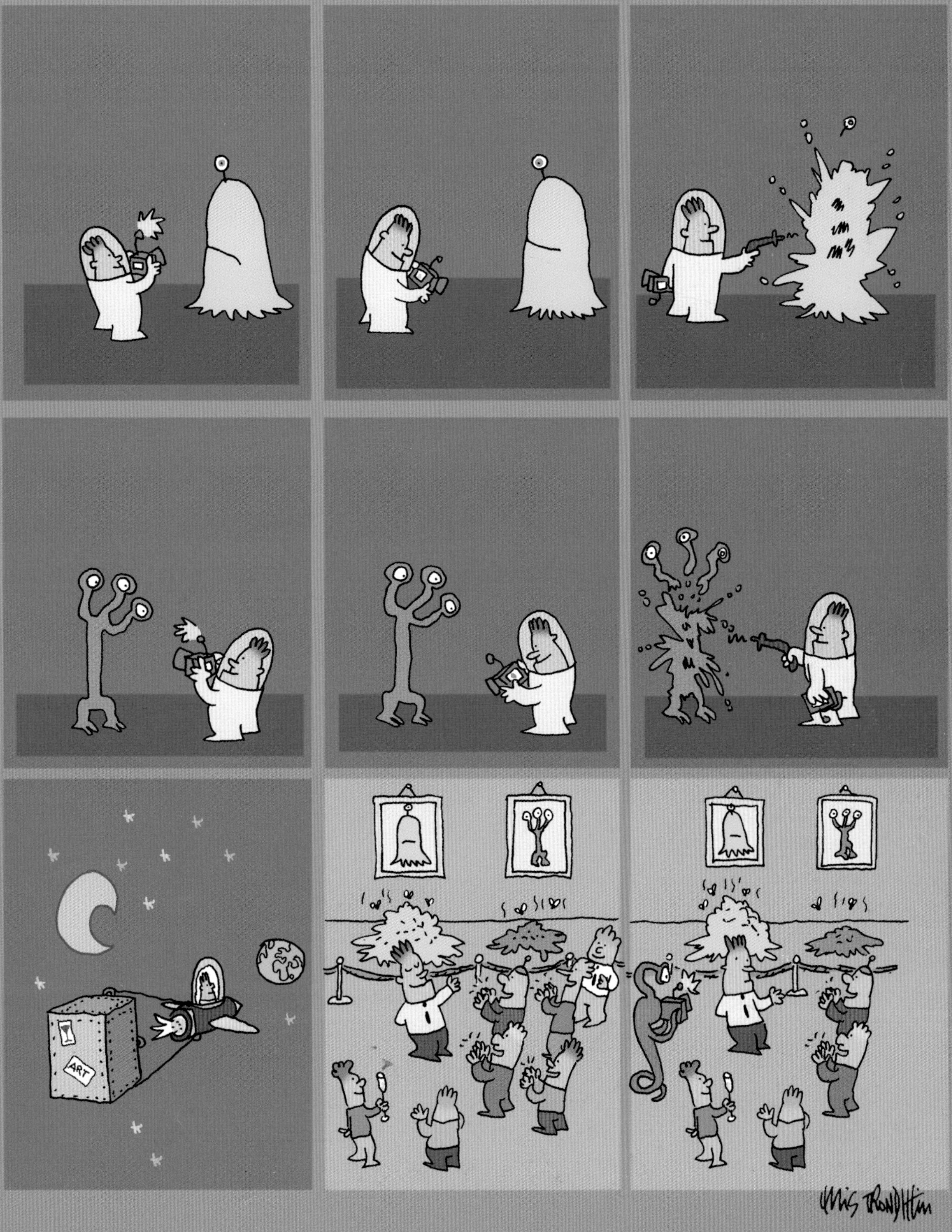
ART
LEWIS TRONDHEIM

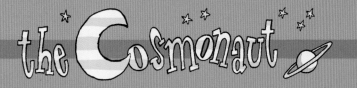

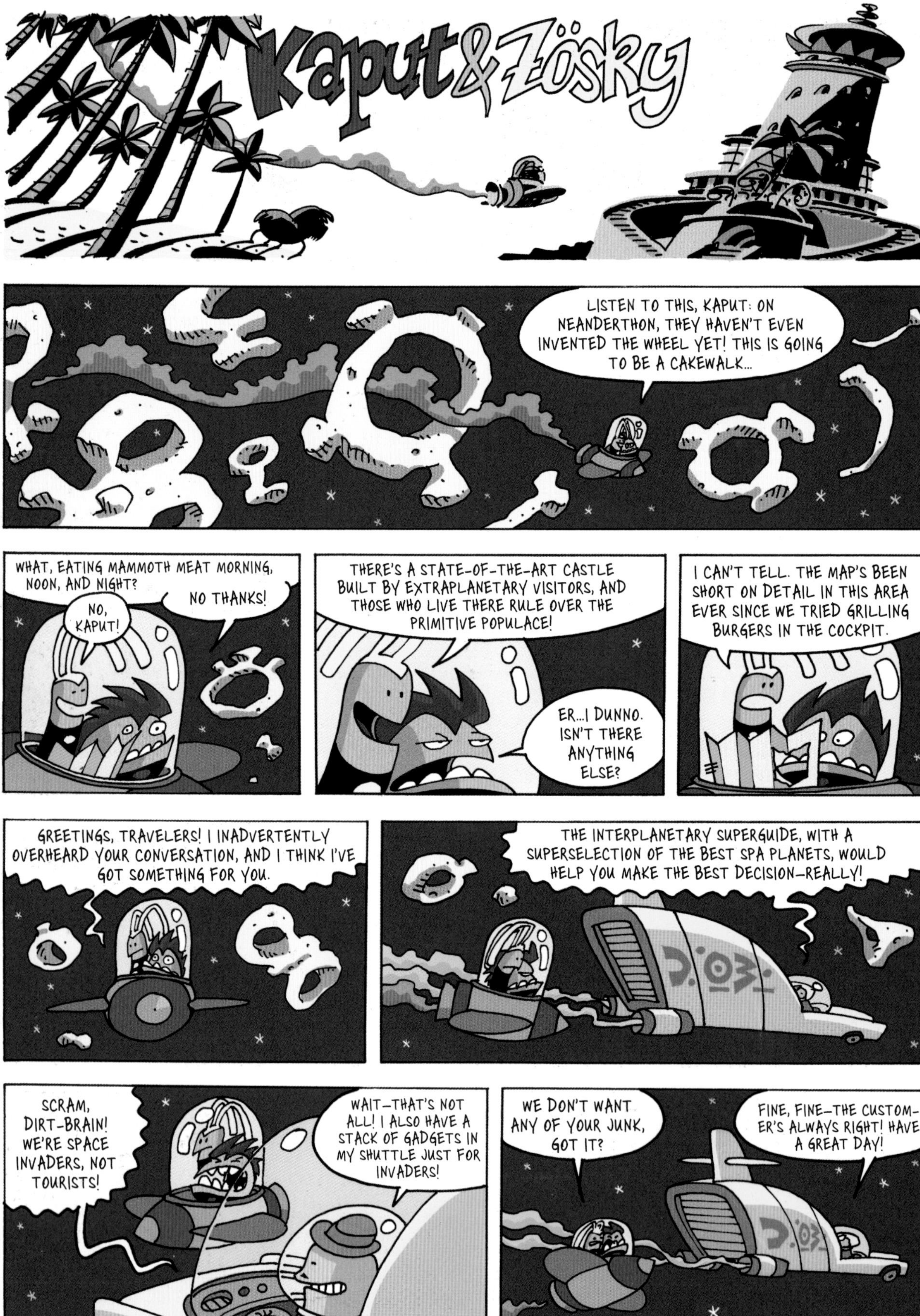
Kaput & Zösky
LISTEN TO THIS, KAPUT: ON NEANDERTHON, THEY HAVEN'T EVEN INVENTED THE WHEEL YET! THIS IS GOING TO BE A CAKEWALK...
WHAT, EATING MAMMOTH MEAT MORNING, NOON, AND NIGHT?
NO, KAPUT!
NO THANKS!
THERE'S A STATE-OF-THE-ART CASTLE BUILT BY EXTRAPLANETARY VISITORS, AND THOSE WHO LIVE THERE RULE OVER THE PRIMITIVE POPULACE!
ER...I DUNNO. ISN'T THERE ANYTHING ELSE?
I CAN'T TELL. THE MAP'S BEEN SHORT ON DETAIL IN THIS AREA EVER SINCE WE TRIED GRILLING BURGERS IN THE COCKPIT.
GREETINGS, TRAVELERS! I INADVERTENTLY OVERHEARD YOUR CONVERSATION, AND I THINK I'VE GOT SOMETHING FOR YOU.
THE INTERPLANETARY SUPERGUIDE, WITH A SUPERSELECTION OF THE BEST SPA PLANETS, WOULD HELP YOU MAKE THE BEST DECISION—REALLY!
SCRAM, DIRT-BRAIN! WE'RE SPACE INVADERS, NOT TOURISTS!
WAIT—THAT'S NOT ALL! I ALSO HAVE A STACK OF GADGETS IN MY SHUTTLE JUST FOR INVADERS!
WE DON'T WANT ANY OF YOUR JUNK, GOT IT?
FINE, FINE—THE CUSTOMER'S ALWAYS RIGHT! HAVE A GREAT DAY!

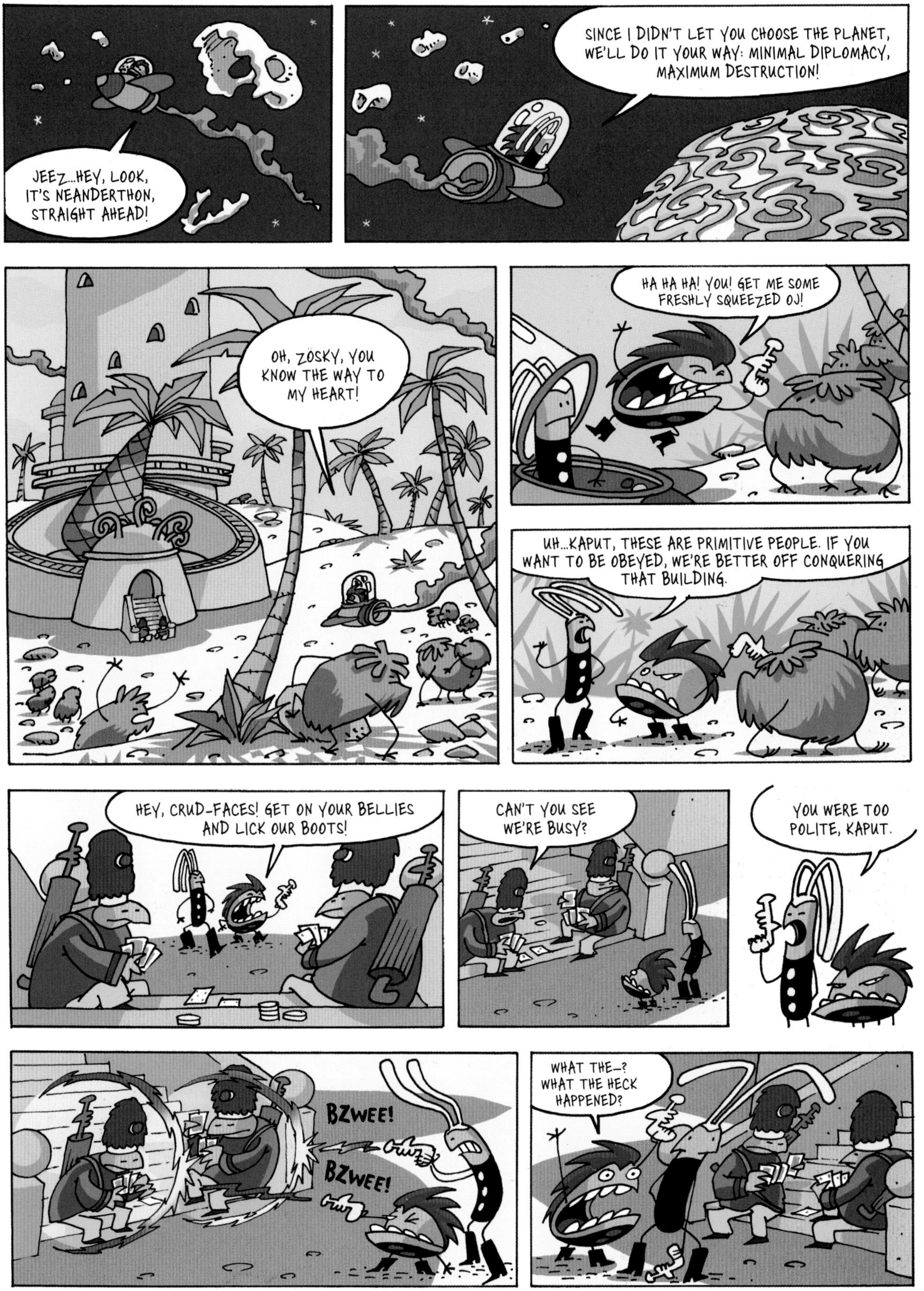
JEEZ...HEY, LOOK, IT'S NEANDERTHON, STRAIGHT AHEAD!
SINCE I DIDN'T LET YOU CHOOSE THE PLANET, WE'LL DO IT YOUR WAY: MINIMAL DIPLOMACY, MAXIMUM DESTRUCTION!
OH, ZOSKY, YOU KNOW THE WAY TO MY HEART!
HA HA HA! YOU! GET ME SOME FRESHLY SQUEEZED OJ!
UH...KAPUT, THESE ARE PRIMITIVE PEOPLE. IF YOU WANT TO BE OBEYED, WE'RE BETTER OFF CONQUERING THAT BUILDING.
HEY, CRUD-FACES! GET ON YOUR BELLIES AND LICK OUR BOOTS!
CAN'T YOU SEE WE'RE BUSY?
YOU WERE TOO POLITE, KAPUT.
BZWEE!
BZWEE!
WHAT THE–? WHAT THE HECK HAPPENED?

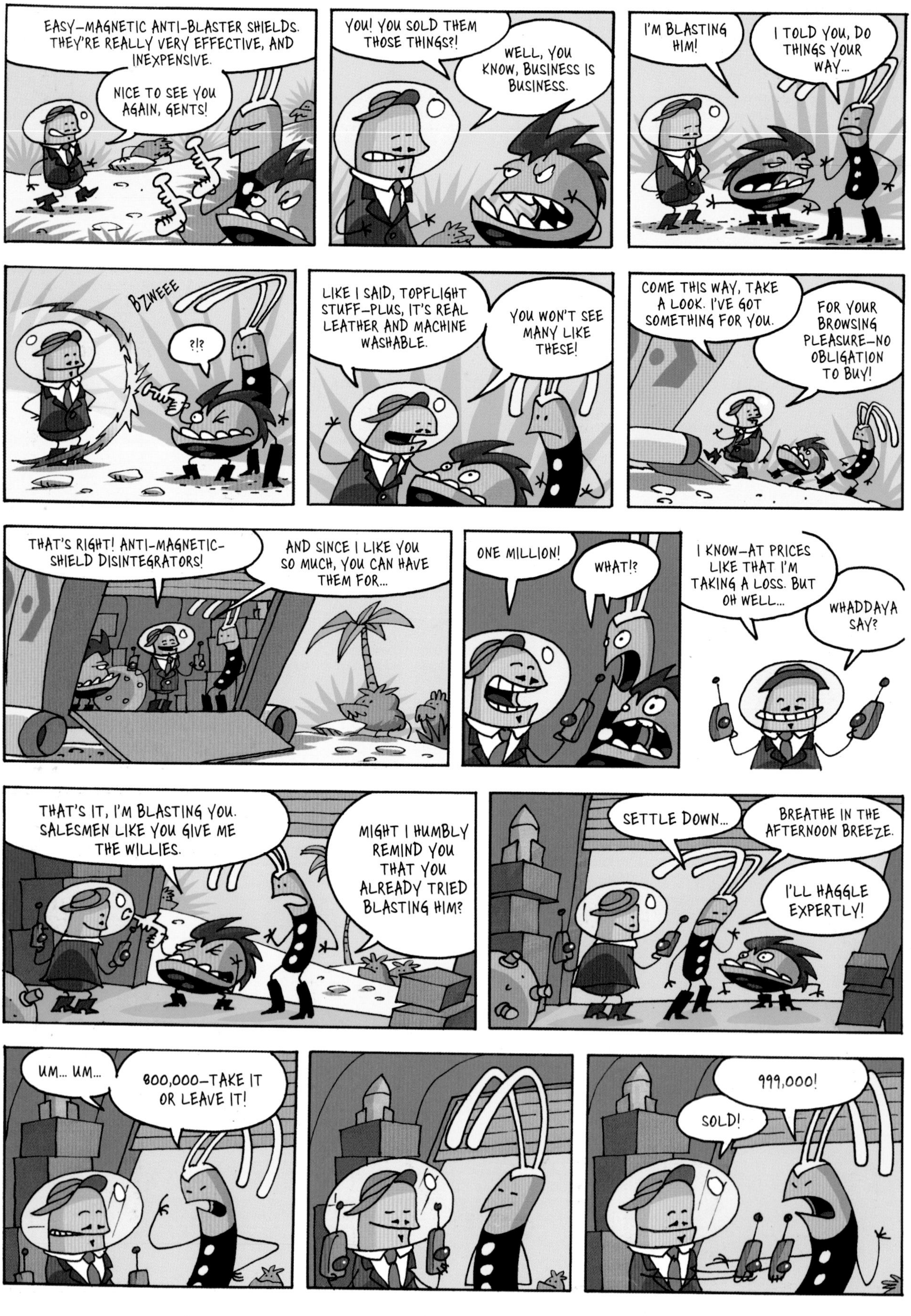
EASY-MAGNETIC ANTI-BLASTER SHIELDS. THEY'RE REALLY VERY EFFECTIVE, AND INEXPENSIVE.
NICE TO SEE YOU AGAIN, GENTS!
YOU! YOU SOLD THEM THOSE THINGS?!
WELL, YOU KNOW, BUSINESS IS BUSINESS.
I'M BLASTING HIM!
I TOLD YOU, DO THINGS YOUR WAY...
BZWEEE
?!?
LIKE I SAID, TOPFLIGHT STUFF—PLUS, IT'S REAL LEATHER AND MACHINE WASHABLE.
YOU WON'T SEE MANY LIKE THESE!
COME THIS WAY, TAKE A LOOK. I'VE GOT SOMETHING FOR YOU.
FOR YOUR BROWSING PLEASURE—NO OBLIGATION TO BUY!
THAT'S RIGHT! ANTI-MAGNETIC-SHIELD DISINTEGRATORS!
AND SINCE I LIKE YOU SO MUCH, YOU CAN HAVE THEM FOR...
ONE MILLION!
WHAT!?
I KNOW—AT PRICES LIKE THAT I'M TAKING A LOSS. BUT OH WELL...
WHADDAYA SAY?
THAT'S IT, I'M BLASTING YOU. SALESMEN LIKE YOU GIVE ME THE WILLIES.
MIGHT I HUMBLY REMIND YOU THAT YOU ALREADY TRIED BLASTING HIM?
SETTLE DOWN...
BREATHE IN THE AFTERNOON BREEZE.
I'LL HAGGLE EXPERTLY!
UM... UM...
800,000—TAKE IT OR LEAVE IT!
999,000!
SOLD!

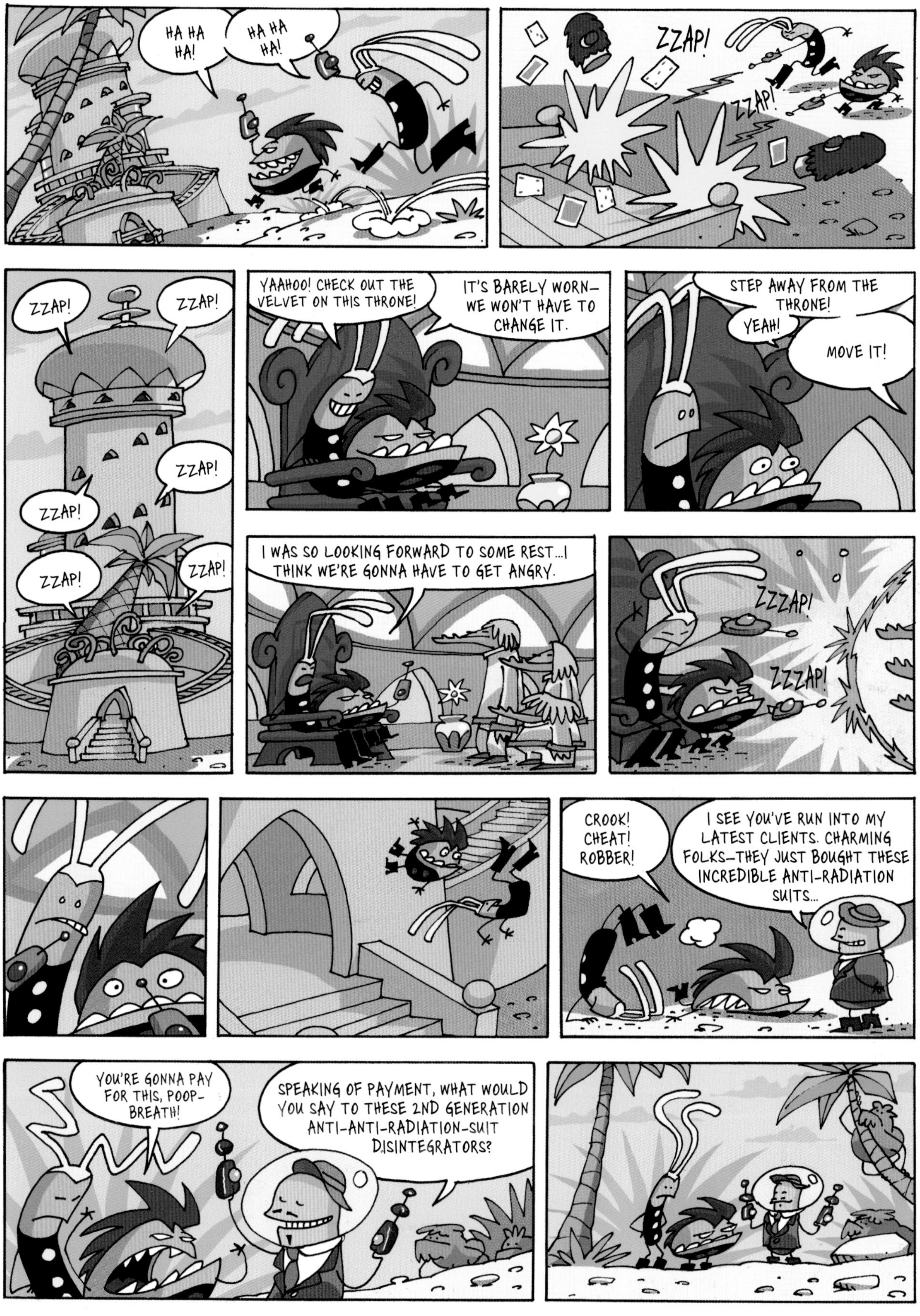

HA HA HA!
HA HA HA!
ZZAP!
ZZAP!
ZZAP!
ZZAP!
ZZAP!
ZZAP!
ZZAP!
ZZAP!
YAAHOO! CHECK OUT THE VELVET ON THIS THRONE!
IT'S BARELY WORN—WE WON'T HAVE TO CHANGE IT.
STEP AWAY FROM THE THRONE!
YEAH!
MOVE IT!
I WAS SO LOOKING FORWARD TO SOME REST...I THINK WE'RE GONNA HAVE TO GET ANGRY.
ZZZAP!
ZZZAP!
CROOK! CHEAT! ROBBER!
I SEE YOU'VE RUN INTO MY LATEST CLIENTS. CHARMING FOLKS—THEY JUST BOUGHT THESE INCREDIBLE ANTI-RADIATION SUITS...
YOU'RE GONNA PAY FOR THIS, POOP-BREATH!
SPEAKING OF PAYMENT, WHAT WOULD YOU SAY TO THESE 2ND GENERATION ANTI-ANTI-RADIATION-SUIT DISINTEGRATORS?

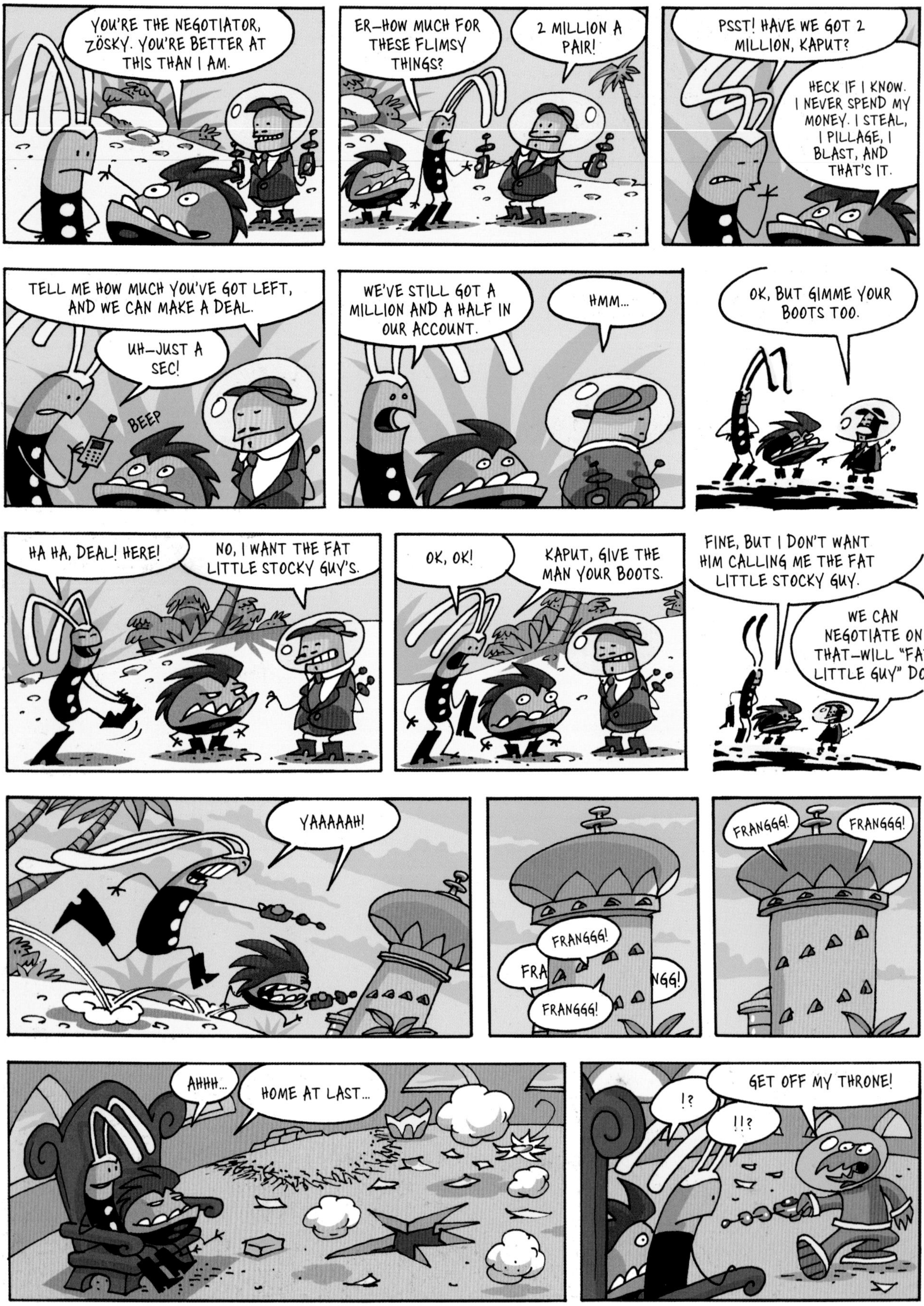
YOU'RE THE NEGOTIATOR, ZÖSKY. YOU'RE BETTER AT THIS THAN I AM.
ER—HOW MUCH FOR THESE FLIMSY THINGS?
2 MILLION A PAIR!
PSST! HAVE WE GOT 2 MILLION, KAPUT?
HECK IF I KNOW. I NEVER SPEND MY MONEY. I STEAL, I PILLAGE, I BLAST, AND THAT'S IT.
TELL ME HOW MUCH YOU'VE GOT LEFT, AND WE CAN MAKE A DEAL.
UH—JUST A SEC!
BEEP
WE'VE STILL GOT A MILLION AND A HALF IN OUR ACCOUNT.
HMM...
OK, BUT GIMME YOUR BOOTS TOO.
HA HA, DEAL! HERE!
NO, I WANT THE FAT LITTLE STOCKY GUY'S.
OK, OK!
KAPUT, GIVE THE MAN YOUR BOOTS.
FINE, BUT I DON'T WANT HIM CALLING ME THE FAT LITTLE STOCKY GUY.
WE CAN NEGOTIATE ON THAT—WILL "FAT LITTLE GUY" DO?
YAAAAAH!
FRANGGG!
FRANGGG!
FRANGGG!
FRANGGG!
AHHH...
HOME AT LAST...
!?
!!?
GET OFF MY THRONE!

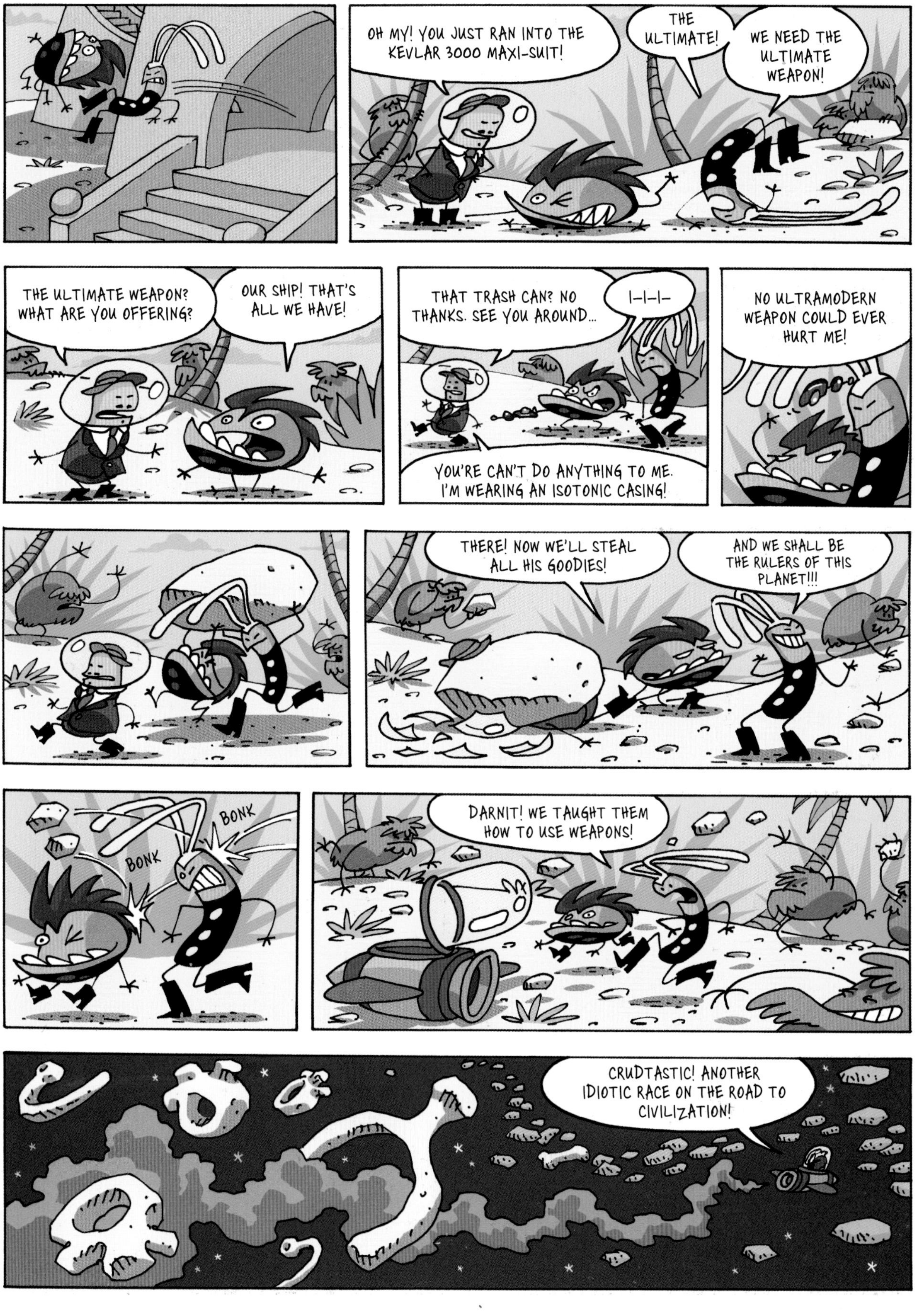
OH MY! YOU JUST RAN INTO THE KEVLAR 3000 MAXI-SUIT!
THE ULTIMATE!
WE NEED THE ULTIMATE WEAPON!
THE ULTIMATE WEAPON? WHAT ARE YOU OFFERING?
OUR SHIP! THAT'S ALL WE HAVE!
THAT TRASH CAN? NO THANKS. SEE YOU AROUND...
I-I-I-
YOU'RE CAN'T DO ANYTHING TO ME. I'M WEARING AN ISOTONIC CASING!
NO ULTRAMODERN WEAPON COULD EVER HURT ME!
THERE! NOW WE'LL STEAL ALL HIS GOODIES!
AND WE SHALL BE THE RULERS OF THIS PLANET!!!
BONK
BONK
DARNIT! WE TAUGHT THEM HOW TO USE WEAPONS!
CRUDTASTIC! ANOTHER IDIOTIC RACE ON THE ROAD TO CIVILIZATION!

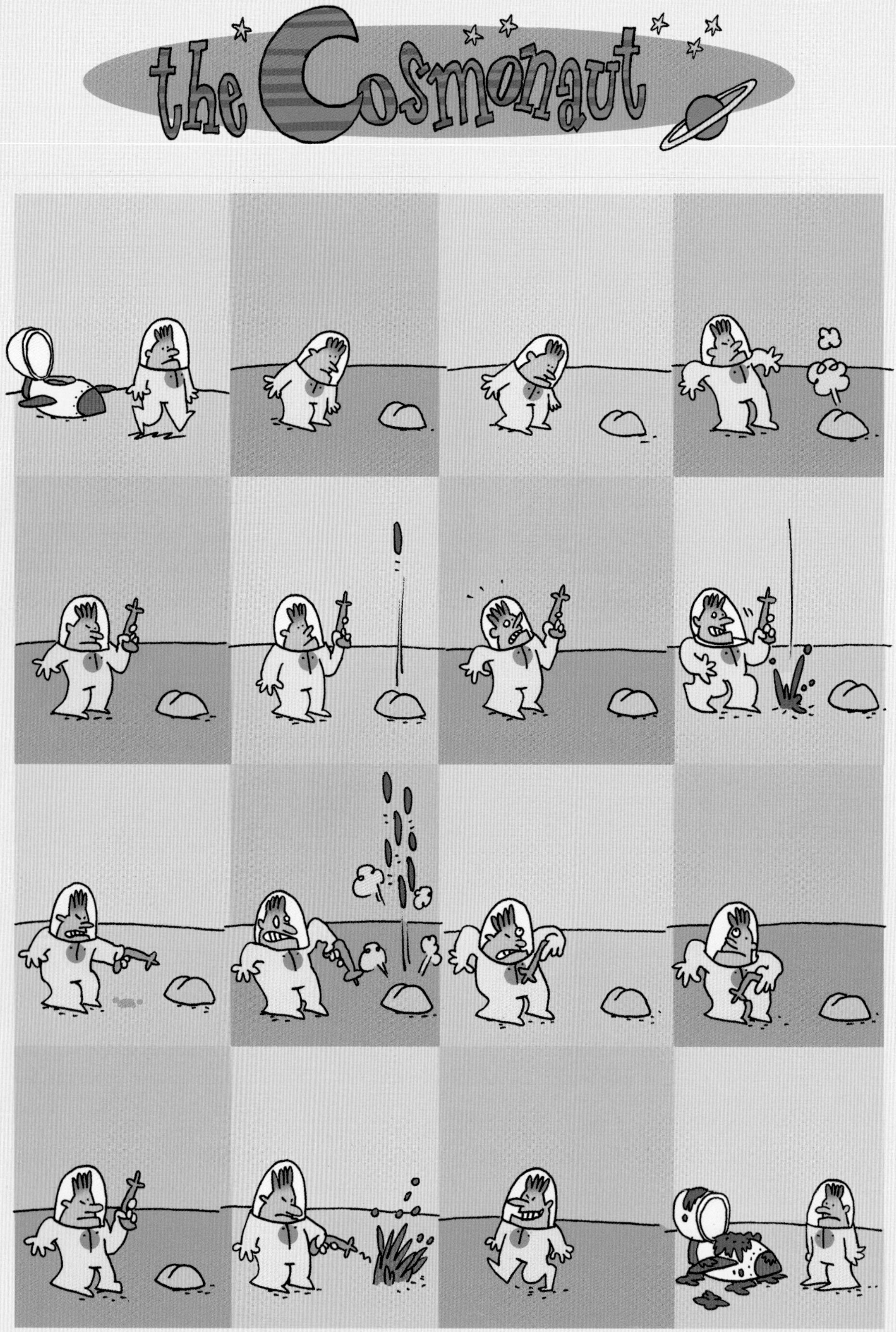
the Cosmonaut

:01

First Second

New York & London

Copyright © MMII by Futurikon / Tooncan
Copyright © 2002 by Guy Delcourt Productions—Lewis Trondheim
English translation copyright © 2008 by First Second
(Pages 5 to 40)

Copyright © MMIII by Futurikon / Tooncan
Copyright © 2003 by Guy Delcourt Productions—Lewis Trondheim—Eric Cartier
English translation copyright © 2008 by First Second
Adapted for TV by Samuel Kaminka & Lewis Trondheim, in cooperation with Sophie Decroisette & Philippe Grimond. Directed by Didier Loubat.
Story 1 [originally *Kaput file un mauvais coton*]: script by Jean-Marc Lenglen, in cooperation with Laurent Turner.
Story 2 [originally *Démocratie*]: script by Sophie Decroisette, Franck Ekinci, Philippe Grimond, in cooperation with Laurent Turner.
Story 3 [originally *Globine 2*]: script by Manon and Huguette Berthelet, in cooperation with Laurent Turner.
Story 4 [originally *Savez-vous planter des choux*]: script by Sophie Decroisette, Franck Ekinci and Philippe Grimond.
Story 5 [originally *Le colporteur de l'espace*]: script by Véronique Herbaut, in cooperation with Laurent Turner.
(Pages 42 to 75)

Supplementary artwork on pages (6, 11, 16, 27, 34, 41, 55, 62, 69, and 76) copyright © 2007 by Lewis Trondheim
Supplementary artwork by Lewis Trondheim on pages (3, 21, and 48) copyright © 2008 by Futurikon/Tooncan
Compilation of Kaput & Zösky and Lewis Trondheim's supplementary artwork copyright © 2008 by First Second

Published by First Second
First Second is an imprint of Roaring Brook Press, a division of Holtzbrinck Publishing Holdings Limited Partnership
175 Fifth Avenue, New York, NY 10010

Distributed in Canada by H. B. Fenn and Company Ltd.
Distributed in the United Kingdom by Macmillan Children's Books, a division of Pan Macmillan.

Originally published in France in 2002 under the title Kaput & Zösky: Les Zigouilleurs de L'infini, in 2003 under the title Kaput & Zösky: Les Flinguizeurs du Cosmos by Guy Delcourt Productions, Paris.

Design by Danica Novgorodoff

Library of Congress Cataloging-in-Publication Data

Trondheim, Lewis.
[Kaput and Zösky. English]
Kaput and Zösky / Lewis Trondheim ; with art by Eric Cartier. -- 1st American ed.
p. cm.
Translation of: Kaput & Zösky: Les Zigouilleurs de L'infini (2002), and Kaput & Zösky: Les Flinguizeurs du Cosmos (2003).
ISBN-13: 978-1-59643-132-4
ISBN-10: 1-59643-132-6
I. Title.
PN6747.T76K3713 2008
741.5'944--dc22
2007023958

First Second books are available for special promotions and premiums.
For details, contact: Director of Special Markets, Holtzbrinck Publishers.

First American Edition April 2008
Printed in China

1 3 5 7 9 10 8 6 4 2

Some fine offerings from **First Second** for young readers of graphic novels...

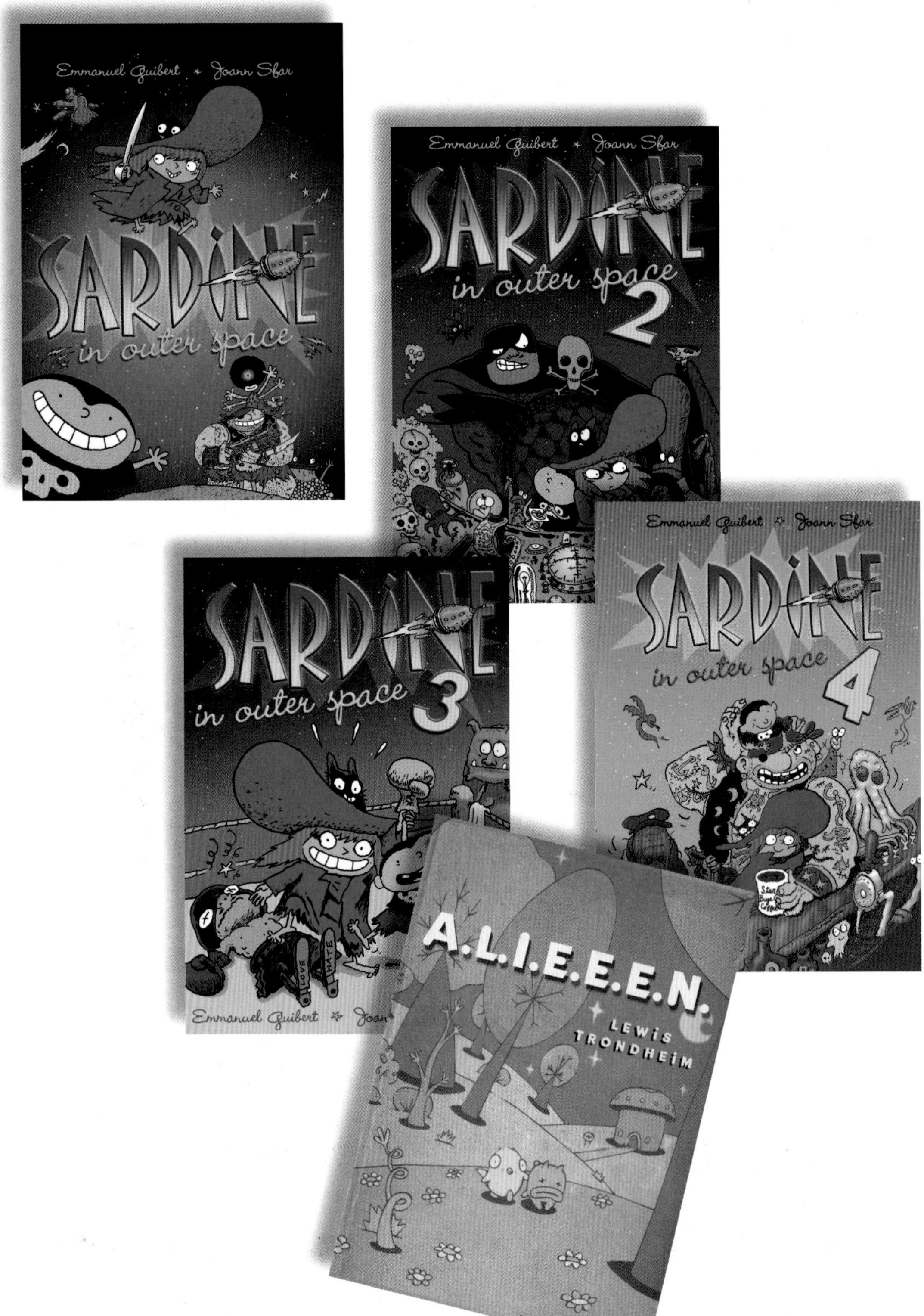

Emmanuel Guibert ✦ Joann Sfar
SARDINE
in outer space
Emmanuel Guibert ✦ Joann Sfar
SARDINE
in outer space 2
SARDINE
in outer space 3
Emmanuel Guibert
Emmanuel Guibert ✦ Joann Sfar
SARDINE
in outer space 4
A.L.I.E.E.E.N.
LEWIS TRONDHEIM